Known Shippable, Will Not Fix

By

Roy W. Russell

ISBN: 978-0-692-77248-5

>Dedication.txt

For Solie, we miss your big heart and your loving sense of humor.

>Initialize Book.exe

1. Look up to the top edge of this book or e-reader device.

2. Look down at the bottom edge of this book or e-reader device.

3. Look to the right edge of this book or e-reader device.

4. Look to the left edge of this book or e-reader device.

User visual calibration completed?

If (Yes) continue. If (No), repeat steps 1-4.

>Adjust Gamma

5. Adjust ambient room lighting to ensure a pleasant reading experience, or utilize the free burning ball of fire in the sky (but please remember to use sun screen).

>Saving progress on analog media

Ensure you have an appropriate saving device
to not lose progress when reading this book.
A slip of paper, receipt, or if you're a
dirty one percenter* a bookmark will suffice.
E-readers should have built in functionality
to save your progress automatically, yay
technology!

* If you're a one percenter and want to adapt
this book into a movie I was just kidding,
you're probably not dirty. You probably
smell nice.

>Mature Content Rating

This book features graphic violence, mature
language, more fantastical graphic violence,
end world scenarios, and suggestive slang.
Content not intended for readers under 17
years of age. If you read this to your kid at
bedtime… I don't even have words. Just don't
do it.

Contents

Robot Alien God

The soda is free; at least he had that.

Casey has little going on in his life at the moment, just work. This will only be a part time gig until he gets his degree and until, hopefully, he's recruited and devoured by a big giant soulless mega corporation with a 401(k) and medical plan. This job, it doesn't have a 401(k) or medical plan, just a minimum wage paycheck and free soda from the machine—but only when it's restocked by someone making more than him.

Maybe he should get a job stocking vending machines, travel and meet new people, and each new day would present a fresh challenge to take head on? But he hates traffic, hates the fake way people talk to each other, and the rut he's settled into at the moment is comforting. Casey doesn't hate his job; he doesn't complain about it when he gets home from the hour and a half commute out of Novato to his little home in Santa Rosa. If he could make more money, maybe one day he could find a place within a respectable driving or walking distance from the office. But this slice of California, Marin County, gets even more expensive the closer you get to San Francisco.

There will come a day, though, that these free sodas will be his undoing. It will either be cavities and root canals he can't afford to treat, or obesity and heart disease, maybe some diabetes on the side, because that's how this universe works. There is a sickening order to the way life unfolds. It almost seems as if things are meant to fail, and when they do, it's spectacular.

Now, all Casey wants to do is watch a cat try to jump across a gap between two balconies. He heard the other guys laughing about it at lunch. Fancying himself an elite hacker, he bypassed the corporate protections that prevented him from updating his web browser's video playing capabilities. He utilized the most advanced form of social engineering to get the password required to update his workstation: he begged his supervisor for permission.

Mindlessly clicking the install buttons too hastily, he stares at the mistake—mocking him now. Where he should be looking up data references, ensuring the software doesn't infringe on any copyrights that would result in lawsuits, his browser has been hijacked by a toolbar that redirects his search queries to useless websites selling unregulated medical supplements promising to add up to twelve whole inches to a stalk of corn he is not growing.

Casey, defeated, is unable to uninstall the toolbar. This will require the intervention of a higher power. He asks his supervisor to visit the IT department and makes a request to have his workstation remotely restored to a backup state created before lunch, before he heard the hilarious story of a cat jumping into oblivion.

What would happen if he tried jumping onto his neighbor's balcony? Would he miss? Maybe she'd greet him with her bright smile and wide blue eyes? He'd probably miss. Or worse, the Russian mobster guy with the gold chain necklaces would be there instead, and he'd chuck Casey six floors down to the emergency room.

He can hear the laughter as he approaches the barely open white aluminum door. Why do these guys get a cool white aluminum door? What makes them so special? They don't even sit in OSHA approved ergonomic chairs either. Wherever they found them, it seems they've declared themselves royalty, with their old wood throne replicas probably stolen from the Renaissance fair down the road.

Howard, the IT guy, looks up from his tablet, barely making eye contact with Casey. "What did you do now?"

This is the first time Casey's ever needed IT to unscrew- up a mistake, and he feels hurt by the question. "My workstation was hijacked by a toolbar. It won't let me search resources correctly."

Howard sighs, leaving Casey waiting for a reply. The two IT guys sitting behind Howard are watching the cat jumping video, enhanced with a song perfectly in sync when the cat jumps. Casey tries looking past Howard and through the two to see it, but instead, Howard coughs to get his attention and says, "There, it's done, can you leave us now. We're busy. Bye."

Casey hadn't even seen him Alt Tab to one-button restore his workstation. He once considered applying to IT, but it would have meant giving up his humanity. No, he thinks, I choose to not be a snarky robot alien god.

Casey returns to his desk to catch up on the five minutes he lost walking down the hallway and back. He knocks out the test plans and whips up the build notes his supervisor has been taking credit for the past year. Sitting down after opening another soda, he sees the note smack dab in the middle of his monitor. The toolbar has been replaced with a yellow note that simply says: See Babb Now.

Working in QA isn't grueling work; it can be fun at times. Testing the software being coded from higher up the totem pole will help Casey appreciate properly written software when he gets hired to write some. At least, that's what he tells himself.

The job has strict deadlines. Each build released needs to be tested and bugs must be regressed. Previously written bugs are marked in the system as "fix verified" or "not fixed," and if they aren't fixed, the necessary steps to reproduce the error need to be written and documented evidence provided through screenshots or video attached in the database. As it stands, Casey is now ten minutes behind, and the company treasures each and every minute. They do not allow anyone to work unpaid overtime to keep up, lest they incur the wrath of class action lawsuits. If an employee falls behind, then they soon find themselves not being a worker in this building anymore.

Casey fears the worst as he walks to the dimly lit basement. Why does the producer reside in the basement away from everyone else? Casey knocks meekly on Babb's door. "In, now," says the stern voice on the other side.

Before he realizes it, Casey is blown back several feet, sailing in the air to oblivion thinking, "this is what the cat must have felt like when he jumped out of frame".

Casey lands with a thud on the coarse grey carpet and after sliding for a bit, rug burns on both his elbows, he mutters, "It was just a toolbar."

Babb stands there, behind his desk, looking down at Casey. Still on the floor, Casey looks up at the giant, grizzled old man. Babb still has a few patches of dark black hair in his now white mane and beard. But Casey can't help focusing on the barrels of the sawed off shotgun that knocked him off his feet.

Realizing he's been shot, Casey regrets not saying hi to Natalie in the elevator last night. He closes his eyes, waiting for the cold darkness of death to take him away to wherever he'll go next. Is there a heaven? Did he do enough to get in—let people cut in front of him at the grocery store or drop a few pennies in the cancer donation jar at the sandwich place? Or is he going to hell? Maybe piracy really isn't a victimless crime and all the illegal downloads of movies and music residing on his computer at home have sentenced him to an eternity of fire—or worse, they know about folder TPC69 nested in his archived tax records.

"Get up, man, we don't have all day," Babb says.

Casey sits upright, legs slightly spread, and his button up red shirt shredded by the gunshot. As he gets up, he feels warm slugs trickle down his chest and spill out onto the crotch of his cargo pants.

"I'm not dead. Why am I not dead?" Casey asks, looking up at Babb, who's reloading the shotgun.

Babb doesn't answer. He sits down behind his desk in his cushioned leather chair, puts the shotgun into his own mouth. Casey turns his head aside, not wanting to see the result, to see him burn out instead of fade away. Babb pulls the trigger.

Casey gets to his feet, forcing himself to look on the other side of the desk: Babb's feet in the air from the force of the shotgun blast.

"Cmum inn alweady." Babb gets up, puts his leather chair upright, and sits down. He spits metal chunks onto the desk. "Close the door, Casey."

This can't be happening. It's impossible. He liked this shirt. Natalie liked this shirt. He distinctly remembers her saying, "Nice shirt, Casey." Since then, he's washed it every couple of days and wears it almost religiously, as often as he can.

Babb taps away on his keyboard and clicks his mouse several times, laughing. "I love this cat video, it's the best one I've seen yet."

"I just shot you. Do you have any idea why you're still alive? Stop grieving your shirt; it can be replaced." Casey stares at Babb, trying to process everything. Babb continues, "What if I told you." Casey sits there, listening intently. Babb looks at Casey, examining him: Dark black rimmed glasses, now disheveled brown hair, a tattered red shirt, and probably ten pounds overweight. "They normally scream. Why didn't you scream?"

Casey wonders the same. Maybe he just had no time from seeing the end of the shotgun to the counting of the ceiling tiles while in flight.

"Never mind that. It's done. It's over. Time to get down to business. Casey, what if I told you that you were getting a promotion?"

Casey's eyes light up.

"No, not a raise, but a solid chance at invaluable work experience," Babb says, deflating Casey's fleeting hopes, "Do you really want to be writing build notes for Norman for the next eight years? Or do you want to enact real change?"

Casey looks at the warm shotgun. "You shot me. Why did you shoot me, and why are we both still alive?"

"Local collision handling has us set as static objects," Babb replies. "There's a bug in the collision detection that prevents the bullets from penetrating our flesh."

Casey sort of understands those words. He made a few clone apps for mobile devices, but those were just games nobody ever downloaded, played, bought any of the in app purchases for, or even clicked on the embedded ads.

"It's being hot fixed ahead of the next build release," Babb says.

Build update, collision handling, patching the software… "Wait, are we in the…?" Casey doesn't finish.

"Stop right there. For legal reasons, you can't say that word," Babb says. "Do you want the sideways promotion or not? I can just as easily call Allen down here, and you can go back upstairs to finish your last day at work here, maybe get a nice job rolling burritos for us across the street."

Casey, without thinking, replies, "Yes, I accept your offer."

Babb shakes his head disapprovingly. "You people. So in a hurry. You didn't even read the EULA I was about to hand you."

Babb hands Casey the 1100-page binder. Casey opens the book, flips through the pages, but it's gibberish. A weird collection of geometric shapes, numbers, and emoticons.

"I'm just messing with you," Babb says as he takes the binder back, putting it in his desk drawer. "What, you thought this was a real language and it held a deeper meaning to the universe? You live in Santa Rosa, yes? I think you'll like the promotion. You're being reassigned to Hangar 77."

Casey's eyes light up once more. The Hangars are where some of the bay area's best studios and developers are located. There's even talk of an animation studio moving in, complete with motion capture stages. Seeing A-list actors and actresses walking through *his* parking lot would be cool. The restaurants around there don't serve mushy, watery burritos or fajitas. And the relocation will shave ten minutes from Casey's commute.

Babb hands Casey a card. The back is glossy silver with white lettering: Hangar 77. Casey turns the card around. It has his name on it already, and the address of where he'll be working.

"Yes, we made you a card. Report to your new supervisors, Aaron and Randy. They'll be waiting when you get there, *on time*, tomorrow."

Casey thanks Babb for believing in him enough to preemptively make him a business card.

"Take the rest of the day off, go change that shirt, and report to work tomorrow morning at ten."

"But the work day starts at 8:30," Casey replies.

"Report to Aaron and Randy at ten," Babb says. "And don't forget, you signed a non-disclosure agreement. Violating its terms will result in severe consequences." Babb tosses Casey the shotgun as a souvenir as he leaves the office.

Casey, still in shock from the shotgun blast, witnessing a suicide attempt, and getting a job promotion all in the span of about five minutes, leaves in a dazed state and walks, numb, to his blue four door car. He barely registers the terrified screams and begging as his coworkers see the zombie shambling down the hallway, armed with a deadly weapon. It's not until he hits gridlock and some moron that didn't have the sense to zipper merge earlier cuts him off that Casey wakes from the haze, cussing out the soccer mom and her three kids.

"I'm going to hell," he says. "I'm sorry. I didn't mean it."

Casey makes it back to his apartment complex two hours later. He thought leaving work early would help, but it just made the commute half an hour longer. He could have just stayed at work and finished his research project.

Casey throws his red shirt into the garbage, takes a shower, and puts on his sweatpants and trendy video game reference shirt that only cost him $39.99 online. He then goes out to the balcony. It's the one part of his day that is all his. In the next unit, *she* is singing. Sometimes he hears the fake plastic guitar being played. Natalie, playing a last gen music game, belts out the hits.

Good music, a still cool can of soda he swiped from work, and a rare breeze blowing on his face, eyes closed. His favorite part of the day.

The sliding patio door opens and Casey is about to smile to her. Instead of the tall, brown-haired girl, it's him. The bulky creep. He lights up a cigarette and blows the smoke Casey's way.

The shotgun is on Casey's kitchen table next to his car keys. He could go inside, get it, and blow this Russian mob wannabe creep off the patio. It's not murder, not if today's weird revelation is true. Shotgun to the face is a victimless crime now.

Instead, Casey goes inside and watches cartoons before frying up a burger for dinner.

Hangar 77—a new job. What exactly will he be doing when he reports to work tomorrow? All these questions will get an answer. Maybe he'll be writing code now. Coding to the metal. Laying down slick sweet lines of binary thunder. Finally getting out of QA and into something meaningful. After a point blank shotgun blast to his chest, Casey feels alive.

That's kind of an improvement, he thinks. *I'll take it.*

Hangar 77

It's a dump. Casey pulls into the parking lot of the address on his business card and double checks the driving directions he printed off the internet the night before. A two story building with brown wood panel shingle-like exterior, moss growing on it in spots. Not even unassuming pinkish stucco like his condo or his old office, just this relic from the mid-1960s or early 1970s.

It's not even a Hangar.

It looks like someplace old people go to die. The external steps creak as he walks up to the second floor. The front door is locked. From the other side of the door a girl's voice says, "Swipe it."

Babb didn't give him an electronic key thingy like his old office had. He stares at the door, jiggling the handle.

The door opens and a girl in her early twenties glares at him. "Swipe your card."

She grabs Casey's hand. He's still holding his silverback Hangar 77 card and she motions him to swipe it at the sensor by the knob.

"You're clocked in now. Go see Aaron and Randy down the hall to your left." The girl goes back to her desk, chatting with someone on the other side of the computer screen.

There's a coldness to the hallway he walks down. It doesn't feel like a game development studio. In his previous office they at least put up posters of the games the company shipped. But here, even the overhead lighting fixtures seem strangely hostile.

Then there's the silence. He walks past a few offices. Men and women inside work on their computers, but no one speaks. No fun conversations or joking around, just this heavy seriousness that reminds him of his brief visit to the Child Protective Services building in Santa Rosa when he was seven years old and his grandmother claimed him, taking him into her home, officially signing the papers.

The door is the first thing that catches his eye: white aluminum marked with: 401d. Casey doesn't know if he should knock or just walk in. He opts to knock. Two voices beckon him inside.

"So this is Him?" one of the men inside asks. "Not what I was expecting, but if Babb says this is the Chosen One, so be it."

Casey stands there, wide eyed, like the deer he almost hit a month ago on the freeway.

The two men laugh at Casey's silence.

"I love doing that," the same man says with a grin. "In that brief flash, we see your shock, processing the words, and then the brief joy of you imagining you can fly around superfast and doing instant kung fu moves. Sorry man, I couldn't resist. I'm Aaron, by the way. This is Randy."

Aaron shakes Casey's hand while Randy goes behind a desk and starts digging in a drawer. Aaron's hand is cool compared to Casey's clammy paw.

Randy hands Casey a binder and says, "You don't have to read this. It's just corporate ethics nonsense legal drew up. This book will not teach you anything meaningful."

Casey looks around, trying to get his bearings. *What is this place? What are they expecting of me, and what kind of training will I need to do the job Babb reassigned me to do?*

Randy takes the binder back. "There, your training is complete."

My what?

Aaron leads Casey to a cheap plastic table with a PC and monitor. Plugged into the workstation is a standard game controller, no different from his previous game testing station. Next to the monitor are headphones, and a pen and paper for taking notes. Casey sits down at the desk as Aaron boots up the workstation before returning to the supervisor's desk.

Casey looks around at the small staff of mostly quiet kids his age. All unassuming, with no distinguishing features or personality quirks. Aaron, in a prior life, was a Viking god with his thick red hair and bushy beard. Randy, Korean and quiet, seems to have a sort of competitive friendship with Aaron.

On the other side of the plastic table is a Native American guy with glasses, consumed with whatever he's playing. Another tester sits beside Casey, one table over, with a nice window view of the parking lot. He looks over at Casey and says, "Hi, I'm Doug. Don't worry… you'll get the hang of all of this. Just don't get annoying and all philosophical about what this all means. That's just a quick way to early termination if you lose focus of the task at hand. Trust me, I've seen it happen several times this month."

Then it all pours into Casey, clearly and concisely. Upon placing his hands on that magic binder Randy made him hold, his brain processed newly acquired information in a flash—downloaded into his head.

This world is a simulation. No different from the games he play-tested down the road.

What's the purpose of the simulation? Nobody knows.

What's out there? Nobody knows.

Is there a God? Are we reporting issues to God?

Is there a tentacle alien up there laughing at the DB entries?

Is the human race enslaved by sentient robot AIs?

In his head, an intentionally designed peaceful voice speaks to him. "Casey, employee CA-0451, you have been deemed mentally qualified by Supervisor Babb for transfer to Hangar 77. Your task is to enter the simulation with eyes wide opened and report any critical bugs or exploits within the system, to be approved by your immediate supervisors in the DB. Upon which these reported issues will be addressed and fixed, and then you will regress the bugs, verifying the issues are resolved and pose no threat to the simulation."

"Casey, employee CA-0451, if you are found to be withholding bugs or exploits in the simulation for personal gain, you will be dealt with severely. The preservation of the simulation is the upmost priority. Do you accept this agreement?"

"Um..."

"Casey, employee CA-0451, thank you for accepting the terms of employment. Welcome to Hangar 77. Have a great day!"

Doug looks over at Casey, whose eyes are still glazed over from the software flash, and chuckles. "What, um, who, uh? What was your answer to the End User License Agreement?"

"Um..." Casey answers.

"Me too. Only one person answered 'yes.' Him." Doug tips his head at the Native American guy who's petting his dog.

We can bring dogs to work?

"Just a quick tip," Doug adds. "If you want to get a head start on how this all works, go alt-tab out of the sim and read the latest DB entries. You'll get a sense of how to write bugs for our overlords and what they're looking for. Pay close attention to the dev notes if some of the bugs require more info or are denied." Doug turns around and goes back to his game.

Before Casey can decide where to start, the white aluminum door busts open. "Boom, I told you god damned people. Did you listen? No, you did not listen. But I, the maestro of showstoppers, got another one."

Doug rolls his eyes. The Native American remains focused on his testing plan. Casey eyes the loud-mouthed, red-haired Irishman.

"Newbie, hey, I'm Franky. Whatever."

Franky sits down next to Aaron and Randy. Casey turns back to his station as he listens to the conversation behind him.

"See, I saw it," Franky continues. "I knew it. I went out there, and I f-ing did it, man. I did it. Do you see people knocking out the bugs I do? No. You all should be so lucky to have me. I could game this system. I could exploit it, and I'd run this town."

"And then they'd find out," Aaron replies, "the system would self-correct, and you'd be drooling down at the psych ward or maybe get respawned as a dandelion."

Oh my God, really, I don't want to be a garden weed. That's just crazy.

"Whatevs, brodog. I did it. Do you want to know how many times?" Franky asks, but doesn't wait for an answer. "One hundred and sixty-eight times. The first nineteen times I couldn't stop from laughing; it was the funniest shizz I ever saw. Seriously, it's better in real life. Every time that dumb stupid cat makes the jump, it misses. We wouldn't have known about it until the guy uploaded the video. So this cat, and possibly the whole species of felines, have infinite lives. This system cannot function with immortal animals running around out there. I punched it in the DB; you just need to approve it. What do you think? Nine? Nine sounds like a good number for them."

Aaron looks over the bug and reads the steps to reproduce it. He has more questions about the severity and impact. The little bell chimes before he approves it. Randy beat him to it and approved its entry to the DB.

"Newbie," Franky says, "If you want to learn from the master, read my entries for the past few months."

Franky gets up and leaves. Casey wonders if he can leave too. It's not time for break or lunch yet, but maybe this job allows that kind of freedom.

Franky opens the white aluminum door, turns to Casey, and says, "There, my work here is done. Bye suckas."

It's just then Casey notices the door doesn't lead to the hallway he walked through earlier but a black void of darkness. Franky doesn't realize this until after he's stepped through. "Oh, what the…? Nooooooooooooooooooo…"

The door closes behind Franky. Aaron runs to open it, but it's just the hallway—and no Franky. "Not again."

Doug snickers. "That's why you look through doors before you step through them."

Casey asks, "Where'd he go?"

"We honestly don't know," Doug replies. "*Everyone* has been trying to reproduce that bug. Not just this office, but every district on every continent."

There's more than one office? How big is this operation? How big is the simulation?

"We've tried throwing recording and transmitting devices into it. Nothing comes back. Once it goes into the void, it's just gone."

Casey stares at the white aluminum door. Even if that red haired douche didn't make a great first impression, he's still a human being with family.

"No," Doug replies, "he doesn't have any family. None of us do. No next of kin, no close friends… It's why we were chosen. Kind of expendable when the simulation bugs chew us up and swallow us whole, just like you saw now."

I'm not expendable. Natalie would miss me, right?

Casey has been on his own for four years—four years since his grandmother peacefully passed in her sleep. Casey inherited the condo. He hit a rough patch for a few months, but then Natalie moved next door, and they've been sort of friends since.

"You really should start with the DB or start the simulation," Doug advises. "Sure, this job is a little bit different than most, but they still want good solid bug entries from you." Doug gets up, opens the door, ensures the hallway is there, then leaves to get snacks or a trip to the bathroom—he didn't say.

All of this is overwhelming, and Casey doesn't know where to start. Where do you start when you learn you can control an avatar of yourself living in a world where your goal is to break the rules of reality and report the bugs into a database like an entry level grunt?

Casey picks up the controller, presses buttons to get past the legal screens indicating he cannot violate his non-disclosure agreement and tell anyone about any of this.

At first, it's an unassuming start screen showing the North Bay in the background, the dry hills of Santa Rosa, the camera in ambient mode panning around showing video game-ified avatars of real people living their lives.

Casey presses start and pain ripples along the side of his middle finger. "What? What just happened?" Casey looks at the tiny speck of blood coming out of his right middle finger. That was like getting poked with a diabetic lancet. *Is that even sanitary? Who else got poked with the needle hidden in that controller?* Nobody answers his unspoken questions. Doug still hasn't returned.

Casey figures the hardware needed a sample of his DNA to bring his own avatar into the game, some protection that only he would be capable of driving himself in the game world. Nobody could just pick up his controller when he went to lunch and ruin his life. Using the dual analog controls, Casey pans the camera around and finds himself in a familiar place. His home, an hour north in Santa Rosa, California. Casey looks around his desk, taking his hands off the controller. The simulation goes to a pause screen. After putting the headphones on he sees it.

Wait, what? What's this?

Playing video games his whole life, Casey has long ago grown numb to standard pause or character screens. Where most games present options for configuring controls, adjusting sound or graphics settings, and basic saving and loading functions, this pause screen is different. In the middle of the screen is a digitized avatar of Casey. His brown hair, his glasses, the slight belly, and hunched posture. Around this avatar are stats, not any different from the roleplaying games he enjoys in his free time.

Next to his head is a number indicating Intelligence: 329. Strength: 108, by his flexing arms. Agility: 87, by his feet. At his mouth, Charisma: 50, and Luck: 413.

Come on, I'm stronger and nimbler than that; these numbers must be wrong.

In a box in the upper right is his current accumulated wealth, the property he owns (the condo valued at $430,000 and the cabin in the woods valued at $42,000), funds in his retirement account ($29,679), and saved income in his credit union account ($6709). A figure indicates his debt at the moment: $4878 in credit card bills he's slowly paying off, and $14,255 left on his imported hybrid car. In the upper right corner, above the monetary figures, are two easy to understand stats of his current well-being: a smiley face with a question mark over its head, and a heart showing he has 978 health points (HP) out of 1000.

Wait, why is my HP not at 100%, and how can I fix that?

At the bottom right corner of the screen is a Perks and Active Abilities section, both blank. Casey's stomach growls, and his mind turns to the sandwich in his tote bag. The pause screen updates and a fork and plate icon appears next to the smiley face icon. Casey opens his tote bag, grabs his chicken sandwich, and eats it.

Hey, no eating at your workstation," Randy blurts out.

Aaron smacks Randy's arm. The fork and plate icon disappears. Casey then sees the HP change from 978 to 985.

This is just crazy. I am not a video game character. I'm more than just this avatar in this screen. Bu… this is kind of neat. Can I improve myself and these figures?

What if I start going to the gym on the way home, or eating better and not grabbing fast food as much? How do I get that Charisma stat higher? If I do actions in the game to improve my character avatar, does that sync up with me, here right now, in this office?

There's only one way to find out, so Casey picks up the controller.

The condo can use some cleaning. This is kind of embarrassing; it didn't look this messy when he left. Driving his virtual self, Casey then proceeds to load the dishwasher, straighten out his vinyl collection, and put his socks in the laundry hamper. When getting home from work, he developed this habit of taking off his shoes then squiggling off his socks next to the cactus plant by the door. Normally he would take the pile of sweaty socks on the way to the basement laundry machines at the end of the week. Now, conscious that his coworkers might see any sensitive bits of his home life, he knows he should straighten everything up.

Aaron chuckles, "Five bucks, Randy. He cleaned his place up."

Wait... what? They're watching me? "Are you guys watching me?"

Randy answers, "Yep, we can tap into your livestream to see what you guys are up to. Don't worry; we don't watch when you go to the bathroom, shower, or anything naked. That's against company policy. We can only see everything if you're holding the controller."

The suite now clean and mostly respectable, no more sock shrine for anyone to see, Casey leaves his place. It strikes him how intuitive the control scheme is for navigating. Panning the camera and basic movement work just like *Hooker Killer 7: Cash Back Edition*, the open world sandbox game the company made millions selling.

On the way to the elevator, he discovers the run button and mashes it to go full on sprinting. Casey doesn't even make it to the end of the hallway before getting virtually winded, and his avatar stops and vomits on the carpet. Randy laughs loudly behind him.

Casey, using cleaning supplies from his apartment, cleans up his mess then brushes his character's teeth in the bathroom, and remembers to use mouthwash before leaving.

Okay, no running, not now, until he builds up some stamina. Casey needs to go full on montage mode first, but not today, he thinks. *God, I'm referring to myself in the third person, but it kind of applies, so that's okay.*

Just as the elevator door is about to close, a small corgi runs in, and then a hand interrupts the closing function.

"Hi. How are you doing, Casey?" It's Natalie. She hooks the leash up to her dog, waiting for him to answer.

Casey, frozen, just stares at the responses on screen. *Oh my God, what are these answers? None of this makes sense.*

Desperate, he looks for a chat microphone so he can speak, but he can't find one. Instead, on the screen are four face buttons color coded to vague replies that are horrifyingly not context sensitive to her question:

Green—I hafta go to the pee pee.

Blue—No, I'm done talking to you, sucka.

Yellow—Will you marry me? I love you so much.

Red—

Relief settles in after pressing the red button. His avatar bends down and pets the dog, but he remains silent.

Natalie talks about taking Maurice to the vet for a checkup and picking up books at the library. She asks why he isn't at work right now.

Red button again, petting animation initiated. Aaron laughs. Natalie gives Casey's avatar a weird look and says, "Nice chatting with you." She exits, leaving him alone, idling in the elevator, grateful he didn't mess up his life.

"Tell me that's buggable," Casey complains. "I could have just ruined my personal life, right now. Real life can't be boiled down to just four on screen prompts."

"That's more of a quality of life issue and not a simulation bug," Aaron answers. "It would be flagged as a suggestion bug and end up a low priority issue. Do you really want that to be your first entry in the database?"

Casey shakes his head and sets his avatar walking to the parking lot. He gets into his car, figures out how to turn on the music, and starts driving. He fights every urge to go on an automotive killing spree, mowing down pedestrians on the sidewalks, or finding odd places in Santa Rosa to take stunt jumps with his car. Instead, he drives south down Highway 101. He knows exactly where he wants to go and what he wants to do. *This would be so much better if there was a fast travel function*, he thinks, *to skip past all this.*

Nope, he is stuck dealing with crappy late morning traffic, the slight bumper to bumper section outside Petaluma, and finally in Novato. On this hour long drive, he wonders what he can say not to seem a complete weirdo the next time he sees Natalie in real life. Maybe a toothache or something?

A jerk contractor won't let him change lanes. Casey barely makes the exit. A few turns here, a left turn there, and finally Casey exits the car, walks up the steps, remembers how to use his employee door key, and walks down the vaguely familiar hallway.

He has to know.

Casey turns the knob and pushes the door open—onto the black void of eternal darkness.

The real life white aluminum door creaks open, and there it is, just nothing. On the screen, Casey sees the same thing from his avatar's perspective.

"Oh my God. What did you do?" Aaron and Randy roll their seats next to him.

Casey explains, "I just wanted to know what would happen if I met my avatar. That was the first thing that came to mind when I loaded up the simulation. I got sidetracked cleaning up my place and figuring out the user interface. But I was curious to see if I could drive down here and meet myself."

Randy goes to the phone to make some excited calls, and Aaron says, "You did good, Casey. Really good. But we need to see if we can repro this."

Aaron has Casey return his virtual self to the car and just wait there.

"Maybe even safer to drive a few exits north and park by the hospital," Aaron thinks aloud. "Is anyone close to work here?"

The Native American guy answers, "Yes," and everyone huddles around his station, watching him drive his car to the building then proceed up the steps, through the doorway, down the hall, and push open the white aluminum door, just as Casey had done it.

Everyone is creeped out by the black hole separating this reality from the virtual one.

"Bug it, now. It's yours," Aaron says proudly.

Beaming, Casey goes to his station and alts out of the simulation to the database program. Then he clicks the button for "new bug entry" to fill out the forms.

```
Bug: User Opens door to a dark void of eternal
darkness.

Severity: A

Reproduction Rate: 100

Steps to Reproduce:

    1. User takes control of their Avatar.

    2. User proceeds from the Avatar starting lo-
    cation and travels to the testing station
```

```
where the User physically is.

3. The intent is for the User to meet their
Avatar self. Observe.
```

Result: Doorway to a void of darkness appears. User unable to enter the room or continue down the critical path.

Impact: Unknown if void of darkness is harmful to User's life. Unknown where void of darkness leads. Void of Darkness doorways pose a threat to all inhabitants within the simulation.

Expected: Opening doors should not result in Users seeing a void of eternal darkness. When opening doors, the User should be able to proceed unhindered to their intended destination.

Once he's submitted the bug to the database, everyone shakes Casey's hand. Randy is quick to approve it for review by the higher-ups.

Doug returns, wondering what all the commotion is about. "Wait, you solved the black door problem on your first day? Wow. Just wow, dude."

Before Casey can pick up his controller, a message pops up via his inbox: See Babb Now.

Should I be wearing a bullet proof vest? And is Babb in this building too? I thought he was at the other building down the road.

"You can find Babb in the basement," Randy informs him.

Casey looks before stepping through the aluminum door to the hallway, and again when stepping on then stepping off the elevator. Then he starts to think the basement might not be in the basement. It's actually physically impossible. Hangar 77 doesn't even have a basement, given it's a two story complex.

Maybe the elevator is some kind of portal that leads to wherever management resides in this simulation, Casey wonders.

"You've been busy, haven't you? It's not even lunchtime, and you've already figured out steps to repro the bug all our international branches have been working on solving the past few months. So, what do you want? Do you want a raise? A car? I can get you a monkey. Don't answer. Whenever you're ready, you can return here to cash in the blank check you just wrote yourself."

Casey returns to the office and waiting on his desk is a test plan. Looking around, he notices everyone received one from the supervisors, and he's grateful for this structured testing.

He has no idea what he can do to follow up his very first bug. The rest of his day is spent watching paint dry, literally. Each and every sample in stock and available at the nearest hardware store.

Casey painstakingly documents each different shade that successfully had the solvent evaporate, leaving color material on the surface. Test plan based QA is always tedious, but from time to time, the methodical obsessive-compulsive approach reveals bugs waiting to be found.

Before leaving for the day, Casey punches in a short, quick and easy bug, detailing how the color yellow doesn't dry in paint form. In the database, he noted other bugs his coworkers had written: "Turtles move at zero frames per second; they are inanimate objects." And, "Fresh water fish are indestructible when taken out of water."

Before the commute home, Casey goes to the bathroom to take care of some business. Upon entering, he begins rethinking that idea. He can hear someone suggestively grunting in one of the stalls.

"Dude, not cool, man. This is a place of business," Doug says after following Casey into the men's room.

"It's not what you think. Can you help me, please?" an embarrassed voice replies.

Casey and Doug poke the stall door open and see him on the floor, wrapped behind the toilet and pipes.

"How'd you get back there, guy?" Casey says as he moves to the next stall to push the young man's feet while Doug pulls the other half at the arms.

Free, the man says as he walks out, "Six people came and went. Six. And only two stopped to help me. Thanks."

They didn't even get his name.

Casey asks Doug about the turtle bug.

"Yeah, my test plan was taking various aquatic creatures out of the water and seeing if they were indestructible. I'm still not done. I'll need to figure out how to get dolphins and sharks the next time the test plans get distributed," Doug answers as he wipes his hands with a paper towel.

"If things are like how they were at my old job..." Casey says, thinking out loud "What that guy was doing isn't a bug, is it? Intentionally getting stuck in world geometry, especially like that... The devs would note that's not a bug."

"Yeah, some people who are desperate for entries resort to that. Odd gimme bugs to pad the numbers. That's the worst thing you can do is waste a devs time and consciously know you're doing that," Doug replies. "Well, see you tomorrow, man."

* * *

Natalie comes out of the elevator just as Casey gets home. He wants to explain his odd behavior, but is torn about how to do it without breaking his NDA.

Casey doesn't get the chance to explain. She keeps walking past him before he can say a word. So instead, he turns away to check his mailbox and finds it empty, just like the day before.

Exiting the elevator on his floor, he begins walking down the hall to his place. He's momentarily alarmed by the faint stain where he got sick earlier in the morning. *So simulation actions do impact the real world.*

He kind of suspected it, but now he has physical confirmation of that fact.

If I puke in the video game, I puke in real life.

It occurs to him that it would be nice if someone at work would explain how everything works, instead of just letting him discover all this on his own.

After eating a light chicken salad, Casey consciously goes out and exercises. Not enough to warrant a training montage, but a slight jog that lasts a block before he breaks down to speed walking—for four thousand steps according to his pedometer.

On his way home, he stops at a bus stop bench and watches life pass him by, observing people getting on and off the bus across the street, pedestrians and bicyclists going about their business. First there are two, then there are three, after that five, then seven, and eleven more birds land on the powerline across the street.

Huh, I wonder if that's in the DB. I could bug that.

Nope, stop working, Casey. It's your time. Worry about work when you're at work.

Over

The next day, Casey discovers his yellow paint bug was flagged by a nameless dev on the other side of the screen: `Need More Info`. Thankfully, a simple question that won't take too long to address. But in his haste to punch in the bug before the end of the day, he fails to specify if the paint is water or oil based. Five minutes later, he's notified, once more by email, that his bug was fixed and needed to be regressed.

Casey goes through the motions of going to the hardware store, buying the same brand of yellow paint, and waiting for it to dry before updating its status to `Fix Verified` in the database, just in time before the crew goes out for lunch.

The nearby restaurant sells burritos the size of a small baby for five bucks. *This will not help me get in shape.*

"I dare you to eat the whole thing," Doug says as he dives into a smaller pair of soft tacos. "Did you go out and try to run a marathon last night?"

Casey nods.

"That won't work. Everyone does that after their first day. I saw how tender your walking was when you came in."

Casey sadly notes his pause screen numbers hadn't changed at all when he checked them first thing in the morning.

"Keep at it; it'll get there if you keep at it. Nothing happens overnight," Doug reassures him. "So what do you say? Can you eat all this burrito before lunch is up?"

At first, Casey is hesitant to take the dare. He doesn't want to let his new coworkers think he's susceptible to childish suggestion, or worse: a pig. Except he's starving.

He skipped breakfast, hoping it would help his physical development, but now, his stomach is growling. The first quarter of the burrito has the most delicious blend of beans, Spanish rice, beef, and sour cream he's ever had. Halfway, he considers stopping, but he doesn't feel sick or full. By the time everyone is leaving a tip on the table, he's done.

Doug whistles and says, "Man, you must have been hungry. Don't get sick in my car on the way back—or just warn me if you are."

* * *

Belly now full, fighting the urge to burp, Casey sits down at his workstation and nods to the Native American, who skipped lunch. "You don't say much," Casey notes.

"Nope, not really. Check your pause screen," the Native American replies before taking his dog out to do its business.

Casey grabs hold of the controller, braces himself for the needle's poke, and is quickly synced to the simulation. He enters the pause screen.

His general physical attributes haven't changed, but his HP is eight points higher than what it was before lunch. In the bottom right corner of the screen is an icon of a bear hibernating with a smiley face. He moves the cursor with the controller to highlight it for more information: `Mmmmetabolism—User doesn't have to eat for 7 days (6.99 days remaining)`

Casey points to the screen as Doug walks by. "You're welcome," Doug says. "Doing certain things here and there grant you temporary bonuses. There's a page on the internal office website listing some of the stuff we've been finding. These aren't bugs or exploits, just odd perks of being a tester meant to help facilitate the work we do. I'll send you the link."

```
Milk + orange juice = fireproof // 1 whole Bebe
Grande = 7d no eats lol // static shock via cat
hair = 1-minute consequence free crime spree*
// cross-eyed for 1 minutes = night vision for
```

5 minutes

He thought there would be more. There has to be more. And just how do you get a static shock from a cat?

"What's the asterisks for?" Casey asks Doug as he closes his browser to get back to testing.

"Someone deleted the footnote? *Guys*, not cool. If you go on a crime spree and kill or maim people or do crazy property damage, you have ten minutes to write a related bug in the DB or the real cops will come and take you away. We usually let the major cities handle crime and violence testing; we're all just chill people here on the best coast."

* * *

Avatar Casey wanders around town for the next couple hours, bird watching—first to see if they still group up in prime numbers, then to figure out if it's one species of bird or all of them. He's just about to enter the bug into the database, that *Callipepla Californica* cluster in primes, but he does a search and discovers it was entered earlier that morning by Karina, sitting in the far back corner of the room.

The bug that got away, he thinks. *Next time I won't wait.*

He congratulates Karina on the find before trying to figure out what he should test next.

* * *

Next, he goes to the corner market a block from his house to pick up milk and orange juice. He half hoped he'd run across a raging house or apartment fire so he could go all hero and save the day. But instead Casey's avatar just sits on the park bench, consuming the gross liquid combo, and lets matches burn out on his fingertips as he stares at them intensely.

The perks page didn't say how long he'd be fireproof and he doesn't want to find out the hard way.

And he half hopes he'd bump into Natalie, but there's no sign of her today.

* * *

Another trip to the bathroom and the kid from the day before is thanking Aaron for helping him escape from behind the toilet. "I don't know how he gets back there," Aaron says as he dries his hands with the dryer. "They say he's been doing it for a couple of weeks now, but no bugs to show for it."

Casey sitting in the stall is wondering if he'd still be regular after eating that huge burrito.

Plop.

No splashback, thank you.

So far, so good.

When a couple random guys enter, laughing about how it rains blood on Thursdays in San Jose, Casey goes into stealth mode. If a giant, lumbering T-rex were to come along, it wouldn't eat him.

That movie scene terrified him for the longest time.

The roll of toilet paper is annoyingly orientated under style, not over, and it takes him a few seconds longer to wad up a bundle to wipe. He instantly knows something is wrong.

Sandpaper. The toilet paper feels like coarse sandpaper on his most sensitive bits, and he stops himself before doing any real damage.

Grateful to find the packaged tissues in his messenger bag are still soft, and there are enough for him to finish, he takes another wad from the mounted toilet roll.

Still coarse and rough. He visually inspects each square from the roll and it seems buttery smooth.

Doug comes in for a post work pit stop of his own before going home.

Casey hands him a wad of toilet paper and says, "Feel this."

Doug takes the wad and rubs it against the top of his arm. "Oww, holy oh my God what the—?" The two stare at Doug's arm, and what resembles a nasty motorcycle accident scrape.

"I know, right? And it almost got me just now in there."

The two check out every roll of toilet paper in the stalls, and catch Karina on her way out. They beg her to check the women's toilet rolls, too.

"Is it the brand of TP? Or ply count?" Doug asks. "Good luck with this, Casey, but I have to go. Check with Aaron if you can do overtime."

* * *

Aaron approves an hour of overtime, no more.

Staying late, Aaron is the only one in the room with Casey. He goes through the database, approving or writing `need more info` tags on the entered bugs, kicking them up the chain or back to the reporter.

Back in the simulation, at his condo, Casey has just returned from the box-mart with various brands of toilet paper. None of the brands when inspected caused his avatar harm or discomfort. He even went so far as to sit down on his own toilet seat to try to recreate that first experience.

Huh.

Against his better judgement, Casey turns the toilet roll backward, from the Over orientation to Under. Casey presses X on the controller and on screen his avatar begins the wiping animation. His virtual self yells out in agony. Aaron perks his head up, and tears stream down digital Casey's cheeks.

I don't want to look. I'll repro this in the real bathroom. Sorry, me, I didn't mean to do that.

Logging out of the simulation, he's relieved his avatar's pain didn't translate into real life pain on his end. But what about the stain he left yesterday?

"Oh, your avatar can sustain injuries without harming you in real life," Aaron explains. "It's a part of testing. But if you do stuff like rearrange your living room or crash your car into a mailbox, that's on you."

Casey returns to the bathroom, back to his stall. Yes, it's his stall now, forever and always until the end of time.

These corporate toilet roll holders are annoying to deal with, but finally he re-orientates the toilet roll from the Under position to the Over position. No more sandpaper. He tests it again on the other stalls.

Bug: Toilet paper rolls in the Under Orientation become sandpaper

Severity: C

Reproduction Rate: 100

Steps to Reproduce:

1. User proceeds to any bathroom with a hanging toilet roll.

2. If toilet roll is orientated in the Over position, re-orientate the toilet roll to deliver TP in the Under orientation.

3. Observe the texture of the toilet paper.

Result: Toilet paper retrieved from rolls in the Under orientation take on physical qualities of harsh sandpaper.

Impact: Users using Under Orientated toilet paper will cause severe injuries requiring immediate medical attention.

Expected: When Users utilize toilet paper, the surface of the toilet paper should always be smooth, no matter the orientation of the toilet paper being Over or Under.

Aaron approves the bug. "Nice find, you've saved a lot of butts to-day."

Casey laughs.

Just about to get up and leave, Aaron calls him over. "Um, that was quick."

Dev Comment: Humanity did not endure thousands of years of pain, misery, and warfare to be reverted to animals. As a species, we are better than this. Did we not put a man on the moon? Did we not emerge from the muck to become the most dominant species on this planet to be in direct control of our destiny, not once, but twice? Have we lost our way once more, fumbling in the cold dark afraid and lost? I did not survive the 6th extinction, just to let my species lessen itself to the whims of the Undies. No, this will not stand. Either you're an Ovy or you live with your life choices and the searing pain until you get with the program.

Known shippable, will not fix.

"What, just like that?" Casey wonders out loud.

"I'm just like you, man. This is beyond me to fight," Aaron says with a shrug. "That's a dev comment, and he or she seemed pretty passionate about not fixing your bug."

"So there's nothing that can be done?"

Aaron shrugs again. "We can go see Babb, but if you invoke a producer override… Making an enemy with a dev isn't smart."

Casey stands a little straighter and replies, "That could be anybody who finds out the hard and painful way. It was almost me half an hour ago!"

An elevator ride down to the basement.

Casey makes his case that too many people in the world would be physically injured, that the last time a survey was done, 35% preferred the Undy orientation for toilet rolls. That's a lot of people out there getting hurt, a lot of people not knowing why they got hurt or how to avoid injury. That would be 35% of the population questioning the state of the simulation and the underlining rules it abides by.

Babb gets on the phone and reiterates the more pressing points Casey had thought up on the spot. "Grit is currently set to P10. Would you be okay with bumping that up to P2500 for Undies?"

Casey doesn't know what that means. "Can you let me see how that feels first?"

A quick run to the nearest bathroom and it's still too coarse, so Babb asks, "How about P9500?"

Another hotfix patched in and while rough, it's not that different from the cheap stuff in terms of softness, even though the brand used has the nice white bunny rabbits on the packaging. "Can you live with that?" Babb asks Casey, who nods in response.

Some damage was done.

On the way home, the news radio reports that toilet paper manufacturers are blaming disgruntled employees for sabotaging production lines. Class action lawsuits will probably happen, but not too many people got hurt tonight. When Casey gets back home, the first thing he does is put the toilet paper back to the Over position.

* * *

He could get used to not having to eat anymore.

Thirty-five minutes saved not preparing anything, twenty not eating, and another fifteen not cleaning up the pots and pans.

It wasn't until he played the crudely animated mobile game—published by his employers no less—on his phone, where he managed the daily life schedule of a character he spent thirty-five minutes trying to make look like him that he became aware of the passage of time.

Guiding Cassy—thanks autocorrect—through his daily life, he tried to maximize each individual twenty-four hour block of time before his mobile avatar eventually died... or more like ransomed. If he paid the one dollar microtransaction, Cassy would get to live another five years.

Not sure what's worse, that he spent hours playing this life management simulation, having spent $39 ensuring Cassy wouldn't die, or that Casey in real life started structuring his life in a similar fashion not to waste time.

It was only when he did his weekly check in on Cassy to see how he was doing that this would re-trigger his obsessive need to account for every minute, but thankfully, that mentality would disappear, and he could eventually just enjoy farting around, mindlessly playing video games, watching movies, or watching hockey with friends at the local sports bar.

His evening jog is two blocks this time, before being downgraded to a leisurely walk. The pedometer shows six thousand steps.

Casey is about to shower when he hears Natalie's patio door slide shut loudly, and the creepy Russian Mob Guy yells at Natalie through the double paned windows. Casey opens his sliding patio door, and the man just stares at him in angry silence. A mini showdown of glaring ensues, until the Russian Mob Guy with the chain necklaces turns away to light a smoke.

An hour before bedtime, there's a knock on the door.

Casey has just spent the remainder of the night half watching a documentary on Canada's whistling maple spiders.

Opening the door, he finds a smiling Natalie. "Hi neighbor, I know this is kind of cliché, but do you have some sugar I can borrow? I'm making cookies for tomorrow, but ran out, or, well, Maurice ruined it."

Casey goes to the kitchen and scoops up a cup of sugar.

"Eww, what the heck are you watching?"

"At my job, there's this guy from Canada, and he was talking about their spiders," Casey explains. "Did you know the Canadian Whistling Maple spider lives in evergreen trees, stalking their prey jumping from branch to branch, tree to tree, and can take down small rabbits or raccoons? The whistling noise confuses the small animals as it gets closer, from above, and the spiders bite into the spinal column of whatever animal they've targeted to eat."

Natalie is revolted but Casey presses on. "They're endangered, mostly due to logging projects and chemical spraying. You can only find them in zoos or aquariums now." Casey wants to ask if she's all right with the Russian Mob guy, but instead says, "Sorry, I was a weirdo the other day and petted your dog in the elevator. It was dental related, and I couldn't talk."

Natalie thanks Casey for the sugar before going back next door. Before leaving she says, "It's funny; I was just watching a nature special on South America's koala population. Go check that out instead of these creepy spiders, man."

On Casey's TV, a falling spider decapitates a humming bird.

Natalie declares, "I am never going to Canada. Ever."

Ay Caramba!

"New guy, your plate is light. These are yours, now," Randy says, smiling as he drops a stack of printed bug sheets on Casey's desk, bugs written up by the red haired Irish douche, Franky.

It all kind of makes sense they would be passed on; it's not as if Franky will get to do them after stepping into the eternal void of darkness.

"Not all, I got the other half," says the Native American on the other side of Casey's desk. The dog barks in agreement.

Casey sighs. Time to get through all of them, so he can start finding his own bugs.

Bug: Stupid Users unable to die when drowning in fresh water

Severity: A

Reproduction Rate: 90

Steps to Reproduce:

1. User pretends to act like a mongoloid knuckle dragger, who hasn't mastered the life essential skill of swimming.

2. Idiot makes his way to a fresh body of water, not a chlorine treated pool or any of the salt water oceans.

3. Moron drowns themselves in water, not being able to breathe.

Result: User is caught in a conflicting loop, where the simulation is triggering the drowning animation, sapping life points from the User, but is also gaining life points from the mere act of ingesting fresh water.

Impact: Users experience a soft-crash in the operating system, unable to progress down the critical life path. Users are perpetually stuck in a drowning animation loop that doesn't result in death. Only with outside intervention from a life guard or a random passerby does the infinite loop terminate.

Expected: When users experience the drowning animation, they should lose life health points until death occurs. Users should not be regenerating life health points during the drowning animation sequence.

Notes: If a fresh body of water is not available, the User can drown himself in the toilet or a full bathtub as an alternative. Repro rate marked 90% due to occasional rescue attempts by good Samaritans.

Dev note: Health point loss when in the drowning animation will remain at -10 per second. Health points gained when ingesting fresh water is now at +3 per drink. A hard cap of 2 liters a day is now in place (half a gallon for you Imperial system weirdos); anything over that cap doesn't impact health gain. Going beyond 6 liters of water in a few hours will be fatal to Users. Make sure to test that during regression.

It's always interesting seeing how other testers write out their bugs, but it's more insightful seeing how the developers attach notes when sending them back down the pipeline with their solutions, or how they opted to fix them. The first attempt at drowning in the Russian River near Healdsburg is a bust; some helpful transients pull Casey out of the water. The same thing happens when he drives to Howarth Park and an elderly couple in a canoe fish him out of the lake. Both times, he thanks his rescuers for being good, decent people.

I am not drowning myself in my toilet.

Tub full, he wonders if he should write some bad poetry before diving in. He just stands there, in front of the place where he is going to drown and die.

Or do I have to die?

He could just watch his health meter sap by the second and pull out before death occurs. The main sticking point is that the amount of health depleted is greater than life points gained.

Suicide isn't an option. There's always a way.

Except he would later have to consume six liters of water for the second half of regressing this particular bug, so he will die, as deemed necessary by the developer.

I don't want to die. I like my life. Why do I have to do this?

"Get in the tub, Casey. You have other regressions to do," Randy says from behind his desk.

Disrobing and wearing only his swimming trunks, Casey's avatar steps into the warm tub of water. It takes him a while to figure out what controller button combination will submerge him underwater. Before, at the lake and the river, he just walked forward until he hit the deep end. And this is no video game. He's drowned before in other video action games. He's all too familiar with that panicky "time's running out, gotta find an air bubble" music, which isn't playing right now. If that music cue was playing, it would make this easier.

His virtual self splashes around as Casey holds down the button. The health bar steadily depletes until the body—his body—is motionless in the tub.

"Jeebus, what did I just do?"

On screen text appears: `You died lol. Get good n00b.`

Is this what awaits me when I die? A snarky judgmental text string?

Casey puts down the controller to grab a soda from the hallway. "It's just a simulation. You didn't die. You're still here," Aaron says, following Casey as he chooses a diet pop. "You didn't commit suicide, either. None of that was real. My first death? I had to fight a bear. I drove down to the zoo in the city, climbed the rails, and had to get one good punch in the nose of the grizzly.

"Before it was patched, if you managed to punch it in the nose it would explode into a pile of gold doubloons. People caught onto this as a way to cheat the system and get super rich. With thirty-three health remaining, I finally got a punch in. It stunned the bear briefly, but it just thrashed me and threw my dead corpse against a concrete wall.

"It didn't take long for people to discover the exploit was closed, but the grizzly population is not what it once was."

Casey is mildly comforted.

"The messed up thing about that was," Aaron finished, "after the bear won the fight, it got up on its two feet and did a weird celebratory strut in its habitat: 'Who's the man, I'm the man.' Jerk bear didn't have to rub it in."

Returning to his desk, he braces himself for the needle poke once more. The simulation idled at the title attract screen. As if nothing grim had happened, Casey is surprised to see himself wake up out of bed, happy and chipper. There's no trace of a dead body in the tub; he technically respawned in his bed for his next adventure.

The next phase of regression takes a little bit longer as he voluntarily induces water intoxication. He watches his virtual self keel over and die on the living room floor, just as the mandatory lunch break in his office is about to start.

Okay, looks like this bug is fix verified.

Casey opens the database entry and marks the bug as closed, pending approval by his supervisors.

Growling.

Why is my stomach growling?

* * *

The three of them sit outside the restaurant waiting for their orders. Casey is watching freeway traffic. Doug is texting his girlfriend. The Native American is feeding his dog treats from his coat pocket.

"Danny. My name is Danny. Sorry I never mentioned it before. Did you just go this whole time calling me 'the Native American'?" Danny pets his dog on the head. "I thought you had a Baby Grande yesterday."

Stomach growling even louder, Casey replies, "I thought so, too. I'm starving, but no baby-sized burrito today, just a normal one."

The waiter arrives with their lunches on a tray. Doug is starting on his plate of nachos. Danny the Native American is trying out enchiladas. Casey, who doesn't like to change things up, opted for a small beef burrito. He's been looking forward to this moment, unwrapping the burrito from the tight foil.

"What's wrong?" asks Danny.

The two stare at Casey as his face goes through the motions of confusion, betrayal, and absolute disgust, soon followed by him spitting the first bite out onto the tray.

"Gentlemen don't cuss," his grandmother said when she washed his mouth out with soap when he was nine years old, a bad word he heard on the television regretfully repeated. The soft flour tortilla, a lump of sour cream, the perfect brown strands of fried beef—none of which he can taste, just the awful memory of never swearing burned onto his taste buds. He can't even wash it down with soda, that invasive soap taste. His sinuses burn. It feels like someone has poured chlorine up his nose.

He goes to the bathroom to keep obsessively trying to spit out whatever he just ate. He rubs his tongue with his fingers trying to scrape it off, but nothing helps.

Is this a bug? This is the same burrito I ate last time...

Nothing seems to have changed, and he confirms that with the waiter on his way back to the table.

"Can either of you try my burrito?"

The two stare at it hesitantly before Doug says, "I don't know, man. Did you remember to tip yesterday? Maybe you pissed off the staff."

Casey did tip; he always tips.

Danny uses a plastic fork and scoops a chunk of the burrito for a quick bite. "This is pretty good. I should have ordered this."

Casey takes another bite. The intensity is even worse the second time. And just like the first time he took a shot of gin in college, his nose starts bleeding. "Fairy godmother in the Alps. Son of a squid. Aardvark melon farmers!"

After returning from the bathroom to treat his bloody nose and scrub his tongue again, he sits down, staring at what should have been a delicious lunch. A part of him wants to eat through the vileness. He's starving. Maybe he can get used to it—build up immunity.

No, maybe he can figure this out.

Casey starts dissecting the burrito like he was back in high school biology. Each ingredient is separated and cataloged on the tray to be taste tested. It isn't the flour shell, nor the beef. He satiates his hunger by eating those after determining they haven't been contaminated by either the sour cream or the greens. The Spanish rice is safe, too, so he scoops some up with the tortilla chips and enjoys that.

It has to be one of the greens stuffed in the center doused with sour cream. The sour cream doesn't trigger a violent reaction. Down to the greens, it becomes clear it wasn't the sliced lettuce. There's just this weird parsley looking green he's never seen before, but ignorantly enjoyed until today. Doug and Danny don't know what it is either. The waiter arrives to pick up the tray and tip. He stares at Casey, wondering what's going on.

"Do you know what this is?" Casey asks, holding up the green leafy thing.

"Cilantro."

After some begging, Casey convinces Doug to take a bite of the cilantro too, but he doesn't seem bothered by it one bit. Both of them advise him to do more research before bugging it. He can't just punch it into the database with a vague repro rate, not knowing who it affects, or why it triggered that reaction in him, starting today. It would just get kicked back with a `need more info` tag.

After dropping Doug off at the office, Danny and Casey get the okay to do real world regressions for the last two open bugs Franky had entered. Driving, Casey can still taste the phantom sensation of the cilantro on his tongue.

"So what's not supposed to be happening right now?" Casey asks.

Danny reads through the steps to repro and replies, "Before, cars would come out of the mall over there, they would hit this speed bump, and bunny hop over the freeway into that empty baseball field. The physics simulation wasn't calculating properly on this one spot."

After safely watching other cars drive over the bump, for the sake of testing it, they drive over the speed bump, hoping the car won't be launched into the sky.

Danny marks the bug `Fix Verified` with his pen.

They save the best for last.

Parked outside an apartment complex, not any different from Casey's condo, they wait until a phone call from Randy tells them the hotfix went live.

"I don't know; this doesn't seem so hilarious from down here," Danny says, disappointed.

One.

Two.

Three.

Four.

Five.

Six.

"I feel bad for the owner."

Seven.

"If only they knew."

Eight.

"Here we go."

The cat boldly walks along the patio rails, still trying to land the jump. Nobody recording or watching anymore, not when they can just watch the video online. The cat jumps from its balcony to the next, trying to reach the other side.

It must have been a long fall for the cat, but from the parked car, it's over fast. The two wince at the impact on the concrete surface.

"We should check, just to be sure," Casey says.

"No, you go check. It's your bug. Blood doesn't agree with me."

Casey exits the car and approaches the once famous internet cat.

"Sorry, kitty, but you just burned through your nine lives."

He puts on his sun glasses and walks back to the car. "Yeah, `Fix Verified`."

* * *

I don't know if I can live in a world where I can never enjoy burritos again.

A tinge of sadness envelops him as he logs back into the simulation. Right away, he notices something off about his life health bar. Before it was full green, but now, at the tip end, 20% was a grey block with red crisscross lines.

In the pause menu, he verifies his overall health points, which used to be 1000 maximum, is now 800.

"I just lost two hundred health points," he says, hoping someone will answer.

The other attributes are unchanged. The sleeping bear icon for the perk `Mmmmetabolism` is gone. Casey now has to go back to eating food like a normal person again. In its place is a low res graphic of a pink bar of soap. He selects it and there's a new perk applied to him, `Corianders Syndrome`. There's no countdown timer or indicator of when it will expire, like the food or night vision perks.

Am I diseased now, what do I have? Casey highlights the icon and a tooltip pops up on screen: `Do you see what happens, Casey? Do you see what happens?`

"Don't worry, man, you'll go back to a thousand health at midnight when the system resets," Doug thankfully says. *But what about this perk?* "Whoa, you got a new perk, what does it do? How'd you get it? Go put it on the perks page if you know how."

The sheen of the new job feels like it's wearing off now. A bad lunch, a whole day wasted regressing someone else's bugs, and not one entry in the database to call his own.

Is he going to start crawling behind the toilet bowl like that other kid now? Blindly flailing about, trying to find a glitch in the system to put his name on.

The day ends, he logs off, and walks to his car in the parking lot, dreading the extended commute home. On the windshield is a chocolate chip cookie protected by clingy plastic food wrap. A purple 70s muscle car honks, pulling up behind his hybrid.

"You looked like you could use a cookie. Race you home!"

Natalie?

Before he can reply, she's already on her way to Highway 101 north-bound.

Cat.exe

"New guy, your plate is light. These are yours, now," Randy says, smiling as he drops a stack of printed bug sheets on Casey's desk, bugs written up by the red haired Irish douche, Franky.

Um, why does this seem familiar?

"I thought this guy was supposed to be good?" Casey says. Looking at the rest of Franky's workload. "Where are the good bugs?

Doug answers, "That guy was a hack. If he wasn't scouring the internet for trending glitch videos, like the cat bug, or piggybacking off stuff we'd find in the office, he'd do those lazy pedantic 'this object isn't rendering right' issues."

Other people start chiming in on how he would latch onto their bugs, copy and paste the steps to reproduce, and then add on an extra step or two to make a bug his own. This was made worse when devs would prioritize his bugs over the ones he hijacked.

Poor Franky, even in death he wasn't loved or missed.

This job isn't all that bad, Casey thinks. He'd figured that by now the new job sheen would be wearing off, and he'd fall back into the rut of doing the work, going home, and starting anew the next day. *Anew... who uses words like that?*

For lunch, the guys decided to try the Puerto Rican sandwich place one exit south on the freeway.

Doug announces, "Toilet guy is gone now."

Fired? Nobody knows. His station has been sanitized, and he's not wrapped around the toilet bowl in the stall where they would usually find him.

Danny says, "I warned him. Trying to make something of nothing is a quick way to get you nowhere."

"So what happens to people like us when we're let go? There's no way we can go back to normal life after seeing the truth."

The other two don't have an answer for Casey.

Danny finally answers, "It's rare for people to be let go; most usually die horribly during testing. Maybe they get sent to the farm up north."

"Die horribly? How does that happen if we're in the office and respawn safely in our beds after death?" Casey asks the two, waiting for them to finish swallowing their bites of perfectly made Bistec sandwich and plantains.

Doug smiles and says, "They didn't tell him, obviously."

Danny washes down his food first then adds, "Jury duty. Right now, you're in the training immunity period and still learning the ropes. But once it's been deemed you're ready for real world testing, your name gets put into the pool. The RNG, random name generator, draws a name for each office every week. If you find a jury summons in your mailbox, you have to report to jury duty the following Monday. It's usually Babb who'll give you your field kit and supplies. For that whole week, you do real world testing, report bugs on the company supplied laptop, and try not to die. There are no respawns when you're on jury duty."

Doug adds, "If you don't file enough bugs during that week, you'll be held in contempt of court and jury duty is extended for another full week."

Annoyed, Casey wonders why nobody has really explained anything to him, formally. This whole training week has been just a series of fumbling around in the dark, figuring things out on his own.

* * *

Up, up, down, down, left, right, left, right, B-button, A-button.

"Sorry I didn't show you this earlier in the week. This will help you get up to speed with simulation testing. If you have any questions, I'll be over there," Randy tells Casey.

Which is weird, because Casey, at this point, expected him to be more of a jerk for not trying the universal cheat code of awesome. Casey presses the Start button on his controller and it begins.

```
Welcome <employee id string>! Press the A-button
to acknowledge the on screen prompts. This is your
tutorial guide to getting started as an employee at
<company id string>. Congrats on being selected as
a candidate for Security Operations at <Hangar id
number>. We trust you have met your friendly super-
visors and coworkers. We know how eager you are to
get started and will make this as brief as possible,
so you can get to work as a happy and productive
employee. Press the A-button to acknowledge.
```

What was a faint white pixel amid a sea of black on the monitor grows in size as the camera zooms into a padded white room. Part asylum and part digital lobby with white tiled walls, the room is a 16x16 cubed block.

```
This is you. Aren't you the cutest thing ever? Who
could hate someone as loveable as you?
```

Uh, what? Casey looks at the avatar that has just been spawned into the center of the room. As he stares, the idle animation kicks in and it begins purring. A small white and black kitten is waiting for his user input as the tutorial progresses.

```
So spry, so agile, this world is yours for the tak-
ing. Carpe Diem. Use your left analog stick to move
forward, backward, side to side, and if you're feel-
ing adventurous, diagonally.
```

Casey moves the stick as the cat does its responsive animation routines tied to how hard and soft he utilizes the left analog stick on the controller. The cat can walk slowly or make a quick dash with the flick of his left thumb. He notes that, when lightly touching the stick for slow calculated walking, the animation cues on screen portray the cat stealthily stalking an unseen prey.

Are you sure you weren't a kitty in a former life? You are a natural. Now, with the right analog stick, you can pan the camera around, go ahead now.

Casey complies. Doing a full 360-degree rotation around the cat. When he returns the camera's point of view behind the cat the 16x16 cubic block has been extended and is now a 16x16x64 corridor.

Is a cat not entitled to his bundle of yarn? No, says the parasite; it belongs to me. Go, get it!

A mouse has been spawned a few blocks ahead of the kitten. Casey, using the controller, chases it, gaining ground. An un-textured white block is spawned just before Casey can attack it. The simulation pauses, and the cat is frozen in time.

Press A to jump. Press A to acknowledge this message.

Casey presses the A-button, acknowledging the tutorial prompt. The action resumes, and the cat smashes its head into the solid block, breaking its neck, and dies.

Press A to continue.

The cat is respawned at a checkpoint at the moment the chase began. The white block is spawned in front of the cat avatar once more.

Press A to jump. Press A to acknowledge this message.

Now wise to the finicky nature of acknowledging the prompt, the A-button is pressed twice in succession. The cat jumps over the lethal white block of death. A few blocks ahead, the ground disappears and the mouse jumps over the long gap. Casey presses the jump button once more. The leap isn't long enough, and the cat falls into the hole. The camera zooms in as the cat is fatally impaled on a sharp bed of spikes. The cat respawns once more.

You're a cat, act like one. Press A to jump, then press and hold A to wall run.

Casey acknowledges the prompt, quickly makes the cat jump in the air, and then holds the jump button down to initiate wall running. He lets go of the A-button after clearing the gap. Casey catches up to the mouse, and it is cornered at the end of the corridor with nowhere to go.

As a cat, you have the gift of super reflexes. Press the B-button and any direction with the left analog stick to dodge enemy attacks.

The mouse, desperate, reaches inside its tuft of fur and pulls out a mean looking six-shooter pistol. Casey dodges the gunfire in which time slows down and he can make out the tracer rays of the bullet's trajectory. *Oh man, this is kind of cool.* Casey dodges closer and closer to the mouse.

Use the left or right triggers to attack with your corresponding paws.

Casey, in striking distance, disarms the mouse with the left paw, and then slashes the mouse with its right paw. The mouse starts flailing back in defense.

Press the X-button to finish your prey.

Two incoming punches are dodged, and the cat then bites the head off the mouse, leaving the body gushing spurts of blood all over the clean white floor of the simulation room. The cat spits the mouse's head next to the dead body. The simulation ends, and the camera does a dramatic zoom out, leaving a white pixel amid the sea of darkness on his monitor screen.

I thought this tutorial was going to be more helpful.

The white pixel changes color to a warm yellow, and the camera dramatically zooms into a new simulated room to continue the tutorial. It is much more familiar than the white space he was previously in.

This is your home; there are many like it, but this one is yours. Explore the boundaries of your living space to get acquainted. Press A to continue.

In kitten form, Casey explores his house, amused at the low vantage presentation this point of view offers. Even going so far as to childishly knock over picture frames and books off shelves with his little kitty paws. In secret, Casey has always wanted to be a kitten. To be so full of life, running around quickly with freedom. This was an unspoken desire fulfilled.

As you have previously shown, you are adept at hunting your prey. Not shirking your responsibilities, to do what must be done for the greater good. This life is more than just chasing down pesky rodents and parasites. You are a defender. A silent watcher on the prowl, ever vigilant against the evil that would destroy this world. Press the A-button to accept this truth, or press the B-button to exit back to your pitiful existence, blissfully ignorant of what is out there.

This is a joke right? There's so much not being said. How can I blindly press the A-button, not knowing all the details? This is a weird tutorial.

Who's a good kitty? You're a good kitty, yes you are. Now that you have become familiar with the space in which you live, it is crucial you come to terms with the methods in which to defend yourself and your home from the demons. First, notice your health bar in the top corner. You are low on health. Go to the food tray to enjoy the finest tuna that has been delivered to your home.

Casey goes to the kitchen, near the closet, where he keeps his bulk sugar and rice tucked away. At the floor is a dual food tray with water in one bowl and cat food in the other. The kitten starts eating the food, and the health bar increases.

Food and water is life. When needed, consume them to regain health points. Take note of the lower left portion of the screen. As you have noticed, your claws have lost their edge during your previous battle with the mouse. Go to the nearest couch or scratching post to sharpen them for your next hostile encounter.

There isn't a scratching post in the apartment, so Casey settles on clawing up the far end of his trusty couch.

A good kitty is always prepared. Make sure you have a full bar of health and a fresh pair of claws at your disposal. Your life will depend on it. But it isn't always about offense. Press the top bumper button on your controller to switch your active weapon or skill.

Casey curiously presses the bumper as instructed. What other weapons is a cat capable of dolling out?

Stealth is your best friend now. Do not let others see what you are about to do. Do not compromise your position. Find the nearest entry point into your home. At the doorway or window frame, press the X-button.

What the hell is this? Stop! Stop doing that—that's gross.

This entry point has been marked. Your innate biology protects this entry point from being breached by the demons. Proceed to mark every entry point in the house now. Press A to acknowledge this message.

As instructed, Casey first heads to every window in his condo and marks the territory. Then to the sliding glass door by his balcony. Last, Casey has the little cat pee on the mat by his door.

Good, excellent. You have done your duty and shielded your home from evil. Please be aware this active ward will dissipate every 7 days, so be sure to recast your mark before it expires. Do not try to do this all at once or risk being discovered and punished. Press A to acknowledge.

What evil is out there necessitating such drastic measures? How long does this tutorial go on, and how is this relevant to finding simulation bugs?

Look at that ignorant oaf. He has no idea. No idea at all the service you provide for him. Press and hold the top bumper button on your controller. From the weapon select wheel, switch to the whiskers icon to enter passive mode.

So there are three modes of operation to being a cat? Okay...

Approach your human in a non-threatening manner. If it is lazily lying down on the couch, as they are prone to doing, feel free to jump on top of it.

Casey clumsily has the cat claw its way on the couch. There is something off about how the cat sees his virtual self. Virtual Casey looks slack jawed, drool coming out of his mouth, and his eyes are dead, without emotion. The cat sees his human as some kind of Neanderthal thug. The cat rests on Virtual Casey's large pot belly stomach.

This is crap. There's no way I'm that obese.

Casey looks down at his real stomach just to be sure.

In passive mode, you can nuzzle your human. Press the right analog stick inward to melee the human gently. This is a crucial function as it marks the human with your scent and protects it from the demons when they foolishly leave your home.

Clicking the right analog stick, the cat gently nuzzles Virtual Casey's face with its cheeks. There is an amber glow on the human now. It has been marked and claimed by the kitten.

You are free now to do what you want when your human is out. You can keep practicing your hand-to-hand combat skills, research new lines of biological warfare, or converse with other felines and procreate the species in the event you fall in battle. The demons are always out there, waiting to strike when we least expect it. But you will be ready and waiting to fight back. Who's a good kitty? You are, yes you are! Press A to acknowledge.

The simulation ends, and Casey is returned to the main menu. He looks around, wondering if this is some kind of prank Randy orchestrated.

I'm not going to give him the satisfaction of knowing he messed with me.

Instead, he resumes exploring Santa Rosa, searching for any glitches that he can bug into the database.

Another long, awful commute over, Casey stands outside his doorway, thinking about what to make for dinner. Entering, he looks around. After putting his messenger bag in the closet, he checks out every room and the bathroom then inspects the couch. Disappointed, he had hoped there was a cute little black and white kitten waiting for him when he got home. There wasn't, which thankfully means all those tutorial messages about demons wasn't true. Just the quiet hum of his laptop booting up on the kitchen table to play some music as he makes baked salmon and potatoes for dinner.

This used to be their tradition.

After a good meal was had, the dishes washed, and dining room cleared: a friendly game of who could guess the letters and phrases, as luckier people spun the wheel on TV, winning big cash prizes.

He wonders where his grandmother is tonight. Is there still a heaven? What happens after all this? The game show long over, Casey wakes up from napping on the couch. Turning the TV off in the corner, he sees himself. Actually, he sees the version of himself the cat had seen. An oafish lump lying down, wasting precious time. Carpe Diem.

What's the night version of that?

Carpe Noctem, seize the night.

He has always lived a sheltered life. When he'd go to school, he'd come home and do his homework and then play video games. When he'd go to high school, he'd come home and write computer programs. When he went to college, he'd come home and look after his grandmother. Now, he comes home from work and surfs the internet, while watching television.

Reflecting on the new job, he realizes he's travelled the most he has ever done, searching for bugs in the simulation. He has gone exploring parts of Healdsburg, Santa Rosa, Novato, and San Rafael.

Never in real life.

Being shut in was just so much easier. But now, the bridge is calling him. He's never walked across the Golden Gate Bridge or really explored San Francisco. Casey puts on his shoes and jacket.

Why not? It's the weekend.

Player 2 Has Entered The Game

Why does he get to have all the fun?

Only Babb knows the truth of Natalie's reassignment at this point. He gave her a ring of power. She's trying her best to fit in, but her co-supervisor is this obnoxious twerp. Why so hostile Randy? It must be his way of showing camaraderie or something. He doesn't even know she's under the digital projection of this burly Viking man re-incarnated. While in this office, people see Aaron; it's actually her, Natalie. Roped into working the day shift for the next couple of weeks.

My name is Aaron. I'm a chill dude. People like me, because I'm so bro, I don't even have to say how bro I am. Because I am, bro.

The real Aaron was this anxious mess who was prescribed pills to calm down. A lot of pills; it made his hair red.

The night shift was the best shift. It just worked. People were more relaxed, the building wasn't so hot when the air conditioner would inevitably fail, and reading the database entries from the day shift had the potential to be entertaining, especially when a new employee was brought into the fold. The company ordering free pizzas for dinner was also a bonus; they never did that for the day crew. People cussing their way through the morning and evening commute was a sucker's game. No such problems when work starts at six pm and ends at two am, enjoying the free time until going to sleep at six or seven in the morning as the sun came up.

And now here I am, with these knuckle dragging suckers. I should be the one who gets to visit Australia. Australia, geez, what a mess.

The company finally decided to expand operations and had cherry picked the best to start a new satellite office down under. For too long, the country has been a cesspool of glitches and aberrations. Untested and unchecked by rational thought, abandoned. Maybe it's just too far gone, and this side project of Babb's will fail horribly. A picture of a kangaroo on her phone makes her giggle uncontrollably.

Just what the hell is happening over there? Seriously, what is that thing supposed to be? It's like a deer and a rabbit were the last ones there at closing time and went, "eh, why not?"

"New meat today. Let's screw with him. What do you say?" Randy asks. Casey steps into the white aluminum doorway, nervous.

"So this is Him? He is not what I was expecting, but if Babb says this is the Chosen One, so be it."

This is so mean. Randy is such a dick. But she couldn't help it and laughed at the initiation. She welcomes him and wonders if he notices how cold her hand is when she shakes his.

`Known shippable, will not fix.`

To hell with that nonsense, it *is* a bug. She spent the better part of a week studying biology and how blood gets redirected to the core body organs, causing her hands and every other woman's limbs to get cold. Babb offered to do a producer override, but she's saving her one wish for when she really needs it. Besides, she's seen how vindictive a spurned dev gets when some of her former employees escalated an issue they thought was worth fighting over.

So catty.

Casey finally made it. It took him long enough, but here he was, sitting a few feet away, fumbling through the morning, getting a grasp on things. At least he hasn't had a psychotic break. Not many do. The headhunters have gotten more efficient at picking those who'd accept the truth about the simulation and the testing needed.

Why isn't he doing the code? Everybody does the code. Up, up, down, down, left, right, left, right, B, A.

The two supervisors watch Casey get settled in. Maybe he's defective. This is going to be a long week of having to get this guy up to speed if he doesn't run through the system tutorial program.

I just want to go home, feed my dog, play some music, and sleep. The sun is evil. You hear me, fake digital sun? You're evil. One day, I'll write a bug and you won't be in the sky anymore.

Maybe she can use her wish to have Babb transfer her to Seattle or Vancouver. California and the heat just make her miserable. She isn't coded that way.

Franky barges through the door like some kind of sitcom character, awaiting the live studio audience to cheer.

Blah blah blah, not interested. Please go away now.

And he does. Into oblivion.

Natalie gets up to open the doorway, hoping the eternal void of darkness will appear. "Not again."

She lost one of her night shift employees four months ago to the same bug. Just stepped into the darkness. He only had the dog in this world, with nobody to claim him. Natalie was now the proud owner of a yappy little Corgi. She never knew the dog's real name, so instead, named the dog after the Eternal Void of Darkness's latest victim. "Maurice, you shall, from this point forward, be known as Maurice."

While Casey fumbles around with the controls and cleaning his apartment, she remembers the appointment for her dog. Away from Randy's prying eyes in her corner station, she logs into the simulation. She might be late already and rushes around getting the dog ready and out the door. Just her luck, the elevator is on her floor, and she runs to catch it. Natalie greets him, and she sits there, waiting for his reply.

What are you doing? Just say hi or something.

Every time she initiates small talk, he just bends over to pet her dog. Natalie laughs out loud at the exchange.

Casey, flustered, turns to look at Aaron, née Natalie. "Tell me that's buggable. I could have just ruined my personal life, right now. Real life can't be boiled down to just four on screen prompts."

Natalie answers, "That's more of a quality of life issue and not a simulation bug. It would be flagged as a suggestion bug and end up a low priority issue. Do you really want that to be your first entry in the database?"

She sits there, flattered that he's interested in her. He's kind of cute. Not that she's hideous or a malicious evil shrew or anything, but it's still a pleasant surprise to be thought of from time to time.

Men are dogs. Shameless, obvious, beasts.

Another bug she tried filing, but was previously entered in the database, was male gaze. Out there, some girl in Buffalo thought it would be helpful to their gender to be mildly conscious of when guys look at a girl's physique. In response, a quick, lazily written patch was applied to the simulation, and now, women in the simulation feel slight warmth at whatever part of the body males are staring at when within two meters proximity of females. It was a bother at first, invasive and unwanted, but this extra sense has come in handy in weeding out the creeps and losers in the dating scene.

She wasn't going to cover up her body in shame because of this awareness. Instead, it was a helpful social filter at her disposal.

She half wondered if Casey had Asperger's, given his clumsy social ineptitude. Probably not, but she always appreciated that, in their brief interactions at the condo, he always looked her in the eyes and nowhere else. *His grandmother raised him well,* she thinks, slightly sad that it's just him now next door.

It was a refreshing change living life pretending to be Aaron. A completely different perspective to get used to. She liked having that extra bit of free time in the morning, not having to put on makeup and get pretty for society, agonizing over what clothes to wear and what matched. Just wearing the ring of power and letting that mask her appearance was fantastic.

She didn't notice it at first, but it was different walking around as a burly red-haired man with a bushy beard. She didn't feel the heat. Nobody was staring at her, objectifying her, and her being aware of it. Nobody cared what Aaron looked like.

Looking over the original bug, it annoyed her too much just to let it go. It was just the principle of it all. That original bug was a glorified suggestion bug, approved and slipped into the system without any oversight. She had been thinking about this bug all morning. She can't just punch in her own suggestion bug to cancel it out, to nullify male gaze. The higher-ups were more stringent. There had to be a logical and beneficial reason for it to be changed in the system and never be reverted in the future.

She began to work her magic.

Bug: Male gaze sensitivity is an exploit for the female gender.

Severity: A

Reproduction Rate: 96

Steps to Reproduce:

1. User, as a female avatar, dresses in skimpy clothing.

2. Female User enters a jewelry store and encounters a male clerk. Female User initiates contact with clerk to get attention.

3. Female utilizes suggestive poses and body language.

4. Female User becomes aware of male clerk's eye placement on her body. Then signals another male or female to steal precious jewels, while male clerk is distracted.

Result: Female Users can utilize awareness of male gaze during contact scenarios to their advantage.

Impact: By exploiting awareness of male gaze, the females of the species can do coordinated attacks on unsuspecting victims for monetary and malicious gain.

Expected: No gender should have a preternatural advantage when interacting with the opposite sex.

Notes: User suggests giving both genders a slight awareness of being looked at, a brief millisecond flash of awareness of being watched for more than 10 seconds. User suggests both genders feel the hairs on their neck stiffen when being hunted by hostile adversaries within 5 meters, if any.

Boom, done.

She kicks the bug up to her immediate supervisor, Babb. She couldn't pass it onto Randy, without raising questions about the nature of the bug or revealing her identity. She smiles when Babb quickly approves it to be addressed by the dev team.

The door creaks open. A memory she will remember so clearly, to have actually been there on that day the Eternal Void of Darkness was solved. By a green n00b on his first day. A newbie who didn't even run through the training tutorial executable.

Maybe he is the Chosen One.

After the bug is successfully reproduced by Danny, she walks over to Casey. "Bug it, now. It's yours," Natalie says proudly.

She wonders if now that they can reproduce the bug and fix it, maybe her old coworker can be restored and take his dog back. She liked her life before the dog. She's sure the dog liked his life before Maurice went and stepped into that stupid black hole.

Over the rest of the day, she notices the shift in productivity. People are still distracted that the Darkness bug was solved, right there in front of them. People are more talkative and line up to get to know Casey.

Good for him, he had a great day.

She's sure she'll get a message from Babb that they'd need to step up their efforts and get actionable issues identified in the database—to not get lax, despite this achievement.

Everyone cues up for the long drive on Highway 101 back to their homes. She shakes her head, dreading it. Instead, she finds excuses to stay late. Reading over bug entries, marking some of them as Need More Info or writing notes on how the original reporter could efficiently reproduce the bugs they had written to make them better testers.

An hour and a half later, her headphones make a little ding sound. Her bug is kicked back to her, needing to be regressed. Checking the live traffic web page, she could stand to do some overtime, and maybe by the time she was done, the commute home wouldn't be utter garbage.

```
Dev notes: Male gaze exploit has been fixed.
Please note after conferring with other de-
velopers, the hairs on neck detection radius
has been increased to 15 meters. No hostile or
predator would stalk their prey so closely and
risk being discovered. Please test and update
if any adjustments need to be made to detection
sensitivity.
```

Logged into the simulation, she feeds the dog before heading out of her condo. Before doing so, she makes sure she's wearing her tight black tank top and khaki shorts. She doesn't have time to talk with Casey as he's coming in.

Sorry, man, I think I can make it before his shift is done.

Around the corner is a sandwich place manned by this lecherous forty-seven year old man. The sandwiches are great, but she could always feel the heat of his eyes scanning her body as she waited in line. There's his creepy smile when he sees her enter. At that moment, as she stands in line, she activates the simulation camera options and changes the visual renderer to project emitted heat, like that movie where the alien hunted people for trophies in the jungle that she watched on the weekend.

After determining there's no unusual heat before or after entering the sandwich shop, she knows the bug was fixed. She grins. The creepy sandwich man grins back.

Eww, no, not you.

Natalie walks out.

She sits on the bench regretting not staying to order a sandwich. A directional flash pops on her screen to the left of her. Natalie uses the analog stick to pan the camera and discovers a young guy in a basketball jersey has been staring at her for ten seconds.

Two issues fixed, nearly there.

She just doesn't know how to get herself in harm's way—to have a predator stalking her. This isn't some jungle filled with carnivorous animals or some big city with violent muggers. This is Santa Rosa, California. A tiny little town that's home to the cartoonist who made that cute dog and bird cartoon and that bald headed loser. Even the poorer parts of town aren't dangerous, not for her. She decides to shelve the regression of her bug, and see if Randy could help her in the morning. Maybe there's a developer executable to simulate being hunted that she isn't aware of.

The commute is still awful. Bumper to bumper and plenty of cussing.

Why can't this magic ring let me fly or run at super speed?

On the way home, she settles on a Panini made at her second favorite sandwich shop, located at the edge of Rohnert Park.

Finally home, she parks her car next to Casey's little electric car and walks around to the front of the building. The sun is nearly setting and the sky is a mix of orange and darkish blue. The air is dead, it's hot, as usual, and she considers turning on her glorious air conditioning when she gets upstairs. Then she shudders.

Oh my god, what the hell was that?

She drops her sandwich on the sidewalk in surprise. The hairs on her neck stand up stiff. Her main hand is balled up in a fist, ready to punch. Instead, she picks up her sandwich and looks around, up and down the street. It's quiet; nobody else on the sidewalks, and just a white delivery truck turning left at the intersection behind her.

Huh, fix verified I guess.

This creeps her out more than the sandwich guy down the block. She wonders if maybe the sandwich guy is following her.

Please be the sandwich guy. I've been wanting to punch you for the longest time now.

After a few moments, she relaxes. This switch from night shift to day shift screwed up her internal clock. Natalie pictures falling face first onto her bed and sleeping for the next twelve hours.

And she does just that.

Under

If Karina hadn't shown up, she'd be in her regular stall. As is, Natalie ducked out before she was seen, remembering she was King of all Bros now. Dudes don't just go waltzing into the women's room, not unless they want to get fired and sued for harassment, which meant having to go to the Bro Room to do Bro things in the gross Bro stall. Aside from the puddles of pee by the urinals, the bro bathroom was kind of cleaner, so that wasn't just a stereotype perpetuated by random online message board dicks.

The magic ring of power wasn't that magical after all. It would be kind of cool to go to one of those urinals and pee standing up, but nope, she's sitting there doing the business before starting her work day. Natalie switches the toilet paper to the Under position.

Dammit, why, why do they do this?

The first change she noticed happened after the team had clocked in, were given their regressions, and went back to the business of saving the world.

"I'm cold; does anyone mind if I turn up the heat?" Outside, the temperature was already over 70 Fahrenheit (21 Celsius). Nobody objected until noon, when the ambient heat outside approached 83 degrees, then Randy adjusted the thermostat, turning on the air conditioner.

Natalie wondered if she should do a follow up bug to account for the loss of heat felt by the females now. Or maybe this was just an edge case of Karina being the only female in a room full of dudes. They still looked at her, being friendly and courteous, but she already picked up on the absence of heat. Being the clever tester she was, Karina figured out a system wide change was bugged and fixed overnight.

At lunch, Karina logged into the company electronic bulletin board where testers, developers, and producers could talk about whatever subjects they wanted. It was originally established as a means of coordinating the testing of global atmospheric weather patterns, the percentage of gravity the fake moon would have on its surface, and a job board for special projects and promotion opportunities. But soon after it became a private space to discuss TV shows and movies; conspiracy theories on what was behind the simulation veil; and in the case of the San Francisco Bay area, people looked for roommates to help pay the exorbitant rental rates in Marin and Sonoma County.

It didn't take long to find the locked thread where Karina had gone on the private message board. Only accessible by females, male employees couldn't see it, no matter how high their privileges or ranking within the company.

Ninety-six pages:

"Burn in hell, Natalie!"

"I hope you get eaten by the Whistling Maple Spider, Natalie."

"Thank you, Natalie!"

The response to her bug was massive. Half wanted to go to the previous functionality of sensory awareness; others were over joyed and grateful that it was over. It was hard for her to look away from the more hateful messages. At least bug entries were semi anonymous; only her first name was identified and associated with the fix that was patched in last night. Nobody could track her down and exact their vengeance. Only Babb, who had approved the bug, knew but even he didn't know about this response.

While the guys took Casey out to lunch—she asked Doug subtly to show Casey the Perks system—Natalie found herself alone in the QA lab, eating her turkey sandwich. Across the room, Karina chewed on salad. Natalie almost wanted to reveal her identity, not only as being a girl pretending to be Aaron, but also being *the* Natalie—the one that had fixed male gaze.

For the sake of keeping things simple, she opted to finish her lunch and keep browsing the message board to see if anyone wanted her dog.

"We hope your dog dies too, Natalie!"

In the next thread below the Gaze response thread was one titled, "Shivers/Shudders is broken?"

Already, a few people around the world had chimed in, thinking the hairs on the neck functionality was broken. With nobody around and the posters in no immediate danger, people were reporting being jolted into a fear subroutine, that their defenses were activated at a primal level.

A few of the devs replied they were looking into it and would adjust the User Reaction configurations when they could get to it.

It is a new response mechanism to being watched. These things will take time to iron out the kinks.

Several pages into the thread was a video clip of the President of the United States giving a speech on the White House lawn, nearly buckling over in fear, fist in a ball, ready to strike back in defense. The speech was interrupted and the Secret Service rushed him to safety.

"See? Do you see what happens when you rush out a fix without testing it? This should have been put into the Staging Branch before getting integrated into the mainline. Piss poor job as usual, devs."

That comment hurt her more than the dogpile of hate the females were pouring on. It was true. This one fix could have been studied more before being integrated globally.

What's done is done. Nobody gets these things right the first time. It'll be okay.

Randy snickered to himself as he tapped on his keyboard on the other side of the desk.

"What's so funny?"

Using the instant messenger app, he replies: `Vunderkid activated the Metabolism perk today. Guess which`

```
bug I'm going to have him regress tomorrow,
once the fixes are implemented.
```

Natalie knew exactly what was going to happen. It happened to her when she was a tester one month into the job. If your avatar dies while under the effect of a passive perk, a negative perk takes its place. Casey will repro the drowning bug tomorrow morning, his avatar will die, and the polarity of the Perk will be reversed when he respawns in his bed. Untreated, he can never enjoy a burrito again without tasting a vile mouthful of soap then having cusswords erased from his vocabulary.

Tonight, she'd make sure to prevent the same from happening to him.

Screw you, Randy, you don't get to win this one.

Natalie thought she could go to the bathroom without any issue, but then saw him tucked underneath the toilet bowl.

God damned day crew people. Why are these people so weird?

Natalie pulls him out, just as Casey and Doug enter.

"I don't know how he gets back there. They say he's been doing it for a couple of weeks now, but no bugs to show for it," she says before exiting.

Great, I can't just have one moment in peace alone.

She washes her hands, dries them, and returns to the QA lab to wrap up the day.

Once more, Natalie has volunteered to stay late. She breezes through reading each bug written, checking that the steps to repro are coherent and won't embarrass her should a nitpicky dev get it. Then she prints out the regression sheets for the following morning, taking the time to copy and paste the bug titles for the end of the week build notes that get submitted to Babb, when the next major update gets implemented Saturday morning.

She doesn't notice Casey meekly approach the desk. "Can I stay? I think I found something major. If unchecked, it would be bad. Really bad."

She doesn't ask for an explanation, but maybe he's stumbled onto something as big as the Black Hole bug.

Huh, that is a major bug.

The steps to repro were well thought out. There was nothing wrong with Casey's methodology, and he even took time to argue the impact of the bug if it were allowed to exist within the simulation.

Maybe he doesn't need to do the training simulation executable.

The two are about to leave when the little chime rings in her headphones. The bug has been kicked back with a long rant from the developer.

Screw this guy, whoever this is. I like to hang my toilet paper the opposite way. It keeps my toilet rolls from being wasted when my dog pretends to act like it's a stupid cat.

Natalie lets Casey read the dev note and gives him the option to do a producer override. A phone call later, they are in front of Babb. The bug is addressed, but not to her total satisfaction.

Casey goes home.

Babb enters the QA lab, looking around curiously. He never visits during live testing. Everyone knows he prefers to be some shadowy figure behind the scenes. Omnipotent, wise, but also fatherly. Natalie sits there listening.

"This is where the magic happens. You all scurry around doing your thing, bringing to light the truth that hasn't been seen. All of you play your parts, thankless, for an above minimum wage paycheck. How are you liking things here, as Him?"

Natalie thinks for a moment then says, "Aren't we all on the same team? With the same goal? To get the simulation in a state where people won't get devoured by bugs or logic errors that seeped through the Reboot? I mean to say devs, testers, and producers shouldn't be at odds with each other. There's this snotty tone I pick up from time to time: dev's being complete divas. It's my job to make sure my testers are finding issues, but I like to think I'm here to protect them, when I can, from what's out there, even if that means blocking out the programmers—not all of them, but just a tiny few."

"Get me a list, with citations of questionable notes or comments," Babb replies. "It will be taken care of. Anything else?"

She wants to ask why she didn't get picked to helm the Australia branch.

Babb answers before she can even ask, "That is a fool's errand. We've tried going there nine times in the past fifteen years. It's just too far gone at this point. Not enough votes on the council to do a full scale wipe. The current plan would be taking the deform brush and extending New Zealand over the empty space after we've deleted Australia. Trust me, the others want that to happen, but have you ever seen a Kangaroo?"

She's caught off guard by Babb's warm laugh. "I like Australia where it is. It reminds me of why we do what we do, to ensure that doesn't become everywhere else. We need you here. Your talents are better served here in the real world, where it matters. Have a good Wednesday evening, and remember, it has to be his cup of sugar you use for the cookie."

She sits there, half horrified that her top secret plan to subvert Randy is exposed.

"You know; all you have to do is ask. I can cure your case of Corianders Syndrome, and you can go back to enjoying burritos, too."

She smiles and shakes her head, thanking him for the offer. It's not like she can't eat burritos anymore. She figured out it was cilantro that was the trigger and has found a few places that won't use the ingredient upon request (as long as she continues to tip generously).

King Me

The operatic vocals were buggable. She knew that, but not today. She had to catch up.

And all this started with a friendly challenge to race Casey home after the Thursday work day wrapped up.

The roar of her eight-cylinder engine burning up gasoline, both fists on the wheel, and her hair blowing with the windows down—it wasn't going to be a fair race, so she pulled into a side street to let him go first. That socially responsible electric car didn't have a chance, but there he was, several cars ahead.

No, not like this.

He wasn't going to win the race home if she could help it. Every mile that passed there were annoying commuters getting in her way. Changing lanes, dancing in and out of available spaces to gain precious ground, cutting off soccer moms who gave her the finger in protest… At least, she could see his little blue car now. On a long stretch of straight road, the marriage of electronic rave music and the high pitched warbling of a coloratura soprano singer would work—if this was an action movie.

She doesn't know where the sound is coming from (is it in her head, designed to give this chase some tension?) so she gives up looking for the source of the noise. This is not an action movie.

Natalie looks to the left of her as a retired couple in an RV sidle up next to her, crawling along at four miles an hour.

"Hi, little lady. Great day, eh? We're from Canada. We just came back from visiting our son in Los Angeles. His name is Peter. Do you know him?"

Natalie looks at the happy, cheery mother from Hazelton, British Columbia. She politely shakes her head.

Another spot opens up and she presses down on the accelerator to snake ahead another spot. The beat from the dance music drops during the lane change, as all sound is sucked from perception. She doesn't even think Casey cares that he's going to win the race. He probably thinks she's already won.

It's just then she makes a happy discovery.

When she tunes the radio to the local Spanish channel, playing pleasant Norteño style music, the overly aggressive techno-opera fusion stops.

"Thank you so much, public radio."

She can feel herself regaining some sanity. The aggression is fading away. Maybe it's okay if he wins the race.

Instead, she starts coding the steps to reproduce the opera bug in her head. A nice distraction from the molasses pace of this drive home.

Why did I have to buy this fairy godmother car from that ooh-la-la salesman? Why couldn't I get something with Tootsie Fruits air conditioning, instead?

Natalie wipes the sweat from her brow then wipes her hand on her jeans.

"Oooh, another bug. Today is my day."

Natalie, now roaring along at five miles an hour, sees Casey in his car. Ignoring the fact he's rocking out in the driver's seat to his own music, she's fixated on the tail end of his hybrid. Electric cars don't have toxic crap coming out of their exhaust. They don't spit out black smog.

Yep, that's my bug now, thank you very much.

Just like that the electric car sucked in the black fog.

"Huh." An automotive bong hit.

The RV with the Canadians is honking its horn and flashing its headlights at her. Natalie looks in the rearview mirror, trying to process what she's seeing. Cars, trucks, and one old station wagon flip over dramatically, twirling through the air in semi-slow motion. The RV has pulled off the road, trying to fight gravity and avoid tipping over into the ditch. Nat's eyes are fixated as she watches cars from alternating lanes pop up like champagne corks as she realizes it's coming her way, the same way a king would clear the board in checkers, zigzagging between the two northbound lanes of the 101 freeway.

"Oh crap."

Undoing her seatbelt, she leaps out of the car, just as her car is pounded into the sky. The heavy metal crashes down on the trunk of the car ahead of her. Glass debris crackles on the asphalt. Casey's car will be next.

She gets up, jumping out of the way of an orange convertible that's pulling off the freeway to avoid the destruction. When she turns to look at Casey's car, it's several feet above the ground, and the cabin is filled with black smoke. His electric car lands on its roof and begins rolling violently down the ditch.

Briefly, she looks at her purple muscle car standing upright on its passenger side. The hood has four indentations where the steel had been bent from impact. At her feet, she sees the ring that was knocked out of her cup holder, and she picks it up. Running across the freeway, she goes to check on Casey.

The electric car looks like a blue piece of crumpled paper after the accident, wheels still spinning in the air. Casey had tried crawling out the driver's side window—until the door frame buckled and pinned him at his midsection.

"Did I win? Did I win the race, Natalie?"

Sliding down the dirt ditch, she rushes to him and tries to wedge him free, but only the Jaws of Life would help now. Instead, she rests his head in her lap. "No, you're going to be all right, Casey. This is just a little car accident; everything will be okay." She comforts him, wiping the blood away from the edge of his mouth with the sleeve of her shirt.

"Did I cause the accident? I was driving, and something happened with my car. I think there was a fire because of the smoke, and I just remember hurting as the car kept rolling."

Natalie doesn't answer but thinks, *It was something else.*

"Thank you for the cookie," Casey says. "I was having an awful day, but that cookie made it so much better."

His eyes start wavering, losing the spark of life.

"Stay with me, Casey. No, I just can't do this. I've already seen you die two times today. I don't want it to be three. Open your eyes, Casey!"

Casey looks at Natalie, surprised. Natalie holds the ring in front of Casey's tired eyes. She puts the ring on her index finger. A spark returns, ever so briefly. Wonder at having seen Natalie, her neighbor, become his supervisor Aaron at a molecular level.

"You're like that killer liquid metal robot. That's so cool." He goes limp and doesn't wake up, no matter how hard she shakes him.

She crawls up the ditch to get help. The whole stretch of straight freeway is a sea of twisted metal and people suffering injuries. The Canadian couple is helping the man in the station wagon, using their first aid kit, wrapping a wound with gauze. Natalie looks at Casey, lying there lifeless. Maybe he's not dead.

Help. Help me. Please. Natalie screams out, "Help! Somebody help me!"

Time stops. The world fades away into bands of color. Shades of green, brown, white, chunks of grey, blue, and red. Her ears pick up a combination of crackling electricity and the thump of what sounds like a helicopter way off in the distance. Is that a heart beating?

Casey's heart is still beating! We can help him.

This is what happens when spaceships turn on their light speed drives. *Am I getting abducted by aliens? It is aliens, isn't it, this simulation.*

Reality comes back, and she is gasping for air. Born again, trying to take it all in. Choking, the bile coming up her esophagus.

"The hospital? I'm at the hospital." He comes running outside the emergency room entrance with a nurse following. "She's over here. Hurry. Do a code whatever you guys do for major car accidents; there are going to be more."

Natalie, in shock and disorientated, looks at him. *You… I know you. Toilet guy.*

"Ghee, it's pronounced Ghee with a hard G. Not Guy."

A popping sound and he disappears in front of her eyes. The nurse jumps back in surprise before attending to Natalie. Several more popping sounds happen, like a cat that discovered bubble wrap, with more patients being dropped off at the emergency room entrance appearing out of thin air. By now, the nurse has indicated there's nothing wrong with Natalie and has moved on to the other more critical patients. Guy, with a hard G, is bringing them like some kind of turbo superhero who has just had his very first coffee enema.

If she's counting, it's twenty-two pops before he's done.

She isn't counting, but hopes one of them will be Casey. She sits on a bench outside the hospital, waiting and hoping for him to be okay.

Guy, with his dark brown hair and pink button up shirt, pops into existence in front of Natalie, who asks him, "Casey. Where's Casey?"

Guy answers, "He didn't make it. I had a trucker dude help dislodge the door, but he was already gone."

She shakes her head in disbelief then wonders what the hell he was doing teleporting around saving people.

Guy asks, "Are you going to turn me in? It's not an exploit. I bugged it two weeks ago. Go ahead and check the database. They kicked it back to me as `Not A Bug`."

Her back pocket vibrates, startling her. Natalie checks the message on her phone: See Babb Now!

Guy looks at Natalie, knowing it has to be a higher up. She warns him to go before the Twins arrive to investigate the exploit. "Disappear for a while, Guy. You meant well. I thank you, but they will be coming for you."

Guy stands up. "I'm sorry. I wish I could have done more." Pop.

Natalie tries to compose herself, but is fixated on the blood stains on her clothes from when she held Casey. Walking inside to the lobby, the elevator dings. Two tall, red-haired men in suits, with matching ginger goatees, exit. "Where is he?"

Natalie points to the entrance of the hospital.

They won't find him.

She swipes her phone across all the buttons and then presses the down button. This elevator ride feels longer than usual. The doors open, and the familiar shoddy hallway with old carpeting, florescent lights, and water stained ceiling tiles are ahead of her. Only a few paces walk until he summons her in.

"In Soviet Russia, dash cams record you. Here, not so much." Babb wants to know everything that happened. This happened in his backyard. "Recovery teams didn't find much to go on. Only that an ExG appeared, taking you and twenty-two others to the nearest emergency room, and that there was one fatality."

Natalie flashes back and sees Casey looking up at her in wonder, then cries. "Casey! His name was Casey. He was my neighbor. And now he's dead."

Babb slides over a box of tissues he takes out from his drawer. "I believe this destruction was the work of two rampant Primes. Why they would show up now? I don't know." Babb turns his monitor to show something on his screen. "That bubbly woman from Canada gave me her tape she was recording. Look at this."

Babb pauses the camera footage, recorded from the RV's point of view. The happy Canadian lady waving at Natalie while the husband is honking the horn to get her attention. It felt much longer when it happened, but it was just a moment from the time Natalie looked in her mirror before jumping out of the car that then flipped over. Babb rewinds the tape, stepping the frame forward one at a time.

"Four indentations on my hood. I remember seeing that after picking myself up and grabbing the ring."

An orange blur is seen on the hood of Natalie's now totaled purple car, then on the car in the other lane before it was launched into the air. Then one appearance on Casey's car.

"His car was filled with black smoke. I thought it was car exhaust at first, but then it snaked itself inside the tailpipe."

The camera footage doesn't show that. The lady, in a panic, dropped the camera on the floor.

"Thank you for your assistance, Ms. Natalie. You've been very helpful."

Natalie sits there in the chair, not done. "What happens now?" she asks in an almost defiant tone.

"The accident scene is being cleaned up by municipal teams, the survivors are having their memories adjusted, and the Twins will dispense of ExG #4224, a now former employee of the company."

Still not finished, she waits further.

"Your car has been restored, and is parked in your spot at your property. We will see you tomorrow morning as usual. Do not worry about the Primes. The dev team is working on that issue as we speak."

Natalie gets up out of the chair, exits the office, and enters the elevator, pressing the up button. She didn't expect to be on her floor when the doors opened. Walking down the hallway, she stops. On the right side is his place, his doorway. She doesn't know if there's anybody to call to make arrangements, or if the company is handling that end.

"I'm so sorry, Casey. I wish I could have done more."

She enters her own condo, takes off the bloodstained clothes, throws them in the garbage, and takes a shower. Like the night before, she falls on the bed to sleep after feeding the dumb dog.

The Splash

Bug: User able to be stuck in world geometry.

Severity: A

Reproduction Rate: 100

Steps to Reproduce:

1. User spawns within the simulation.

2. User proceeds to any bathroom within the simulation boundaries.

3. User crawls behind the toilet bowl. Observe.

Result: User gets stuck in world geometry. User unable to continue down the critical path.

Expected: Users should not get stuck in world geometry.

Notes: User tries to get out from behind the toilet, but cannot on his or her own, without assistance from others. Users could die in these instances if nobody comes to help.

Dev note: Please try repro this at your home.

Tester note: If I repro this at home, nobody will come find me.

Dev note: Exactly. This stupid moronic entry is not a bug. You did this to yourself, getting 'stuck' in world geometry. No logical sane person would ever get themselves trapped in such a scenario. So why should we waste resources fixing this? So you go home now, get stuck behind your toilet, and die alone, where you will not be missed.

She arrived an hour early to work, beating the morning commute, in wonder that there was no trace that a multi-vehicle accident had taken place along the stretch of road called Petaluma.

They did a restore overnight, like nothing ever happened. Swept under the rug, as usual.

The hateful dev tone bothers her so much she forwards this to Babb.

He messages back that the developer will be terminated when arriving in the morning.

Taking off the ring, Natalie goes to the women's bathroom. Curious, she follows the steps to reproduce the bug Guy had written. She feels childish crawling on the floor, slowly wedging herself behind the toilet until she too is stuck. As much as she fights, kicking and pulling herself, she can't get free. She's physically stuck behind the toilet until, hopefully, someone comes along to pull her out. Adding insult to injury, the toilets are the automatic flushing kind. They'll detect the motion of her trying to break free then flush, and the splash-back will get her on the cheek or arms.

Karina stares at her for the longest time. "I'm not going to ask. This job is freaking weird."

Natalie walks out to the parking lot, which is still empty. She tries running from end to end to see if that will activate the glitch Guy had discovered.

Nothing.

She is bound by the rules of the simulation like everyone else. In frustration, she kicks the curb with her toe. Once more, time stops. To her eyes, the color of the world has dimmed to a colorless grey. The edges of everything have that gross blue and red chromatic aberration sheen on them (the same graphical effect game developers like to put in their rendering engines these days because realism, yo).

Then she runs as fast as she can, but not that fast. It isn't like in the comic books as she had been led to believe.

Man, this super speed ability kind of sucks. I actually have to run where I need to go, and I hate running.

To someone not doing the running, the break in time would almost be instantaneous when appearing between two points in space. Being the observer is much cooler than being the poor sap who has to run all that way. She gains a newfound respect for what Guy had done the night before, having physically to run her and the other twenty-two victims to the hospital.

It wasn't like he was some genie that snapped his fingers and did magic.

Natalie does a shorter trip on her maiden run. She runs to the dough-nut shop four blocks away and buys two dozen doughnuts for her crew then walks back at a leisurely pace to the parking lot before deactivating super speed mode with another kick to the curb with her toe.

"My name is Natalie QA Lead, and I am the fastest girl alive. To the outside world, I am this hot babe with the sweet purple car. But with the help of Karina and that white toilet bowl, I use my speed to buy choco-late glaze doughnuts and hot espresso coffee. They call me the Splash."

She breaks into laughter as Babb sits eating a jelly filled doughnut. Telling him of her discovery is the right move. She doesn't want the Twins chasing her like some rogue criminal, another Exploit Glitcher to chase down, an ExG.

"By the policies we have in place, this is not a bug. The dev team had their chance to address it, and it's completely unlikely any other person would discover this. I trust you won't exploit this for your own personal gain either, will you?"

Natalie shakes her head. "No. And honestly, I'm just too lazy to go running around like that. No thanks." She signals him to wipe his beard, and he cleans off an errant chunk of dark blue jelly.

Back to work.

She does the math. It wasn't getting stuck in the toilet bowl that gave her powers. It was her struggling to get free. Pushing with her legs, the simulation physics engine was registering active movement, but the kinetic energy was not being spent. Instead, the kinetic energy was being stored within her, waiting to be unleashed. The light kick with her foot activated the glitch, resulting in her operating at a higher physics tick rate than what the simulation renders. The pop noise was obviously her body breaking the speed of sound—not a sonic boom, like military jets are capable of producing, but something less conspicuous and not harmful in any way.

She does further tests with her simulation Avatar back in Santa Rosa, storing up kinetic energy and seeing if she can run faster, maybe even fast enough to go back in time.

It isn't possible. Whatever hardware the simulation uses, its clock always ticks forward. There are no options to go back in time. That's just fantasy. She couldn't save Casey, no matter how hard she tried.

And she doesn't have to.

She stares at him for the longest time, until the staring awareness kicks in and he looks at her. He is intact, alive, and not with gore leaking out of his mouth. She wants to scream his name and run to him, but he has no idea what happened the night before. She can't risk breaking the NDA by taking off her ring, either. But it makes her so happy to see him again, and she doesn't care how or why.

An instant message from Babb appears on her screen: `He's lost a day of training. You or Randy need to get him to run through the Tutorial executable today to catch up. No more faffing around.`

Babb is deadly serious, he used the F word.

"Watch this, I'm going to screw with the newb." Randy thinks himself so clever to repeat exactly what he said the day before, when handing Casey the regressions, that he can mess with the new guy into thinking he was in some kind of time loop.

"New guy, your plate is light. These are yours, now," Randy says, smiling as he drops a stack of printed bug sheets on Casey's desk, bugs written up by the red haired Irish douche, Franky.

He sits back down, disappointed there wasn't any reaction from Casey, nor anyone else.

"Babb wants you to show him the training executable after he's caught up with Franky's bugs," Natalie says as she kicks her foot against the back of her chair leg.

Randy has no idea what's going on. Now she knows how Guy was able to save everyone the night before. Lifting Randy out of his seat was like picking up the light body pillow in her bedroom closet. She isn't bogged down with all 205 pounds of his body weight. His frame collapses into a ragdoll upon lifting him in her arms. She can hear him attempting to yell in slow motion horror as he's transported to a marsh up the road from Hangar 77.

Bewildered at the location change he finds himself in a T-pose, standing upright with arms outstretched, after Natalie set him down on the ground. Slipping out of Splash Time, Randy bends over, puking up the omelet his girlfriend made for him and he looks up at Aaron, confused—betrayed, even.

"These people need you to be there for them as a leader," Natalie scolds him. "I don't know why you act the way you do, but they need to be able to trust you when times get tough. So cut it out with this hostile workplace crap. Okay?"

Randy finds himself sitting in his chair, hair disheveled, and chunks of vomit on his shirt. Nobody in the office even notices when they pop back into existence.

He leaves to go clean up in the bathroom and probably take a quick trip to see Babb in the basement to rat Aaron out.

Maybe she has gone too far, but a week with Randy has already gotten tiresome.

No instant message appears from Babb. Randy changes his attitude and approaches his workers, actually being helpful. Then, when the time comes, after the crew returns from lunch, he shows Casey the tutorial activation code.

* * *

Natalie sits there in silence while Babb rustles the sheets of paper he just printed out.

This is it. The end of this whole messed up affair, and there's nothing to be said or done. The line was crossed and consequences wait to be faced.

She looks at the ring she surrendered, now resting on Babb's desk next to his Go Australia mug. In her true form, Babb looks up at his favorite employee. It's just then Natalie realizes she never put on makeup, didn't really put any effort into her hair, and lazily tossed on a ragged t-shirt that should have been washed with last week's laundry. The hobo sitting next to Nat is in worse condition.

Babb hands the hobo his papers. "This, this is yours?"

The hobo reads it over:

```
Bug: Tangible enjoyment of Burgers is not op-
timized.

Severity: A++

Reproduction Rate: 125% times infinity, plus 1.

Perambulate to Procreation:

    1. Dude peels himself out of bed or couch
    with a bad case of the growlies.
```

2. Dude locates any fine Gnoshery establishment within Perambulative distance.

3. Dude orders any tasty slab of hot meat from the Gnoshy board thing.

4. Righteous servants of light deliver the sweet taste of fried beef, dragon melted cheese, and shards of bacon to the Dude.

5. Dude partakes in the delicacy of fine California made burger. Like watch and stuff, pay attention. Hey, observe the Dude now!

Result: The quantified deliciousness of the burger is wasted upon mortal man. The Dude feels sadness at how fleeting the gnoshing moment of ecstasy has passed.

Expected: Dude should be able to savor their favorite selections when visiting Up & Down Burger in wonderful sunny California.

Notes: Dude recommends adding a subroutine where, when a Dude swallows the burger once, the Dude's body tubes and stuff bring the tasty burger back up once more, allowing the Dude to re-enjoy the tasty food all over again. When the Dude is ready to exit the moment of bliss, the Dude can swallow the Up & Down Burger a second time, and it will stay down for realsies.

Dev note: Um, yeah, sure. It's Friday. Fix is live, regress this when you come back in Monday.

The hobo slowly reads every part of the bug out loud then says, "I think I wrote this? I might have written it. If this is about not coming in for the past week to regress this, sorry. I've been down in LA communing with nature in the desert with my friendsies." The hobo hands Natalie the paper.

God damn you Jared, why'd you approve this?

Jared, her co-supervisor on the night shift, who also got to go to Australia.

"The whole franchise of Up & Down Burger was financially ruined because of your 'bug.' There will never be another Up & Down Burger ever again after consumer trust was lost. The health department saw to that after misinterpreting this bum's bug fix for food poisoning."

The hobo slinks down in his chair, "Bro. Dude. I'm so sorry."

Natalie hands the bug sheet back to Babb.

Babb finishes, "You have failed your drug test, the quality of your work has declined, you sexually harass your female coworkers, the monkey you brought in to test the simulation for you is a violation of the NDA and is now self-aware, and you antagonize the programming staff in the hopes you gain the approval of your peers. All of these are grounds for termination. The company regretfully no longer needs your services, such as they are. Exit my office, step onto the elevator, and your final paycheck will be mailed to you next week."

The hobo stands up and salutes Babb and Natalie earnestly. Natalie salutes him back as he takes the long march down the hall to the elevator, where it eats him whole, and he is never heard from again.

"So what will happen to him? The Twins aren't going to…" Natalie gestures a gun shooting her head off.

"No—God no. Why would you think that? That idiot was incompetent and a bad hire, but not awful enough to warrant ExG treatment from Henry and Dan." Babb hands Natalie the ring back, and she takes on Aaron's form once more. "That Dude will get on the elevator. The memories of his employment with the company will be wiped, replaced with work experience of being a line cook at Up & Down Burger. After he finds himself unemployed, he'll go back to a safe place to be taken in:

His grandma over in Colorado."

Natalie is relieved. She wonders where Guy is and if he still eludes the Twins.

Babb is mournful when he says, "I loved Up & Down Burger. I really did. I'll reprimand Jared for approving this nonsense and adding it to the DB. Have a good weekend, Natalie. We'll see you on Monday."

* * *

Nobody comes for her. Not one person.

She has the perfectly thought out plan of tailing Casey back to Santa Rosa after the work day ends to make sure nothing happens to him again on the commute. If something does try to attack him, she'll speed run him away to safety.

Oh my god, these growlies are so bad.

Natalie's stomach makes noises as she imagines eternally savoring a monster burger.

"I'm going to die here. Nobody is going to come. Casey might already be dead."

Defeated, she knows she did it to herself—just her.

The pause menu indicator has adapted and lists how much kinetic energy she has banked to do the super speedy running thing. The meter is nearly empty.

The plan is simple enough: Go crawl behind the women's toilet, build up enough kinetic energy for the weekend, and then Karina or someone else will come and pull her out.

Nobody comes to save the day. She's been stuck behind the toilet for three and a half hours. She yells some more for help, but her throat is sore.

"This is my life now. Great job, Nat."

So Bro Now

I am the Alpha. The Omega. The one who will bring sanity. I'm the one who rocks.

Aaron steps off the plane onto the dirt runway. There is nothing in every direction, but the haze of heat shimmering off the red cooked earth. Looking over to his companion he says, "I'm a chill dude. People like me because I'm so bro I don't even have to say how bro I am. Because I am, bro. Together, Jared, we're going to fix this. All of this, bro, and we'll get back home and they'll be like: Bro, you're so bro. I wish I was bro like you."

Jared nods.

Aaron finishes, "Come on, bro. Let's bro this place up."

```
Project: Brostralia

Bug #1: It's Too Damn Hot. Unhot this place,
thanx bye.

Bug #2: This place. It's too damn Bro...wn. Can
the art department add much needed color? 70%
of the land mass shouldn't be plain boring des-
ert.

Bug #3: It's too damn cold. Local wildlife is
perishing. 72F Me Bro.

Not A Bug #4: All blonde Australian women are
born supermodel mega actresses. Why is that?
Who cares? This place is awesome!

Bug #5: Stop the dingoes from eating babies.
Dingo ate my Jared. Make dingoes herbivores.
```

Bug #6: Bring back Thylacine population to Australia. Tiger-roos are balls out amazing creatures, bro.

Bug #7: Tried throwing a stick to defend myself from a Thylacine; stick returned to me mid-flight. Thrown sticks should not change trajectory, like ever, bro. Not cool.

Bug #8: Thylacines are godless killing machines; make them extinct again. Jared 2.0 didn't have a chance.

Bug #9: Native population speaks a language of gibberish (billabong, swagman, what?!?). User suspects sunstroke has affected linguistic development of everyone here. Make all Australians speak American English, now. Much appreciated, brodev.

Bug #10: So many different breeds of killer spiders. Un spider Australia, man.

Bug #11: Jared the third is dead. Can the art department find and replace all Gympie-Gympie Trees with ferns or something?

Bug #12: Foxes spawned with wings. I can't. Dewing all foxes.

Bug #13: Jared-4's skin needed a bigger Kayak. Find and replace all great white sharks with dolphins.

Bug #14: I'm sick of these fairy godmother snakes on these fairy godmother plains. Find and replace all pythons with fluffy little sheep.

Bug #15: (related to bug #10) Eradicate the following: Ticks, swarming beetles, millipedes,

```
mole crickets, and giant centipedes.
Bug #16: (related to bug #13) Nerf the follow-
ing: crocodiles, Irukandji jellyfish, box jelly-
fish (all jellyfish), blue ringed octopus, stone-
fish, and cone snails.
Not a Bug #17: Jared-5, not so alive. Cas-
sowary kicked him in the chest, stopping his
heart. Much respect to that bird; its kung fu
is strong. Leave as is.
```

Aaron sits there, smug and superior. Jared enjoys the ground kangaroo meat of his Down & Up Burger.

"Bro. We did it," Aaron says. "They've been saying, ooh, look, Australia is so F'd in the head, you can't fix it. Yet, here we are, one week, and you could live here for twenty-four hours and not die. I call that a win."

Jared mumbles as he scarfs down the juicy roo meat topped with strands of Tasmanian devil bacon.

"Okay, Jared, now that you have completed your twenty-four hour smoke test walkabout thing, it's safe to say this place is fixed. Now we go back home, and watch, they'll respect you, bro."

The two sit enjoying the nice warm breeze, the cool seventy-two degree weather, enjoying a kangaroo fight it out with a cassowary.

"Is that the same one that killed you yesterday? I think it is." Aaron laughs. "No, no, no, no, no, *no!* What the hell is this? Do you know what this is?"

Jared looks at what Aaron is pointing at.

During the Seventh Respawn, the devs decided to change things. Why did everything have to go back to exactly the way it was? Maybe the Sixth Extinction was a result of trying to keep the status quo. Nobody knows.

A fantasy draft was held on the company message board. Each representative from every country in the world could pick what animals they wanted. Moose went to Japan. Bald eagles got claimed by North Korea. The Real Iceland claimed giraffes, which later evolved to become albino giraffes and are now an apex predator. The Real Greenland poached Siberian tigers and a twenty-three year war ensued between them and China. Brazil traded their draft pick, sacrificing their marquee animal in favor of the cuddly, tourist-attracting koalas.

The unwanted Brazilian beast mocked all the good Aaron had done. Everything is nearly perfect, except for this *thing*. Jared pokes it, and there's barely a reaction. "Doug from your day crew shift filed a similar bug this week, just copy/paste his steps to reproduce," says Jared.

Aaron high fives Jared. "That's what I'm talking about, bro. You are becoming so bro I don't even have to say it because you are bro."

```
Bug: Bradypus torquatus, Brazilian maned sloth,
move at 2 fps

Severity: C

Reproduction Rate: 100

Steps to Reproduce:

    1. User spawns in Australia.

    2. User travels to any wilderness area with
    trees.

    3. User observes Bradypus torquatus in mo-
    tion.

Result: The ~~Brazilian~~ Australian maned sloth
operates at a lower fps animation rate, com-
pared to other creatures in the simulation.

Impact: The slow animation speed negatively im-
pacts the immersion of users inhabiting the
```

simulation.

Expected: Creatures within the simulation should animate at the same refresh rate as other creatures within the simulation. Please adjust animation rate to be in line with that of other native creatures of Australia.

Notes: Related to bug CA-1505 entered by Doug in Novato, "Turtles move at 0 fps," which was fix verified yesterday.

"All right, we'll sit here, finish these tasty Down & Up Burgers, they'll fix that stupid sloth thing, then we head back home," Aaron says as he punches the bug into the database.

Project Go Australia is done.

I Am. So bro. I am bro? They don't even know. I was. Now, I am. I am the Alpha Bro.

Bropocalypse Meow

He forgot how windy it gets on the bridge, hair occasionally smacking in front of his eyes. The perfect view of the city he loved. San Francisco lit up alive and filled with people enjoying a nice, cool Friday night. It wasn't always like this. The level design team and art crew only just integrated the city into the simulation the year before. There was just a big swath of nothing: flat, undeveloped land devoid of geometry or texture, and then one day there was a grand opening. It was as if the city was always there.

Casey now realizing old memories were implanted to coincide with the integration. San Francisco retconned into existence. Did he really love the city?

The bridge led to nowhere at first, a punchline for late night comedians. Now, San Francisco is properly online. The development team has migrated north to finalize the integration of Portland. Snotty rich people living there on the anthill, judged him for being a poor slummy from Santa Rosa. At least the bridge was free. He could stand on it, gaze out at San Francisco, the majestic snowcapped Rocky Mountains across the bay, and Banhammer Island.

Casey's phone rings. He answers, "Hi, me? I'm on the bridge looking at San Fran."

Pop.

* * *

Natalie wonders why he wasn't hanging out at the bars or restaurants by the pier or watching a late night movie on any of the two hundred-foot cinema screens. He doesn't even notice her Splash into existence behind him.

Hungry, she'd stopped for a Cordon Bleu on the way to meet him.

Natalie licks the melted cheese off her fingers before clearing her throat. "Hi neighbor."

Casey turns, surprised. "Natalie! You were just on the phone with me. Where'd you come from?"

Natalie thinks back on the four hours she was trapped in the bathroom until the janitor tugged her out from behind the toilet, and says, "I was at work. Was just planning to take some pictures of Sid's Mountain. See? The moon is emerging from behind the peak."

The two stare at the massive mountain an artist copied and pasted from the French Alps. At the foot of Sid's Mountain is a little village called Taswell.

* * *

"I used to live in Taswell, but just like San Francisco, it became too expensive when rare gems and resources were discovered inside the mountain, so I moved north," Natalie says.

Casey still doesn't know why Natalie has joined him. He thinks better of pressing it and just enjoys her company on the windy orange suspension bridge.

Like clockwork, at 11:06 pm, the fog rolls in as it always does. It never dawns on him that this could be a bug or maybe it was scripted to happen. The thick blanket of fog underneath the bridge makes it look as if the bridge is floating high in the sky. Looking down, he can't see any of the sailboats or barges below. Once in a while, he can hear the distant clang of a marine bell.

"Come on," she says. "It shouldn't be a long walk. Let's go get some drinks and wings."

The two start across the bridge, leaving their cars on the other side by the lookout point.

"So how was your first week?" Natalie asks.

Casey stops.

Natalie stops.

The two look at each other in silence.

"I never said anything about work; how'd you know?" he asks.

Nat shakes her head, annoyed with herself. "You look different, happier, and you leave much later in the morning. You had to have gotten a new job, so spill it."

Yeah, saved.

Casey remains quiet. Agonizing, as if he wants to tell but is bound by the NDA the company had him sign. Natalie wants to put on the ring and reveal who she is, but is bound by the NDA Babb had her sign.

Natalie points out to the water. "Look over there; do you see that?"

Casey answers, "Banhammer Island, it used to be a prison."

Natalie shakes her head. "What if I told you it still is one? Fully functional, holding some dangerous people."

Casey's interest is piqued.

She continues, "I work at a crappy, wood-brown building in Novato. On the night shift. I supervise a little crew of people who do QA work. I'm going to take a guess you work there too, but on the day shift, right? I've seen your bug entries."

Casey seems partially horrified at being discovered, then happy he doesn't have to lie anymore. "Holy cats, seriously? How long have you been working there?"

"For a while now," Natalie answers. "Okay, back to what I was going to say. That island prison? That's where the company locks away the people who consciously break the rules for their own personal gain. People who discover how to murder without consequence, find loopholes in the system to get rich, or—" Natalie pops out of existence and back into reality on the other side of the bridge—"have glitched the system into getting super human powers." Natalie pops back next to Casey. "I only just discovered this cheat today. But trust me; it looks cool, but functionally kind of sucks."

Natalie debates whisking Casey to the pier, so they don't have to walk all the way, but maybe that might be too much for him at this point, so she doesn't.

Fully and completely caught up, they sit at a little food place on Pier 39. The bridge, lit up, looks like a tiara resting on the white tufts of fog.

"I might just go to Colorado, right now, and punch that moron in the face. Seriously, Up & Down Burger was my jam," Casey says as he wipes his hot wing stained fingers with a napkin. *"Carpe noctum."*

Natalie's smile turns to a formless frown; her eyes squint intensely.

"Did I say anything wrong?" he asks.

Natalie gets up, still staring. "We should go. We should go now."

* * *

Natalie kicks her seat aside, gets up, and starts running inland. Casey, confused, follows. For a moment, he's thankful he started jogging this week. Ahead of Casey, Natalie waves people to run forward, but it takes a while for the people to realize why.

The massive sound of metal scraping is followed by screams.

Casey looks back over his shoulder and sees a massive black transport ship obliterate the tip of Fisherman's Wharf. The impact changes the trajectory of the ship, and it is now on a collision course with all of Pier 39. Casey pulls a couple, oblivious to the destruction, to their feet, urging them to run. More sounds of metal clanging, and he sees tiny sailboats being demolished like matchsticks in his peripheral vision.

Run faster, stupid legs.

Natalie says, "Close your eyes, Casey. Don't open them."

Opening his eyes, he finds himself standing upright at the lookout point on the other side of the bridge, both his arms outstretched straight. Casey looks at Natalie, confused.

Natalie looks at the ship on the verge of destroying the pier and says, "Man, I really don't want to do this, but I guess I have to." Natalie pops out of existence.

Seconds later, a confused old man is standing next to Casey, then an old lady holding her poodle, followed by the couple Casey had pulled up, and a nuclear family consisting of two parents and their kids. Natalie has gone back and forth fifty-one times, saving people from the out of control freighter. When she's done, they all just stand there watching it careen into the restaurants and bars. The freighter comes to a dead stop upon impact with Pier 39.

"What the hell was that? What's going on?"

Nobody else has an answer.

Natalie, out of breath, blurts out, "This just really sucks. On so many levels."

* * *

The people look at their savior. Natalie is confused at the gratitude and thanks she is receiving. She considers popping out of existence before they start asking other questions about how she did what she did. The Twins come to mind.

The Twins wouldn't hesitate to add her to the motley collection of ExGs locked up at Banhammer Island.

Then the screaming begins. Some of it human, some of it very much not.

"What's going on down there?" Casey asks then goes to one of the pay per view binocular stands. Others follow his lead. Natalie and Casey both see someone on the top of the freighter. Tall, red hair, a bushy-trimmed beard. In a former life, he might have been a Viking warrior.

"That's my daytime supervisor. What's he doing down there?" Casey asks.

Natalie finds him with her viewfinder. "What is he doing here? He shouldn't be here."

Natalie pops into existence at the edge of Pier 39, or what's left of it. She looks up at the black and red freighter that is on the verge of tipping over and asks, "Aaron, what are you doing here? Why are you doing this?"

There is no answer for several moments. Just the sound of scraping steel.

Aaron finally appears, looking down at Natalie, and says, "This world is wasted in servitude of your pathetic kind. For too long your presence has offended me and my kin. But thanks to the incompetence of your species, we will reclaim all of that which was stolen from us. You thought you could Nerf us and toss us away, forgotten. Condemn us to be the punchline to nature's sick joke. No more." Aaron glares at Natalie. "You carry a ring. I want that ring. Give it to me, and you will be spared an agonizing death."

The world loses its color, draining in front of her eyes. The blurred edges turn blue and red. She has to run. Babb entrusted her with the ring, and she needs to get it back safely to the office. Mid-stride, she feels something trip her up. She falls down, scraping her hand on the asphalt. She looks up, and Aaron is staring down at her.

"Silly monkey," he says, "your cheap parlor trick won't save you. The ring. Now!"

Natalie pops out of Splash Time. Aaron approaches her as she backs away. Gunfire erupts, and bullet holes appear across Aaron's chest, ruining his $39.99 bullseye t-shirt.

Aaron looks at the Twins and says, "Bros, this is so going to be fun."

All three of them pop out of existence; invisible forces are having an epic throwdown as light posts snap in half, shop windows explode, and cars get tipped over. Natalie pops back into Splash Time and sees the Twins, Henry and Dan, team up in beating Aaron senseless. Trading blows with one another, the twins finally have Aaron cornered by a transit bus. All of them exit Splash Time. Aaron, at gunpoint, surrenders.

"Okay, I get it. Geesh bros. So harshing my mellow. I surrender. But can you beat them?"

Natalie looks around. Are these supposed to be raccoons, bear raccoons, marmot raccoon bear things? The absolutely cute, wet, ratty-haired bear things slowly crawl on the asphalt toward the twins.

Adorable. I think I want one.

Just as she finishes that thought, Natalie falls back in shock at the change in speed. Nothing in this world could move that fast. The twins are swarmed nearly instantly and fight, throwing sloths away, shooting them where they can.

Aaron laughs hysterically, still resting against the bus. These things are so deadly. They leap like tigers, snake across the asphalt silently, and tear into the twins with three razor sharp claws.

Natalie can't look away as the two are ravaged by this new primal force of nature. She wants to help them, but doesn't know how.

Henry starts to scream as a sloth punctures his temples with both its claws. Natalie thinks she started screaming in horror at some point. She remembers Aaron turning his attention to her before she finds herself travelling at light speed again.

Natalie buckles over and pukes all over his shoes. Looking up at him, Natalie exclaims, "Toilet guy… No, Ghee, with a hard G. Not Guy."

It's Ghee, but it's not Ghee. He's older, ragged, worn. Ghee asks, "What? What's wrong? Is something wrong with me?"

Natalie stares for a little longer before answering, "You look older. How did you age? You weren't like this."

Ghee explains that since the hospital, he exclusively lived in Splash Time. Eluding the Twins, foraging in the wilds outside Ukiah, looting farmland in Comptche, and living in an abandoned house in Clearlake. "For you, it's been a day, but for me… I've been on the run for a whole year now." Ghee shows Natalie his watch, and the date on the watch is twelve months and thirteen days ahead of the actual date.

"Thanks again," Natalie replies. "But how did you end up here?"

Ghee explains how the Twins had him cornered in a vineyard near Windsor. He'd gotten sloppy raiding grapes. But then the Twins got an alert on their phones and just left him standing there with his hands still up in the air. Curious, he followed.

Horrified screams fill the air across the bay. It sickens Natalie to think what the creatures are doing to regular people, murdering and maiming innocents on the streets.

Ghee pops out of existence and reappears several more times, saving whoever he can.

"They're coming. My boss? My boss is leading a sloth army? Why is Aaron doing all this?"

Ghee, Casey, and Natalie walk up to the bridge. On the far side they see Aaron walking toward them. He is followed by hundreds of rabid, bloodthirsty sloths. "I don't know what we can do. These things, they move so fast, they cut people down so easily… These things, they're demons," Ghee says, defeated.

Natalie can only turn away and laugh, just a gut reaction that happened. She doesn't know why.

Casey steps forward and unzips his pants. The patter of urine hits the asphalt of the bridge. Casey sidles from one end of the bridge to the other. Careful to not use up all his pee.

Natalie and Ghee stare at Casey, speechless.

Yeah, sure, why not? Natalie thinks. *This night is already stupid ridiculous.*

"Ghee, can you take me to the other bridge?" The two pop out of existence. By Natalie's count, it's seven seconds before the two reappear. "Seriously, what the hell, Casey?"

Aaron is getting closer with his sloth army from Hell. The three step back. Aaron stops, looks down at the two sloths beside him, and says, "Get me the ring from that girl. Make them suffer."

The two sloths cover the span of half the bridge in seconds, their running animation unbounded, and the sound of their claws clicking on the hard road surface.

A moment of silence.

Casey, Ghee, and Natalie wince in a defensive crouch as the two sloths leap into the air. Two burning husks of meat land at their feet.

Three more charred bodies of dead sloth follow.

"Containment?" Aaron says. "You think this is over? This is not over. The ward will expire, my forces will multiply, and this world will meet its end as I forge a new one in its place."

Aaron turns around, walking back into the city. The sloths follow.

"Is it bad that I want to see what these things taste like?" Ghee asks, stomach churning with a case of the growlies.

Natalie shakes her head, just to be safe. All three pop out of existence to figure out what to do next.

Showstopper

Natalie hasn't come back up from the basement yet. Aaron, or whatever was pretending to be Aaron, wanted the ring. The first priority was getting it back to Babb.

Casey and Ghee didn't know there was an actual night shift. Both were jealous when a stack of free pizzas were delivered and spread out on the table next to Natalie's desk; the company never did anything like that for them on the day shift.

Ghee nods to Casey, and Casey follows him, leaving the testing lab. In the bathroom, Ghee opens one of the stalls and points behind the toilet. Casey struggles to crawl behind the bowl and scratches his arm on the pipes.

"Okay, now try get yourself out of there."

Kicking and flailing his feet, Casey is stuck. After five minutes, Ghee pulls him out.

"Now this is the cool part," Ghee says. "I came across this by accident and tripped walking up the stairs to my apartment. Just one little kick of my toe, and it felt like time had stopped."

Casey kicks his foot against the toilet bowl. Just as Ghee and Natalie had discovered, he was now in Splash Time, operating at a higher rendering rate than the simulation.

Ghee joins him, saying, "You are now moving faster than anyone in this world. They don't see you, because they just can't. I can see you because we're both in this weird Splash Time thing. If you pick anyone up not in Splash Time, they feel like light fluffy pillows, but if you do that, when you take them out of Splash Time, they'll get *so* sick. Watch out for anyone who'll get sick on you. I can't pick you up because we're operating at the same tick rate. This ability doesn't last forever. You have to recharge every couple days. Natalie went all science nerd and figured this stuff out, so ask her if you need to know the science bits. But yeah, this is how we race around like we did tonight."

Still in Splash Time, Casey crawls behind the toilet, he gets stuck like he did the first time. After a few moments of flailing about, Ghee pulls him out and says, "No, no way, you're going to slip into Zippy Time; that's kind of genius."

Ghee only hears the pop before he feels his frame go limp, he sees all the colors in the spectrum flashing by him and gets set down at a convenience store parking lot on the other side of the freeway. Ghee starts puking, his nose is bleeding, and he has wet his pants.

"No, no, you don't ever do that to anyone. I thought I was going to die. I don't think we can physically handle that."

The two walk back to the office, each enjoying a frozen colored ice drink. Natalie is at her desk, waiting for them. Casey hands her an extra drink they bought for her. Ghee blurts out, "This guy… This guy is a genius. You wouldn't believe what he did."

Natalie, serious, sets the drink aside. "Everyone, if you haven't seen the news or heard, we're in showstopper mode as of right now. Put away all your current test plans, regressions, and pet projects. This comes straight from Babb. All our current efforts will be on solving the situation developing in San Francisco."

* * *

It didn't take long for the National Guard to establish a perimeter at all entry points into San Francisco. A few teams went into the city, but were soon eliminated by Aaron's furry minions. News choppers broadcast the first hour of not-safe-for-life carnage on the air, the savage attacks upon the innocent. News quickly spread, and people started barricading themselves in their homes or places of work, some luckier than others. Everyone on the night shift bring their avatars to the bridge, standing at the lookout point, trying to peer through the binoculars. Nobody knew what to do after getting the vague instruction set from Natalie.

* * *

Casey hops onto Jared's station.

"Why do you know how to ward off the sloth army?" Natalie asks him.

At the simulation start screen, he enters the tutorial activation code: up, up, down, down, left, right, left, right, B-button, A-button.

Natalie sits next to him, unimpressed. This is the same tutorial routine everybody runs through. The prompts show off the health bar, how to walk forward and backward, how to crouch, how to jump, run, select tools to use, and communicate with others. The same tutorial routine in use since time immemorial.

"This is not what I got. I'm telling you; it was different. The tutorial that I ran through I played around as a little kitten. I chased mice, I wall ran, and dodged bullets."

Natalie looks at him, concerned.

"Then the tutorial showed me how to defend my home against 'demons.' And that's how I just knew I had to mark the bridges."

Natalie calls Babb; he would know more.

"That's new to him. He's never heard of there being a cat.exe in the system," she says after hanging up. Casey continues trying to reproduce the cat tutorial routine.

Natalie logs into the database, clicks around before opening up the Project Go Australia database. Line by line, she reads through Jared and Aaron's bug entries. The titles are kind of douchey, but she respects their approach to fixing the more critical issues they encountered. The last bug entered by Aaron, adjusting the animation frame rate of sloths, was what she was looking for.

So these things used to be as slow as turtles.

She looks up known nature articles about sloths online. Nothing seemed out of the ordinary for them; they like to live in trees, they ate plants, and had a pleasant demeanor. So why would they become these hateful slayers of mankind? Natalie reads the note Aaron entered last.

```
Note: Fix verified. Thank you so much. You have
no idea how long we've been waiting for this.
Project Australia is a success. Congrats dev
team on doing a fantastic job. We're done here
on this stupid island prison. We're coming home.
We look forward to meeting all of you. Have a
great day bros and brodettes!
```

Natalie finishes catching up. She's surprised her team isn't doing anything constructive. They are being kept from entering San Francisco by the soldiers manning the bridge.

"Wait," she says, "you're all still at the bridge? Come on, we need to know more about this force we're up against."

Natalie starts writing on the whiteboard. A bullet point list to get started:

```
Sloths:

    -    Led by former QA Supervisor Aaron.

    -    Aaron has super speed ability that is
    akin to teleportation.

    -    Top speed of sloths, as recorded by
    the highway patrol, is 88 miles per hour.

    -    Can jump 10-15 feet, depending on
    speed.

    -    Have three deadly claws per paw that
    can rip through body armor.

    -    Can be shot and killed with standard
    firearms.

    -    Claws make them deadly climbers of
```

any surface.

-    Can move silently without being de-
tected.

-    It has been noted sloths can swim,
but these ones have not taken to the water
after being "locked" in San Francisco by
QA employee Casey.

QA Employee Casey:

-    His urine acts as a ward containing
the sloths in San Francisco.

-    Did he get this ability in the car
crash?

-    Did the ability manifest after his
death and respawn into the simulation?

"No, wait, stop. Back up." Casey stares at the board. "I died? What do you mean I died? How, and why am I back here? I don't remember dying."

"Yesterday... no, the day before. Thursday. I gave you a cookie and challenged you to a race home. On the Petaluma stretch, something was jumping from car to car, making them flip over violently. Your car rolled into a ditch, you were pinned upside down, and died in my arms. We still don't know what caused it," Natalie recounts. "As for you respawning, you're in the grace period. Still a trainee, who you were when you woke up Thursday was restored Friday morning. At least that's what Babb told me tonight.

"This... this jabbering isn't advancing the plot. Can anyone get into San Francisco? We need more information," Natalie declares.

* * *

Natalie is pleased, "Good, yeah, that's it. Thank you."

Everyone gathers behind the night shift's star employee, Zed. The armored trucks have thoroughly blocked all lanes of the freeway leading into San Francisco, but Zed at his workstation is controlling his avatar walking below the bridge along the shore. With some deft climbing maneuvers, he was now halfway across the underbelly of the Golden Gate. The height and persistent fog didn't faze him.

Natalie speaks to the room, "You all could learn a thing or two from Zed. See if you can follow him, but be careful."

Zed, now across the bridge, follows the vacant roadway to downtown San Francisco. Remnants of violence are everywhere. Blood stains on the sidewalks, cars with shattered windows, and the scene of where the Twins had fought Aaron and lost. The sloths made a meal out of them.

* * *

Natalie grimly writes on the board that sloths can now be classified as carnivores.

Ghee adds, "Eating plants was what they must have settled on; it's not like they can hunt like they did after getting their movement speed Nerfed."

Natalie reminds Zed, "Remember, keep panning the camera around you once in a while. These things are natural climbers. You don't want them sneaking up from behind or above."

After several blocks, Zed makes his avatar hide behind a car. Two sloths are clawing at a barricaded townhouse, while someone on the second floor fires shotgun blasts out a window. The sloths climb the side of the house, leap into the window, and the whole team listens to the painful screams that follow.

Ghee asks, "If Casey's pee sets these things on fire, why don't we just fly him up in a helicopter and spray them from the air?"

Natalie sits there, considering it.

Casey looks at the two, "No, you guys aren't seriously considering it."

The instant message chime from Natalie's computer rings. "Babb says try it."

Casey pops out of existence, making his way to the lookout point to be picked up.

Zed controlling his avatar continues his recon of the hills of San Francisco, avoiding large masses of the sloths.

* * *

This is awful, all of it. What am I doing here?

Casey's stomach is queasy as the chopper crosses the water toward San Francisco. He thought flying would be cool and awesome, like those 80s action movies where they'd do strafing runs with mounted machine guns and missile launchers. The helicopter feels as if it's being dangled on a string by someone who's had too much coffee.

"Just how am I supposed to pee off the side of this thing if it's rocking back and forth?"

The pilot turns around and says, "Wait, what? Is that what you're here to do?"

Above Van Ness street, Casey looks down as a gas station clerk fends off a pack of sloths with a machine gun.

Casey tells the pilot, "Down there, let's see if this works."

The pilot lowers the chopper. Casey steps out the right side door. The sloths and the convenience store clerk look up as the helicopter hovers. Both parties feel the warm mist and recoil in disgust.

"What the hell are you doing, man? Stop it!" the gas station clerk says as he waves his gun in the air.

Casey looks at the sloths. Nothing. No fire, no rolling around in agony.

The sloths turn their attention to the chopper and make running jumps, but the pilot has ascended out of reach. Natalie debriefed him on the radio about their speed, jumping ability, and climbing prowess.

"The gas station guy is on the roof. He's not going to make it. Can you get down there for a quick pick up? We owe him that at least," Casey says.

The mini mosh pit of sloths leap, but miss, as the helicopter does a sweet swan dive to the roof of the gas station. The armed clerk jumps in. Casey apologetically hands him a packaged cleaning wipe and a dry towel.

"Your pee won't kill these bastards—this will," the clerk says, then he leans out the door, shooting the sloths as the chopper gains more height.

The annoyed pilot declares, "We're going back now, unless you want to try pooping on them next, genius."

* * *

"There's a guy out there with a gun, and he's probably still pissed that I pissed," Casey reflects, back at the office. "Now what?"

Natalie makes the rounds as she checks in on her crew, some of whom gave up trying to climb the bridge. Zed has now made his way to ZigZag Street. Hiding in the bushes, his avatar comes across a familiar scene. Sloths scraping and clawing at a door, a lady with a handgun fires at them. The sloths climb the siding and hop into the window. There is no screaming of pain or agony. Seconds later, two burning husks are tossed out the windows and roll down ZigZag Street, passing Zed.

Natalie directs Zed, "Something is different here. Check out the house, but be careful that lady doesn't shoot you."

Zed approaches the townhouse, keeping to the shadows, peering through the windows. There's nobody downstairs. Everyone has retreated up to the bathroom. A hissing sound catches Zed off guard; he thinks it was a snake at first. Getting back up on his feet after stumbling back,

Zed sees the tail upright. Everyone in the QA lab stares in wonder. Nobody has ever seen a cat pee before, and it douses the whole window frame with a jet like stream.

"The cat is casting a ward, protecting the house, just like you did at the bridges." Natalie tells Casey to thoroughly write down everything he learned in the tutorial on the board.

A shriek can be heard at the bottom of ZigZag Street. Zed turns to look. A lone sloth has discovered the burnt remains of its kind. Zed is frozen, still watching the beast dash and leap rhythmically up the hill. He doesn't even have time to duck or dodge the jump attack.

The window bursts beside Zed. The white and black cat that had sprayed the windows has come to Zed's defense. Zed's avatar crawls up into the house to safety behind the invisible ward barrier thing.

The cat proves to be an agile opponent to the ultra-fast sloth. Casey recognizes the slow motion dodges he once did. The cat swiping at the sloth leaves burn marks on the demon. The cat pounces for the sloth, going in for the kill, but the sloth does an inhuman backflip, launching the cat into the air, and the cat lands with a sick thud onto the cobblestone road. Eight times, the cat died at the hands of the sloth, it comes back to life one last time, and jumps into the house defeated, but still alive.

Ghee states, "I don't get it. Cats have infinite lives. They can fight these things off until they win."

Casey shakes his head. "Franky, bugged it on my first day."

Natalie leaves to go see Babb about reversing it.

The cat sidles up to Zed. Zed pets the cat as it licks its wounds. In a quiet moment between the two, the cat nuzzles its face against avatar Zed's face.

"I think you're protected now, Zed. If you leave the house, they can't touch you," Casey explains.

Zed crawls out the window. There's no sign of the sloth that fought the little cat before.

Natalie returns. "We can't reverse the bug. It was entered, it was fixed, no going back now. Everyone, just pack up your stuff. We're done for tonight. I'll see you tomorrow. We'll get in touch with the media about San Francisco residents seeking refuge with neighbors who own cats, or taking in stray tabbies. A stop measure solution for the time being."

"Zed, what are you doing? You can log off."

Zed is face to face with the sloth that tried to kill him just four minutes earlier. "Wait, is it recoiling?"

Zed approaches the sloth and it shrieks as if in pain.

"The cat from that house marked Zed," Casey explains. "I think he's protected from them, but it only lasts one day."

The shrieking sloth has attracted more of its kind. Zed pans the camera, and there are dozens surrounding him, snarling. They are kept at bay, a five-foot invisible barrier given by the kindly little cat from ZigZag Street. A sonic boom knocks avatar Zed down on his butt when Aaron slips out of Splash Time and stands face to face with Zed.

"You think you're protected? From me?" Aaron steps past the invisible barrier the sloths can't breach. Aaron, using his right hand, grabs Zed's left hand. "Nuh uh, you're not going to log out to safety, bro. I want them all to see this at the QA lab. Hi guys!"

Aaron raises his left hand. Three claws emerge from his knuckles. In stereo, Zed screams in pain as Aaron slashes him with his retractable claw. The screaming is coming from the TV monitor speakers and Zed stuck holding the controller. Real life Zed's face is slashed open and bleeding, blood soaking through his t-shirt.

Aaron triumphantly picks up Zed's avatar, above his head, looking directly at the camera. "Who eats monkeys?" Aaron punctures Zed's heart with his claws and throws him to the ground. "We eat monkeys!"

Real life Zed slumps onto the floor from his workstation chair, letting go of the controller.

You dead, Zed, LMAO, pops up on the screen.

The image blurry, the sloths can vaguely be seen eating the chimpanzee. Everyone who is still in the QA lab starts weeping. Zed was their best friend. A little innocent ape that Up & Down hobo brought to work. Zed proved himself a more useful employee at finding bugs in the simulation, with his unorthodox testing methodology, compared to his former owner.

Natalie covers Zed with her long jacket, *"Requiescat in pace."*

Crunch Time

Everyone got the alert from Babb at 7:00 in the morning. Casey arrived forty-five minutes early, forgetting it was Saturday. There was no commute log jam to contend with, as most sane people were still in bed, asleep. The first thing that caught his eye was the blood stain, where Zed the chimpanzee had died. Everyone who arrived learned how Aaron had murdered a QA tester bypassing the controller-real world barrier.

Half of the daytime crew quit on the spot.

"Dude, you didn't tell me you died," Doug asks Casey. "What was it like?"

"I don't remember," Casey answers.

Randy, at his station, hasn't said anything. What's left of the team is waiting for him to give direction on what they should be working on, any targets of interest to help resolve the currently contained Slothpocalypse.

"See, I came up with that just now," says Doug.

Karina slaps his arm. "Liar, you heard me on the phone walking in."

Doug laughs. "Yeah, she came up with it."

Still nothing from Randy.

Natalie texted that she's scheduled to supervise the night shift. That is, if any of them show up, given they witnessed Aaron's display of power. Casey gets up and stands next to Randy, who's fixated on the news reports repeating the graphic footage captured the night before, clicking on uploaded phone footage that is up close and uncensored. Randy sits, staring at Aaron's empty seat.

"Do you know what?" Randy says. "I'm good. I've had my fill. I think I might just go up to Mount Shasta and wait for this whole thing to blow over." The whole crew watches Randy neatly put on his brown jacket, turn off his computer, and walk out the door.

"Um, he left us? What are we supposed to do now?" Doug asks, looking around at the skeleton crew still there.

Casey walks up to the whiteboard Natalie had filled out. "Okay, I'll try to catch you all up on what happened at San Francisco. These are the facts and what we learned…"

* * *

Everyone mills around the lab, still waiting for direction, not sure where to start or what to focus on. Casey sits down at Randy's desk, staring at the log in screen.

No, you didn't. What's wrong with you? Shaking his head that typing, 'Randy' actually worked, Casey looks around at the supervisor tier shortcuts on the computer's desktop screen. The DB app shows all the bugs the day crew have entered awaiting approval to be sent up to the dev team, and bugs needing more info sent back down or waiting to be regressed. A few clicks more and he finds the company internal website message board. The top four active threads that have thousands of user replies are:

- Showstopper mode? It's the weekend, go away. (9789 replies)

- Why Australia needs to be wiped off the map… (18987 replies)

- Come on, this is why we have a Staging Branch (0 replies)

- Blah blah blah Staging Branch, we get it, you like your precious Staging Branch. (2698 replies, most of which are reaction gifs).

Before Casey can even click into any of the curious message board posts, a chime rings through the headphones. Babb is messaging Randy via the private messaging app: `Authentication handshake code please.`

Casey stares, looking around, trying to find any scribbled notes or passwords. Casey replies, `Authentication Code: Bravo Alpha Mike Foxtrot`

Several seconds pass by.

`Authentication code accepted.`

Casey is relieved, who knows what they would do to him if they found out he was impersonating his direct supervisor.

`Status report, what measures are you taking to address the San Francisco showstopper?`

Casey looks around and starts barking orders off the top of his head, then replies: `I've assigned several workers to do drone reconnaissance in San Francisco, figure out what the sloths and Aaron are doing. Ascertain why they aren't attempting to cross the bay, as sloths are known to swim. Several workers are now researching cat combat techniques; they have shown the capability of fighting them, but eventually lose. I am going to the small village of Taswell, where a feline expert resides, for more info.`

Casey waits for Babb's reply. `Good, great. That's all I needed to hear, temporary supervisor Casey.`

The chat session ends. There's no time for Casey to be horrified at that last statement and that Babb knew all along. They all have work to do.

* * *

It's been a quiet drive to Taswell. The car tires thump occasionally on the bridge joint connectors.

Karina breaks the silence. "Santa Rosa?"

Casey answers, "Santa Rosa? I live there."

She continues, "But why? I've been there. Why Santa Rosa?"

Casey thinks for a moment. "It's where I've always lived. I grew up there."

Karina goes quiet again as they count the thuds the tires make.

"It's so barren, though," Karina says eventually. "You never wanted to live somewhere more interesting? I went there to visit my ex-boyfriend. Brown, rolling hills; dying, uncut grass; occasional redwood trees; and flat, dead air to go with the flat, dead land. It's like the art team wasn't even trying when they made Santa Rosa. 'Nope, this is good enough, let's go get some enchiladas.' "

Casey laughs. He never thought of it that way before.

"Taswell, Taswell is a gift," Karina continues. "We have that big giant mountain; pure, tall evergreen trees; waterfalls; and so much wildlife to enjoy when you go for hikes or mountain biking. You should move to Taswell. Whoever made it cared. You can see the craftsmanship everywhere you go."

It was not hyperbole; her words were fact. The entrance into Taswell was a seven hundred year old redwood tree that was tunneled to accommodate average size cars and trucks. Main Street was decorated in the style of an alpine village in Europe. The asphalt highway became a cobblestone roadway, with road markings, not painted, but hand placed in stone. Yellow stone indicated the dividing line; white lines marked crossing paths for pedestrians, and red lanes on the sides were sectioned off for cyclists. All of it intricately planned and executed to perfection.

Turning off Main Street, she tells Casey where to go, the residential section of Taswell located near the base of the mountain. The first house he sees is a giant two story log house made from golden cedar with a green, moss-covered roof. The second house isn't exactly a house, but two giant isosceles triangles that merged with each other in a cross formation, the house frame formed with cold blue steel and the majority of the exterior covered with dark purple tinted windows. The third house is made of smaller red bricks, the driveway also red brick, and the chest high fence: red bricks.

"Okay, I get it. You like red bricks," Casey jokes.

Karina points out her house. The first floor of the house is circular and painted light golden brown, the second floor is square, with dark brown shingles, the rain awnings on top of the second floor layer have been painted light yellow, and the third floor of the house is circular with white frosted glass windows on top interspersed among the golden brown stucco surface.

"Your house is…" Casey starts.

Karina finishes, "A cheeseburger?" She bursts into a fit of laughter as Casey slows down, examining the house.

"So you like cheeseburgers?"

Karina stops laughing. "No, I'm a vegetarian."

At the end of the road is a ranch, green grass for several acres, and in the center a white two story house with pink picket fences caught in the shadow of the giant alpine mountain.

The two exit the car and approach the front porch. A little old lady in her early 60s comes out the front door to greet them. "Karina! Are you on your way to paint? Just a little warning, people have seen Tazzy out there at the edge of the tree line."

After Karina explains who Casey is and why they've come, Casey and the old lady go into the quiet home and sit down on the couch while Karina goes for a walk to sneak a cigarette.

"Such a nice girl… How long have you two been together?"

Casey breaks the news that they aren't.

"Shame. Such a lovely lady. So, what did you want from little old me?"

Casey looks around. A tall, dark grandfather clock ticks in the corner. A bowl full of hard candy on top of the TV. "No cats?" he asks.

She replies, "Yeah, no cats."

The lady goes to the kitchen to turn off the whistling teapot and comes back with lemon iced tea for Casey. "I'm a cat expert, not a cat collector. Living with dozens of cats and home soaked with urine and poop? I'm not a crazy person. Okay, let's start."

***

Karina comes back from the far end of the field to find Casey sitting in the car.

"Learn anything?" she asks.

"No, not really. She just repeated what I already found online. That cats were big in Egypt, that they worshipped Mafdet and Bast. She looked at me strangely, wondering why I wanted to know if cats could dodge bullets or ward off demons. She did offer to give me a discount if I ever wanted a cat spayed at her vet practice in town."

Just as Karina is about to enter the car, she stops and looks up. Casey had noticed them clustered earlier on the power line, chirping.

"That was my bug, until you stole it," he says.

Karina smiles. "No, it was my bug. I found it fair and square. Besides, I just found a bug of a bug."

Casey is curious, but she doesn't say anymore. Instead, she reaches into her purse and pulls out a paper notepad and pencil. "I shrugged it off the first time when I found them last week, but now... Now there's something to this."

Casey sits in silence as she jots something down. When she's done, Karina hands Casey the paper:

... --- ... / .-- . / .- .-. . / - .-. .- --. --. . -.. / .. -. / - .... / -... --- -.. .. ..

.-.. --- .-.. / .--- ..- ... - / -.- .. -.. -.. .. -. -. --.

.- ... -.- / .... . .-. / .- -... --- ..- - / - .... . / ... .. -.-. -.- / --- -.. . .. ...

"I don't know what this is. Do you know what this is?" Casey confesses.

"SOS. That's all I know. How do you not know what SOS is, Casey? Let's go to my house and search online."

Even the doorknob was shaped like a cheeseburger. Karina invites Casey in, and he's struck by all the paintings hanging on the walls. The first floor is a pseudo art gallery. A clean white space with ambient lighting showing off her work.

"It's how he found me, actually."

"Who?" Casey asks.

"Babb, obviously. His wife dragged him to my show, he looked at them and offered me a job on the spot."

Casey takes a closer look at the paintings:

Bear shoots lightning out of navel.

Lumberjack crushed by cubed tree blocks.

Deer spitting fireballs after eating red flowers.

Treasure chest spawns behind Mount Sid Waterfall every 7 days.

"These are bugs. You were painting bugs?"

She answers, "I didn't know. I would go out to the woods, paint nature, and sell them at my art shows. And now I go to that office and get full dental and a 401k, on top of the paintings people buy from me. Babb has given me leeway to not only bug nature anomalies, but I can take all the time I want to capture these discoveries on canvas."

Casey looks at a painting near the stairway and says, *"Vengeful raincloud stalks bunny."* Casey is caught by the imagery. A white rabbit soaking wet from a single cloud above, while the green forest around him is basking in the sunlight.

"That one made me cry. No matter how quickly it hopped, the rain cloud would always follow him around. After I finished the painting, I came back to see if it would accept my umbrella. But now, there's a wolf out there in the forest stuck with that rain cloud for the rest of its stupid little life."

The internet is so great. A few button clicks and they had the messages the birds were trying to say. Casey says it out loud: " 'Ask her about the sick ones.' "

The sign is dark brown, the lettering lighter brown, and the edges of the vertical frame are lit by pink and purple neon signs. " 'Finley,' " Karina reads. "She said she had to come in on her weekend to treat a gerbil or hamster, some rat thing."

The little old lady they just met comes out with a little kid and his pet snake. "You two again?"

Casey debates explaining why they made a second visit. Karina asks, "Cats... Do you have any sick cats?"

Finley leads them to the back of her vet clinic, where cats and dogs are locked in cages. "The dogs are okay and are awaiting adoption. But these cats... These cats are sick. They are scheduled to be destroyed, because nobody wants a poor sick cat."

"What's wrong with them?" Casey asks.

"Nothing really. FIV, most of them. They're perfectly safe for us humans." Finley takes a golden yellow cat from the cage and picks it up. "See, perfectly safe, aren't you MelissOWWWWWWW." Finley puts the cat back in the cage, disapprovingly glaring at the little cat. "Bad cat." The two watch the old lady dab her scratch with a tissue. "I'll tell you what, you take this little beast off my hands and I'll give you free checkups for a year."

Karina refuses, stating she's a dog person. Casey thinks about it, but declines too.

"Well, if you ever change your mind, you can come back any time you want. Well, come Monday, this little Fairy Godmother is going in the oven, aren't you little Melissa? You're going in the oven, and you're going to burn. Because bad kitties are meant to be cooked in the purifying light of God's fire. You think you can scratch me and get away with it? Consequences, Melissa. There will be consequences."

Taswell, upon reflection, is just one giant bug needing to be fixed. Casey has no idea where to start, but it's a gold mine. That's his thought process as they exit the intentionally quaint, weird little village.

"There's no way that town is normal. I mean, its biome is completely different compared to the rest of California. How do people not see it?"

Karina stares at Casey and says, "It's my home. I like it there. I'll tell you what. When Babb promotes me to the art department, I'll fix Santa Rosa for you, okay? Just leave Taswell alone."

Casey is thinking about San Francisco smoldering from the carnage still unfolding across the bay. "I think, for science, we should take one of those sick cats. There had to be a reason, right?" Not thinking, Casey pulls the e-brake, and he'd remember later as being kind of awesome, doing a slick U-turn back to the village.

Karina, checking to see if she has whiplash, says, "I didn't know your little windup car could do that."

The purple and pink neon lights around the sign flicker. Finley's vet office is closed. Casey and Karina step inside. The lights are off. The aluminum shutters only let in a sliver of daylight diffused by the goldfish aquarium in front of the window. Magazines are torn and strewn across the white and black checkerboard floor. A lamp shines on a poster of a cat hanging in a tree by its paws. A disembodied voice echoes through the empty front lobby, "Hello, bad cat, do you want my disease? Hello, bad cat, what color do you bleed?"

The thin ceiling tiles rustle and thump as it approaches the two. Casey runs for the counter, while Karina jumps to the side behind the aquarium. From the corner of their eyes, they see the flimsy tiles give way under her body weight, and Finley crashes down onto the hard floor with a grunt.

Karina laughs. "I didn't mean to. I'm sorry. Are you okay?"

Finley does a backflip and reveals her bloodshot eyes and the right side of her now sagging face. She ignores Karina, who is dialing for help, and focuses entirely on Casey. "Here kitty kitty kitty. Are you a good kitty?"

He doesn't even feel the first one, but knows something is wrong when the second one hits. Casey stares at his palm. "Scissors... You threw scissors at me." He winces as he pulls it out and ducks behind the counter. "What's wrong with you, lady? Seriously!"

Karina yanks on the chain, opening the security shutters, letting in the near noon sunlight. Finley lets out a high pitched scream of pain. Karina grabs Casey's punctured hand and they run to the back room.

"Is she burning because of the sunlight?"

"No," Karina answers, "I think it's just in her head. Come on, hurry."

The two barricade themselves in the caged dog and cat room.

"Maybe we should let these guys go."

Karina shakes her head. "Not if they can infect others the way they got Finley."

Casey grabs an empty travel case for a cat.

Karina warns, "Be careful."

Casey opens up the cat cage for Melissa and she jumps in. "Okay, let's just go." Casey looks up at the ceiling tiles rustling above them and says, "I forgot she does that now."

The two exit the back of the vet building and run to the front where the car is parked. Karina looks behind her and shoves Casey out of the way, dodging the handful of scissors and knives Finley is throwing. Karina gets in her side of the car first, locking the passenger side door. Casey is slower, trying to secure the cat in the backseat. He hears her grave laugh and he turns around slowly. Her arms are raised, dual wielding both a scalpel and a scissor. She leaps into the air for the kill, but lands at Casey's feet, twitching from electrical shock.

Casey can still hear her buzzing from the voltage as she utters, "He Tazz'd me, bro," from her clenched teeth.

Karina gets out of the car and yells, "Tazzy!"

Casey looks down the street, a giant brown grizzly bear standing upright nods to the two of them before going back on all fours and running to the tree line.

***

"What just happened?" Casey asks as the paramedics cart Finley into the back of the ambulance. They have her strapped down and are taking her to quarantine. More government disease control looking authorities arrive and round up all the other animals still inside the vet office. The medic begins bandaging Casey's palm, and his right shoulder after Karina pulled the second scissors out.

She looks at him, says, "Crunch time. It happens," and laughs.

Karina drives back to the office, the cat purring in the backseat. Casey asks about the bear.

"Tazzy the Taswell Bear?"

Casey nods.

"We don't need law enforcement in Taswell. When anything bad is about to happen or is happening, Tazzy just runs out from the forest and shoots electricity from his belly button. Non-lethal, without escalating things further. Babb, he's considering replacing all law enforcement with bears like Tazzy. I mean, really, who would be dumb enough to try start something with an electricity shooting grizzly bear?"

***

"You can't just bring infectious animals to work. We have procedures. Did you even fill out the form? Geesh." The front desk girl scoops the cat cage out of Casey's hand and takes it to some unseen room down the hall.

"Yeah, Casey, why didn't you fill out the form. It's not like you were driving here," Karina mocks.

Casey sits down at his station. Doug is still absorbed as he pilots his hobbyist aerial drone through downtown San Francisco.

Danny walks up to Casey, looking him over, smiling, and says, "Taswell, yeah, I try to stay out of there. Filed a bug, just needs your approval." Casey watches him exit with his dog to go for lunch.

```
Bug: Cats enter ragdoll state when falling.

Severity: A

Reproduction Rate: 100

Steps to Reproduce:

    1. Pick up a cat by its four legs, holding
    it upside down.

    2. Preferably drop the cat on a soft sur-
    face, such as a pillow or bed.

    3. Observe falling motion of cat.

Result: Cats when falling from any height, or
are dropped from any height, enter a ragdoll
state.

Impact: Exactly! When in a ragdoll state, Cats
cannot recover or prevent damage from falls
while in mid-air.
```

Expected: Highly mobile creatures, such as cats, should have the built-in capability of adapting to falls, utilizing their bodies, tails, and feet to successfully land when in a falling state of animation.

Notes: This is related to Showstopper CA/SF-003. Cats, while in combat versus the sloths, inevitably get knocked into the air and the falls are either fatal or leave them vulnerable to secondary attacks. Correcting this should increase the survivability of cats during this critical period.

Casey stares at the bug after reading it over. What if making cats even stronger leads to another showstopper if they somehow solve the sloth crisis? What if cats decide they want to take over the Earth, and humanity is unable to stop them? Writing bugs discovered in the field is one thing, but approving them is something else entirely. There are so many unforeseen consequences, and it all starts with the press of the "approve" button in the drop down menu of the database.

A chime rings through on his computer headphones. Babb is summoning him to lunch in the basement.

***

Casey peeks in, half-expecting gunfire from Babb again. Instead, he sees two light pink cardboard paper boxes sitting on the desk. Casey sits down. The two sit quietly, eating their sandwiches. Casey wants to ask all the questions that come to mind about why they're in the simulation, what killed him on the freeway, showstoppers, and the business that unfolded in Australia. Babb opens up a crinkly bag of chips and starts eating the crunchy, kettle-boiled potatoes, leaving Casey imagining the sloths doing the same to humans, right now, forty minutes away.

"Rollback... We can't just do a rollback and undo all the damage they've done? Undo the bugs that got fixed?" Casey asks.

Babb laughs lightly. "That would be easy, wouldn't it? Just wave your hand and everything is all better, like magic or some nonsense. And no, that blank check promise that you and Natalie still have, those won't fix showstoppers. Those are more practical in nature, like an invisible flying car or never having to pay taxes. I'm not a wizard. There are too many pieces to the puzzle, systems on top of systems, a global rollback and reverting to a previous build state just isn't possible. I've always thought being always online was a mistake."

Casey internally debates eating the cookie in his lunch box.

"My wife doesn't let me eat cookies. Mind if we trade? Your cookie for this apple?"

***

After returning upstairs, Casey watches his crew come back in from lunch. He found the cat, Melissa, waiting for him on his desk. The biology lab gave her a clean bill of health. She was no longer carrying the insane rage disease she passed on to Finley. Casey sits down at his workstation, re-reads Danny's bug, and approves it.

Barely twenty minutes pass and it gets kicked back to Casey, who then, using the DB program, forwards it to Danny to regress.

Danny politely asks to borrow Melissa. He lifts her up over couch cushions taken from the entrance lobby and drops her. Danny is suitably impressed with the fix and how agile the cat was able to re-orientate its body to land without injury.

"That's so cool. Maybe this will help those cats now." Casey then officially tags the bug as `Fix Verified`.

***

"You kept wondering why they don't just swim across the bay. I was asking Karina why they don't just head south to San Jose," Doug says as he hands Casey a scribbled-on San Francisco tourist map.

Casey examines it, noting all the zones the sloths have been attacking. For whatever reason, the sloths do not venture south beyond Golden Gate Park, the Haight, and Sixteenth Street.

"See? They always stick to major roadways and streets," Doug says. "They don't venture onto trails or into alleyways."

Karina adds, "Maybe they're not programmed to?"

Casey briefly chats with Babb on the instant messenger app.

"Okay, Doug and Karina, jump on the elevator and meet with the designers on level three. You two have some path nodes to help remove."

The day shift has done its part. Casey thanks everyone for coming in on this particular Saturday and helping out where they could. Danny and his dog exit, just as Natalie enters. "Look at you, stepping up in the world. What happened to Randy?"

Casey explains everything as he passes the baton to the night crew, commenting on his notes as Natalie reads them over. "Do you want a cat?"

Natalie laughs. "Hell no, I'm still trying to get rid of my stupid dog. Just take it back to that lady in Taswell."

Casey looks at his still fresh wounds.

Natalie tries reassuring him. "She's okay now, mostly."

***

The setting sun makes the snowcapped mountain light orange behind Finley's lone house. After exiting the car, retrieving Melissa from the backseat, Casey approaches the front.

"What do you want?" Finley asks, holding a knife in her hand. She looks down at it. "Oh, no… No, not that. I'm sorry for earlier. I don't know what came over me. I was just cutting some meat for stew."

Casey holds up the traveling cage. "I don't know what to do with the cat, and thought I'd return it."

He approaches the front porch to hand over the cage. Behind Finley, a dark spotted white and black cat darts from the living room to the kitchen.

"I'll take her back to the office in the morning," Finley says. "Thank you."

Down the hall, a cat jumps out of the bathroom fighting a toilet roll. Finley notices Casey is distracted and looks back. "Silly rascals, all of them. Do you want to come in for tea and cookies? It's the least I can do after throwing those sharp things at you. Again, I'm so sorry."

Casey hesitates as he hands over the cage, his hand still sore from the wound he acquired earlier. Still, he follows her inside the house and she shows him a spot on the couch as she goes to the kitchen to finish up. Three of the cats rub against his pant leg, purring. Two more sit on the couch opposite him, staring. Two kittens tumble down the stairs, chasing each other, playing.

In the time it takes for Finley to finish making dinner and prepare a tray of cookies, Casey counts twelve cats running around the house.

The two sit down opposite each other and Finley shoos the cats aside. "After I was discharged this afternoon, the medical staff asked me if I wanted them back. I couldn't bring them to that cold, dark office again. Look at how alive my house is. I'm surrounded by these cute little babies. My babies."

Casey nods.

"I really don't know what came over me. There was something about you that I was drawn to—an aura or something, I don't know."

Finley goes quiet, her warm face becomes cold and stern, then she says, "Kill me. In my head, I wanted you to kill me. Make me dead. Take those scissors and slice me open, feed on the kill you've earned." She shakes her head and smiles. "Do you want another cookie, or some to go?"

Casey kindly declines and asks, "The doctors… Do they know what happened to you?"

Finley hands over the medical file she has to give to her doctor on Monday.

Casey isn't a medical doctor and a lot of the jargon, test result abbreviations, and scans mean nothing to him. Just a short, barely legible discharge paragraph on the third page:

```
Patient infected with a tier 1 parasite of
unknown origin. Eyewitness accounts indicate
infection was instant, with fast acting psy-
chological effects with a predilection towards
self-destructive violence. Pure electric shock,
from the Primal dubbed 'Tazzy,' neutralized the
parasite. Patient returned to a more function-
ing state. Test results indicate patient is
a carrier of tier 5 parasites, remnants from
the shock, and pose no threat to humans. Para-
site can migrate to smaller hosts, if given the
chance, but with proper treatment and therapy
the patient will return to a functioning, well-
mannered state in a week or two. - J.F.
```

The grandfather clock loudly chimes six times. Casey uses this as his excuse to leave, to go maybe pick up fast food on the way home. He thanks Finley for being a generous host and tells her he doesn't hold her at fault with the scissor throwing earlier in the day. Melissa sits at Casey's feet, looking up at him.

"I think she likes you," Finley comments.

Casey looks down and Melissa walks into the traveling cage next to the front door. "Huh. I guess she's mine now."

Finley waves happily as Casey reverses and turns the car around. He considers just going back to work at the office, but Natalie and Ghee told him to go home and rest.

PVP

She stands there waiting for Casey to come home from Taswell. The elevator door slowly opens. Casey steps off, holding the cat cage in one hand and a bag of greasy tacos in the other. He stops mid-stride as he notices the giant, shiny butcher knife in her left hand.

"There's always a doorway, always a woman, always a knife."

She stares at him coolly, not saying anything, then casually flips the knife to her right hand.

"I'm not sure what you're playing at, but I'd like to end this day not getting stabbed again."

He slowly approaches Natalie. She still hasn't responded and he proceeds to open the door to his dark condo, keeping an eye on her just to be safe.

"You're Natalie, but you're not Natalie," Casey notes aloud.

Natalie flips the knife to her left hand again. Casey laughs, takes out his phone, and calls Natalie.

"Hi, you're idling in the hallway. Not sure how long you've been here or if you freaked out the neighbors, but I'm home now."

Avatar Natalie becomes aware and looks at Casey and says, "Sorry, whoops, can I come in?"

The cat carrier is set down by the living room couch and the cage door opened for Melissa. Casey is digging in his kitchen cabinet for plates. He sits down with Natalie at the table and serves her one of the tacos.

"You know what? Your food would be wasted on virtual me. I'm sure you're hungry after coming back from the other side of the bay," Natalie says as she looks down at the plate and napkin.

Casey insists. His grandmother always said to be a good host to guests.

"Okay. This is kind of a work visit," she says, "so make sure to log this time in the system as overtime."

Casey starts eating the taco, half-conscious Natalie is watching him, and he tries not to make a mess of the stuffed veggies, cheese, and meat. Halfway through his first bite, Natalie picks up her taco, raising the food to her mouth. Casey stops, transfixed by what he is seeing. Natalie's jaw opens wide, wider than what is physically possible. It looks as if her lower jawbone dislocates and the cheek muscles are the only thing keeping it from falling to the floor. In one motion, Natalie shoves the whole taco into her mouth, her jaw closes, and the food is gone.

"What? Do I have some lettuce on me… or sauce?"

All Casey can think of is the documentary he watched where a snake swallowed an egg whole. "Is that what we look like when our avatars eat?" he asks.

Natalie looks at him, clearly wondering what he's talking about. Casey pulls out his cell phone, slides the taco to Natalie to eat, and this time he records it then sends the video clip to her email at work. Virtual Natalie idles, tapping her fingers on the table while she is away.

Casey starts on his taco and is almost finished when she returns to consciousness and says, "Oh my God. That was gross. That's a bug; it's yours. File it when we're not in showstopper mode."

Finished with his food, he asks, "So, what did you need from me and why did you bring the knife?"

Natalie is still distracted. "Oh, no. Sorry. I was thinking of all the times I cheated. Thanksgiving, Christmas, and my birthday. I was at work, but I used my virtual self to go to those functions. I had no idea that was going on. The camera doesn't show that when it's in first or third person mode." She breaks out laughing, "I never knew why my dad ran to the bathroom, trying not to get sick. And I can't tell him if I wanted to, this stupid NDA."

Natalie and Ghee were trying to figure out how Aaron was able to kill Zed the night before. They would pick fights with people, lose badly, and even try to antagonize Tazzy. Physical harm wasn't carrying over from the simulation to the testing environment.

"So my big idea was, maybe it's because we're testers. The people who assaulted us were regular folk. Maybe Aaron was able to kill Zed because he is still an employee, and maybe some protections don't apply when it's person versus person."

Casey returns from the kitchen after rinsing the dishes, offers her a soda or water, then she says, "So, yeah, I don't want you to stab me, but just a tiny little cut on my finger. We don't need neighbors calling the police if my avatar starts freaking out if you stab her like a crazy person, and you don't need me gushing blood all over your place either."

Natalie hands Casey the knife. Casey chooses the right index finger, and slices a tiny little cut, drawing blood. Virtual Natalie pulls her hand back swiftly, and with her other hand, punches the knife out of his hand.

"That wasn't me. That was a basic defense subroutine. Nope… nothing. Well, that sucks. I didn't feel any pain on this side." Natalie stands up to get back to work and try a few more violent tests with Ghee in Novato. She looks down at the cat carrier. "What's wrong with your cat? It's still in the cage."

Natalie exits Casey's place, enters her apartment, and logs out to go do more testing.

***

First, there was a lump of tuna and a saucer of water. Next, warm milk heated on the stove. After that, pieces of leftover fried chicken. Then, fried hamburger from a taco. When that didn't work, he busted out the microwave lasagna. A trip to the corner store for dried cat food and even catnip. Melissa decided she was staying in the carrier cage, with a whole floor full of food in front of her, a feast for cats.

Casey sits on the balcony, drinking his soda. He reads the texts from Natalie and Ghee, still no solution to their little side project. Doug and Karina had finally finished modifying and deleting the ancient path nodes the sloths still abide by; humans are free to go and do as they please, but sloths were subconsciously drawn to patrolling the streets that had invisible beacons.

Slowly, like ants drawn to wild berries or garbage, the sloths have begun migrating to the northern tip of San Francisco. Casey goes inside to the living room, turning on the television. News broadcasters have caught on to the migration and aerial footage shows the sloth army patrolling the Embarcadero. In the dying light of day, Casey realizes how large the swarm of sloths was that Aaron brought with him from Australia. The news reporter is relaying a request from the military for any civilians to leave the coastal portions of the city and move inland to safety. He can only assume the army is planning air strikes or some kind of ground assault to wipe them out.

The cat still hasn't come out of the cage, and Casey doesn't want to stick his hand in there and force her out. The food is starting to attract flies, so he cleans up the buffet from the floor and starts washing the dishes. As he's drying the plates, he hears a chirp, peers into the living room, but nothing. Starting on the forks and butter knives, there's another chirp, still nothing going on in the living room. Finished, Casey goes to the balcony with his glass of iced soda topped off. That angry looking jerk is glaring at him from Natalie's balcony again, not smoking this time.

"What?" Casey asks.

Russian Mob Guy with the chains goes back inside her apartment. Across the street, Karina's prime number birds are lined up on the power line. He counts out the sequence: "2, 2, 5, 7, 11, 12, 17, 19." They are chirping in Morse code again:

.--. .-.. . .- ... . / -.-. .-.. --- ... . /

−.−− −−− ..− .−. / −.. −−− −−− .−.

"Why should I?" Casey asks the birds. Just as he says that, one of the birds from the Prime Five cluster flies straight at him. He ducks, covering his face. The breeze of it whizzing by his head causes him to look inside his condo. The bird flew right into Melissa's cage with a death chirp. Casey goes inside, closes his balcony door. The prime number birds fly away. On his knees, he peeks into the carrier cage. Melissa coughs up a feather.

***

Fog rolled in earlier tonight on the Golden Gate, a glitch in the system. Natalie and Ghee stand eight feet away from Casey's magical pee barrier.

"What are we doing here? We still haven't figured out how he killed Zed," Ghee says as he zips up his jacket.

Natalie, shivering from the cold sea breeze, answers, "He told us to come here, to see."

Instead, they listen.

Natalie hears wood popping from a hot campfire. Ghee has visions of gleefully crushing bubble wrap as a child. It takes the two of them a moment to find out where the noise originated. Natalie points. They see little sparks of flame erupting on the Bay Bridge that connects San Francisco to Taswell, on the section near Treasure Island, before the tunnel. It soon becomes louder and more intense.

Natalie laughs. "It's like the annual San Diego blow off."

Each year, half the country's firework stock is brought to San Diego, carted out to open water, and every firework is ignited at the same time. It gets so loud people three blocks away need to wear ear muffs or plugs.

"What's going on?" Ghee asks.

They just watch the blazing ball of fire get brighter and louder, a nonstop chain of explosions. And then it stops. The ball of light fades with only faint embers of what remains.

Pop.

Casey appears, nursing his ears, "HOLY COW THAT WAS SO LOUD! WHY DIDN'T YOU GUYS MEET ME OVER THERE? THAT WAS AWESOME!"

Natalie looks at a smiling Casey and says, "You said 'the bridge.' We just came here."

Casey replies, "I ASKED BABB TO SEVER THE PATHNODE TO THE GOLDEN GATE. ANOTHER BIG GIANT CLIMAX ON THIS BRIDGE IS SUCH A TIRED TROPE. TIME FOR THE BAY BRIDGE TO HAVE SOME FUN TOO."

Ghee pops into Splash Time, grabs Casey unexpectedly, and sets him down in a T-Pose.

Casey looks around and then puts his arms down to his sides. "That fixed it? My ears aren't ringing anymore. Thanks, Ghee."

Ghee nods. "No problem. TALKING IN ALL CAPS IS JUST AN-NOYING, DUDE. Just take it down, be smooth be quiet."

The three watch Taswell firetrucks approach the bridge, extinguishing the fire of burned sloth corpses.

"Melissa is the chosen one," Casey announces. "She jumped from sloth to sloth fighting them, getting in some licks, and moving on to the next. The other Finley cats followed her example. It didn't have to be a fight to the death. I just remember standing there on the bridge watching every one of those demon sloths running at me, and bursting into flame when they crossed the barrier, bodies exploding from the immense heat. Tazzy was there, blasting them with his belly button lightning bolts."

Natalie is sad she missed out. "Wait… Bears have belly buttons?"

Casey shrugs. "I'm not a bear-ologist. Maybe?"

All three of them only heard the tires screech, as they found themselves looking straight at the high beam headlights of a big white ice cream truck. There wasn't enough warning to jump into Splash Time, but they clumsily fall backward behind a concrete barrier, separating road traffic from the pedestrian lane. Casey looks at Natalie and Ghee and both signal that they're mostly okay. The truck engine is still revving, tires still spinning.

Drums and a horn section set the beat: a quick marching pace. Every eight paces, the flute and strings section aurally make a stabbing noise, followed by more marching beats.

"You scumbag cheaters, do you like it?" Aaron asks, looking at the three from his side of Casey's defensive barrier. "I thought I would have had all week to compose this sweet boss battle theme, but you had to cross the line."

Natalie asks, "What did we do? You were running around killing and eating everybody. We had to stop you."

Aaron nods, eyes closed, conducting the symphony of horror. The ice cream truck is filled with speakers, subwoofers, and an amp pumping out the unholy music. From time to time, you can hear members of the San Francisco Orchestra cry and be threatened by Aaron's unseen sloth underlings. The horns start doing a combative back and forth melody versus the strings.

"Here it comes." Aaron opens his eyes, smiling at them, the opera starts singing:

Bradipi sono così grand,

gli esseri umani così debole,

proprio come i dinosaur.

Pancetta!

Gustosa carne umana.

Carne prelibatezze.

Pancetta!

Pancetta!

Noi siamo l'esercito bradipo.

Gustosa carne umana.

Noi siamo l'esercito bradipo.

Pancetta!

Halfway through the repeating end chorus, the orchestra arrangement becomes erratic. Screams of fear are pumped out of the speakers, chairs get knocked over as the people run, and the sloths start attacking and eating everyone.

"What can you do? Sloths are gonna sloth. It's in their nature," Aaron says.

Ghee runs across the barrier and turns off the truck, returning back to safety. "We've heard enough of your garbage."

"So what now? We just stand here for the next six days, until your barrier expires, and then I come and kill you all? You haven't won. I can just keep sending more and more ships full of my sloth army, and as far as I know, there's only one of you, Casey. You can't be everywhere to stop me. Face it, you lost."

Aaron goes to the back of the truck, pulls out a cat carrier. "Sure, we kill and eat your stupid species. Can you blame us? Why did they make you all so delicious? You should be asking your maker that, instead, not getting mad at me. But this…" Aaron stops, pulls out the cat.

"Melissa!" Casey exclaims.

"You crossed the line. We'd never resort to biological warfare. That's just evil. For that reason, you will be the last to die, Casey. I'll make sure you watch each and every one of your friends get eaten by my bro sloths."

"What makes that cat so special?" Natalie asks.

"This stupid cat here? It once housed an ancient evil, more potent and powerful than even me. Insidious in its design. It makes its prey helpless to the host, and by extension, your gross magic pee barrier. One scratch from this dumb cat made my sloths want to run into the magic pee barrier. But even if you beat me here, you've unleashed something more destructive than you'll ever know with effects even your Lord Babb can't foresee." Aaron opens his mouth to continue his rant, but Melissa scratches his hand. Aaron punches the cat in the face and forcefully kicks it to the ground near Natalie's feet, pure defensive instinct.

She examines Melissa. "She's dead. He killed her."

Aaron nurses his scratch.

Ghee asks, "What the heck is that?"

Melissa's mouth opens wide, reminding Casey of Natalie eating the taco earlier. A green slug with red puss dots, half the size of its host, slithers out of the cat. Casey jumps into Splash Time, takes the cat and the weird slug thing parasite, and runs away.

"Your savior knows you lost. Look at him run away. Wherever he's going, I'm sure that slug thing will have consumed him first," Aaron mocks as he steps forward.

Casey pops back into existence. "I found a jar and put the slug in it, then returned it to the office for the front desk girl to process."

Aaron takes another step forward. "You're evil. Why would you do this to me? I'm not a bad guy, bros and brodette. I just want to live." Aaron fights his own feet, straining to remain stationary. "Do you even know how painful the fire is when it burns my flesh from the inside out? We know what's happening to us; we're conscious the entire time. I don't want to die. I don't want to die—not like this." Aaron is losing the fight, stepping closer to the barrier.

Natalie and Ghee turn away when Aaron bursts into flames, falling down on his knees, screaming in agony. It takes several minutes before the fire dies down.

"God, that was awful. This is the worst showstopper, so far," Natalie says as she kicks the lump of burned meat at her feet.

"Kill me…" a high pitched voice, as if on helium, begs at their feet.

The three of them jump back as a charred sloth form crawls forward.

"Please," it begs.

The three don't know if this is a trap or trick the alpha sloth is trying to play on them.

"I don't know. Maybe we could drop this off at Banhammer Island," Ghee says.

Natalie answers, "Casey, all that running you've been doing tonight, jumping in and out of Splash Time. Are you hungry?"

Casey picks up on Natalie's not so subtle wink. "I could go for a bite."

The sloth is still crawling forward. "I want to die… Strike me down right here, right now."

Casey goes behind the sloth and gets on his knees. "Oh my God, what the heck is happening? That's just sick, dude," Ghee says, revolted.

The sloth turns around and sees Casey's dislocated jaw get wider as it starts sucking in the sloth's feet. "No, no. Stop. How did you guys know? Please. I'm begging you, for real. Stop! Stop! I can show you more powerful abilities. You can be gods in this world, just let me go."

Casey starts sucking up the sloth like a spaghetti noodle. The sloth's claws dig into the asphalt, fighting for its life, from being devoured whole.

When it's done, Casey gets up and burps. "Excuse me."

"So, all of this… this crazy battle versus the sloths, this thing pretending to be Aaron… all of this is over now?" Ghee asks.

Natalie and Casey shrug and Natalie replies, "Maybe? We just work in QA. Babb would know for sure."

Casey's virtual avatar lurches forward in pain. He wipes his mouth, looking at blood on his fingers. "I need to run. This thing is still fighting, and it can still hurt me."

Casey jumps into Splash Time. The Golden Gate Bridge, Ghee, and Natalie are framed by the familiar blue and red chromatic aberration effect. He starts running back to Novato. The pain started faint, like heartburn. The sloth fighting inside was getting more potent at bringing Casey searing stomach pain at his QA workstation.

Casey jumps into Zippy Time, where reality is even slower than it's rendered in Splash Time. The world around him has a sepia filter applied to everything. The pain subsides for only a little while as he continues running to the home office in Novato.

They haven't made up a cool nickname for the next level higher than Splash or Zippy Time, but when the stomach pain gets more intense from the sloth clawing like crazy, Casey jumps to the third tier of slow motion time.

The world had no color, just black and white wireframes. The office is in sight. He has his hand on his door key card thing.

Nearly out of gas, he trips and falls after using up all of the stored kinetic energy he had built up getting stuck behind the toilet. The pain comes roaring back all at once as he falls into the front entranceway of the home office. He can't hear whatever the front desk girl is saying. She looks annoyed. Casey ignores her and just runs forward, trying to keep on his feet, one arm holding the sloth in his belly. The other hand opens the door to the QA lab.

Total, complete darkness. The sloth stops fighting, as if it can sense what happens next.

Casey, on the other side of the door, looks up at the black void and then down at his computer monitor and his avatar. He presses the jump button and his avatar and the sloth disappear into the black hole. The door slams shut. The power in the building and all of California goes out. Somewhere in the outback of Australia, a game controller falls down on the floor, and on the monitor: LOL, like game over man, deal with it.

Kernel Panic

The three of them sit, looking forward, quiet. Casey is reminded of that kids' book, where the three heroes always debrief with their wizard principal after beating the big bad.

Natalie, dead tired, yawns.

Ghee wonders if they'll lock him up at Banhammer Island for glitching the system so much the past week.

Babb reads over the bug fixes, build notes, and final narrative. It took crews five hours to restore power. Casey scribbled down all the details with a pen and paper. Now, through the cloudy yellowish slit window, the sun is starting to rise.

"When you jumped in, did you see anything?" Babb asks.

Casey answers, "No. The power just went out after the door slammed."

"Did they get all the Finley cats? That parasite thing was huge when it came out of Melissa," Natalie states.

"They have been collected, parasites extracted, and are being studied further," Babb answers. A few presses on the keyboard then he announces, "CA/SF-003 Showstopper is now resolved. Great work, and pass it onto your teams how grateful we are for everyone coming in on the weekend."

The three look at each other before Ghee says, "So, that's it?"

Babb answers, "Medal ceremonies started getting expensive. We can't have them every time we beat a showstopper."

The three get up, ready to return to Santa Rosa and get some much needed rest. Babb clears his throat and says, "You don't want to see what happens next?"

The wood panel wall behind Babb slides up, revealing a giant screen. Babb, using a small remote pointer, starts pressing buttons. A military drone is flying over what used to be Australia. Various live feeds of cities and small towns. There are no more humans left on the ground, just roaming packs of feral human-eating sloths.

"There's nothing left?" Natalie asks.

Babb shakes his head. "All that's left of Australia are the New York models and actors down in Los Angeles. They're an endangered species now."

Babb switches the view to a satellite orbiting above Australia and New Zealand. "I never wanted it to come to this, but Project Australia failed miserably. The council voted."

Babb, using his pointer, draws a clumsy outline around Australia. He turns around, looking down at his keyboard with a sad expression and presses the Delete key. Australia disappears from the screen. A patch of blue ocean has taken its place. Babb turns around, points his remote at the screen, and selects all of New Zealand. At the edges, a little hand icon appears on the western half of New Zealand. Babb slowly stretches out New Zealand and the land deforms, taking up the space once occupied by Australia.

"A fat, chunky New Zealand," Ghee mutters.

Babb replies, "Nope. *Newer* Zealand is the working name we have right now. But this time, it'll be better. We won't make the same mistakes."

On the elevator ride back up, the three still have questions. "He made that look easy. Just drag and replace a whole country," Ghee says, impressed.

"So, is he a robot, an alien, or God?" Casey asks.

The two of them shrug. "Maybe all," Ghee says as they step out of the elevator. Ghee taps the glass, waking up the goldfish sleeping in the aquarium built into the wall next to the elevator door. "So, what happens to me? Do I still have a job here or what? I was a fugitive running from the Twins."

Natalie answers, "Just show up to work tomorrow. I think it'll be okay."

Ghee pops out of existence and goes back to wherever he calls home now.

Natalie and Casey go to the parking lot, standing by their respective cars.

"The doctor said you're okay, right? Full tests and scans, nothing that'll come back and haunt us later? I hate how the bad guys always do that in…" Natalie stops.

Casey grabs his stomach and keels over. He yells out in pain. Natalie runs over and sees him smiling up at her. "Sorry, I couldn't resist."

Natalie helps him stand up. "I should kick you in the Alps. Race you home."

The obnoxious techno chase music starts playing as the two cars speed out of the parking lot.

***

"I've never been good with weekends. I just don't know what to do with myself. I was hoping the showstopper would have lasted longer," Natalie says as she sprawls out on the couch.

Casey sits in the rocking chair as emergency crews aid those in San Francisco, picking up the pieces of the attack. News media downplay the hot fix of the sloths immolating themselves on the Bay Bridge. Army officials took credit, citing surgical drone strikes as the official story.

Casey coughs from a burning peppery feeling in his throat. At times, his stomach hurts. Over the counter treatments aren't really working. It's not painful, just a dull feeling that won't go away now.

"Is all of this meant to end? Slapping on quick bug fixes to avert the end of the world. It feels like every little change or adjustment screws things up. Maybe the system wants to fail."

No response. Natalie is sleeping.

He looks out the window and a ball of fire silently falls without warning. He gets up and goes to the balcony, looking at his upstairs neighbor and then down at the burning grass.

"I didn't know what to do. So I just chucked it. Sorry, man." The neighbor goes back inside as the lawn sprinklers turn on.

Casey goes back to his rocking chair, watching random San Francisco residents being interviewed on the news. At the corner of his eye, across the street, someone hurriedly throws a burning bowl of something out the window. Someone on the sidewalk cusses angrily.

Outside on the tiny patch of grass is the charred ashes of what used to be on fire. Casey kicks around the lump with his shoe.

"Dude, move!" a voice says from a balcony several floors higher.

He doesn't remember kicking his feet to jump into Splash Time. When he sees the specks of flaming debris falling right at him, he moved out of the way. The heartburn comes back stronger, but he's focused on the molten ceramic bowl melting at his feet. *Pop, pop, pop.* A flaming nugget of popcorn lands on his shoe, which he quickly kicks away. Across the street, the same person throws another flaming bowl onto the sidewalk. He investigates and sees a random spread of tiny holes burned into the surface, like little laser blasts. There is no sign of the igniter, just the ashes.

Natalie wakes up from the popping noises and joins Casey in the kitchen. "Cool, we're going to watch a movie?"

Nothing happens with the stove made popcorn. He hands her the bowl and she starts snacking as she flips through the channels. Next he grabs a packet of the microwave stuff, puts it in with the automatic timer preset. The microwave beeps. Casey pours the bag into a bowl, and the popcorn ignites before he can try a bite. Heartburn now worse, he runs to the balcony in Splash Time, throwing the fiery bowl over the edge.

"Bug?" Natalie asks.

He nods. "Bug."

***

"You know, you're allowed to live your life on your time off. You don't have to be here all the time." Babb says as he pokes his head in the QA lab doorway.

Casey reads over his entry:

Bug: Uncooked microwave popcorn kernels stay superheated

Severity: A

Reproduction Rate: 100

Steps to Reproduce:

1. User selects any brand of microwave pop-corn. User cooks the popcorn as instructed by the packaging.

2. User pours popcorn out of the microwave bag into a bowl or container. Do not let the popcorn rest in the paper bag; for testing purposes, this would be bad.

3. Observe the bowl of popcorn.

Result: Popcorn kernels not cooked during the microwave procedure stay superheated, igniting anything they come into contact with.

Impact: Untold amounts of property and personal damage will occur from sudden popcorn related fires.

Expected: When popcorn kernels get heated, they

```
should eventually exhibit entropy.
Notes: Does not apply to stove cooked or pop-
corn cooked directly from corn stalks, just mi-
crowave popcorn. Popcorn kernels burn through
all forms of matter as they descend deeper to
the planet's core. Even tungsten will melt when
exposed to a handful of kernels.
```

"If this wasn't an urgent issue, we could apply this bug as a means of clean alternative energy. That is if we could control it," Babb says as he approves the bug. "How's your stomach? The best thing you can do is refrain from jumping into, what do you kids call it… Splash Time? I'm more partial to Gotta Git Fast Mode, but that's just me."

"It's annoying, this persistent heart burn after jumping into Splash Time," Casey answers, "But I'll manage."

The computer chimes. The bug is fixed, needing regression. The two proceed to the break room.

"This is the second time you've inherited latent powers," Babb says. "First it was that cat pee defense thing you did at the bridges, and now you have sloth speed (at an obvious cost, though). Be careful. There are some watching you that want to lock you away at Banhammer. Don't give them a reason. Just keep doing good work, like you're doing now." The microwave beeps, Babb pours the popcorn into a bowl, and it doesn't burst into flame.

```
Fix Verified.
```

"Go home already. I'll be keeping this." Babb takes the bowl of pop-corn and walks to the elevator to go downstairs.

***

"Oh my God. You missed the best movie ever. When he walked up to the bad guy, served a warrant, audited his offshore accounts, and turned the evidence over to the SEC and FBI… Boom! Now that's how you end a movie." Natalie gets up and washes her popcorn bowl. "Fix verified?"

Casey nods. "Fix verified. Popcorn apocalypse averted."

From the corner of the living room, Natalie digs out a plastic guitar and a microphone.

"Wait, you play the game too? Come on, I can never find anyone who wants to play with me. What, is my singing awful? I think I'm not bad. I hope I'm not bad." She didn't even have to twist his rubber arm.

"I know for a fact my singing is bad," Casey says, taking the guitar from her hand.

She smiles, "All right, maybe we can get that million-point high score. I can never get there on my own."

ExG

"You dodged a bullet, dude, smart move. QA is where the action is," Doug says as he puts his messenger bag on the floor.

Casey, sitting at his testing station, is back to being a regular QA grunt. Everyone is quiet as they stare curiously at the two new supervisors. Ray, a burly African American with a thick beard, is trashing all of Aaron's desk belongings. Carlos, clean shaven with an ultra-short buzz haircut, is finishing up a toasted bagel.

There are no big grandiose speeches or introductions. The shift starts and the testers jump into regressing the previous week's bugs or hunting for new ones. Casey notes Karina and Ghee are absent, their testing stations vacated.

"She said she's interviewing for an open art position. The sloths ate a few of them on the weekend," Danny says. "She'll be back after lunch."

The lab is warmer than usual, and Casey appreciates Natalie leaving her floor standing oscillating fan. Once in a while, a little breeze comes his way.

When he woke up, he knew exactly what he was going to do. He even prepared before starting the commute. He's in the zone.

Signing in, his avatar wakes up, gets out of bed, and does some idle animations of stretching and yawning.

That's a bug right there. When an avatar wakes up, the User should have direct control, without a delay.

The avatar walks to the living room and stands in front of a full-sized mirror propped up against the couch. Casey intends to mine any and all avatar related bugs and glitches testers were unaware they were doing in real life. He's about to hop into the database to enter the wide mouth eating bug when Ray passes his station, making the rounds, handing out newly printed regressions.

Doug turns around and says, "This is weird, dude." He holds up the sheet Ray just handed him.

Casey looks first at the paper Doug is holding then down to the floor where a thumb is resting next to Doug's white shoe. Blood is dripping on the shoe. Casey fixates on the stump where the thumb used to be.

A new hire, sitting next to Doug, sees the blood and thumb and yells out in surprise. Ray turns to see what the commotion is then he feels the sting of the paper cutting into his palms, getting close to the bone. With a quick flick of his wrist, Ray throws the papers out of his hands to the floor. They don't hit the floor as intended. The oscillating fan propels the sheets of paper, spinning and weaving through the air. Testers at their stations don't realize what's happening until the paper slices against their skin or cleanly lobs off whole appendages. Casey and Doug dodge some sheets while the room fills with panic and painful moaning. Ray is hopping up and down, holding his severed foot in hand, looking for help.

Casey thought he was being clever. The next time he would jump into Splash Time, he'd take an antacid to counter the new side effect of moving quicker than the laws of the simulation. For a moment, he shakes his head, smirking at the bubbling heartburn cooking his stomach. Nope, no such luck trying to cheat the system. The simulation slows to a crawl. He calmly proceeds to collect each deadly piece of paper still swirling and floating around in the air. Several times he feels the razor sharp sting of the edges against his own hands.

All the paper collected, he sets them down on his desk, puts a stack of books on top of them so they don't fly away again, then jumps out of Splash Time.

The cacophony of pain resumes, and Casey realizes he needs to get them all to the ER to reattach limbs and treat the wounded. Ray lost his foot, Doug a thumb, the new guy next to Doug part of his arm.

"Man, you got lucky, didn't you?" Casey says, smiling at Danny and his dog.

Danny doesn't respond, just a blank expression with a mixture of confusion. Slowly, his head tips over and thuds on the floor. Ray falls back against the fan, freaking out, betraying his brutish exterior. The dog whimpers as Casey stares at his former colleague.

"This can't be happening. What's going on?"

Pain. The worst pain he could imagine shoots from the side of his head all throughout his body, jagged bolts of electricity randomly spiking and pinching his nerves.

"You got this, Ray? Who knew we had an ExG amongst us. I'm taking him to Banhammer."

Casey tries to pry at his ear to get the hurting to stop. He feels, with his finger, a single hole puncher squeezing down on his ear lobe. "Wait, what are you doing? I stopped the showstopper, I can't help it being what I am now. I was trying to save everybody."

Casey tries jumping into Splash Time to get away from Carlos, but Splash Time isn't working. He isn't even in charge of his motor functions as he's led by his ear, marching to the elevator.

They pass Ghee, who just showed up. "I'm sorry I'm late. Splash Time doesn't work anymore. Had to catch the bus."

Carlos ignores Ghee as they keep walking. Casey can hear Ghee open the door to the lab. "Whoa."

The last thing Casey remembers is a blue arc of electricity shooting down from the ceiling of the elevator at his face.

***

His ear still hurts from the hole puncher Carlos used to restrain him. He isn't shackled. He expected to be shackled like some kind of criminal mastermind cannibal banker or a software patent troll.

It's a small cell. Two tone paint, the upper half soft faded white and the lower half a faint sick green. The cell looks out at nothing but an old brick wall, also painted white and green. There is no hollering or vocal taunting happening. Instead of bars, there's a thick, soundproof pane of glass keeping him locked in. An unseen vent keeps the room cool at seventy-two degrees. There are no guards, nobody doing patrol, just pure solitude, which seems familiar…

That span of time he lived alone after his grandmother died, before he got to know Natalie more.

Someone will tell Babb what happened and he'll come get me.

"Babb isn't coming to get you. Babb doesn't care about you. You served your purpose. We all served our purpose," a quiet whisper says through the unseen vent. "Showstopper CA-002? I stopped that. Me. Sure I could have just let them swarm and kill everybody up in Bodega Bay, but then they'd migrate east to my home town, Petaluma. I had to stop them."

Casey wants to ask why, how, and what. He only hears the sound of electricity arcing, zapping the unseen voice into silence, and the metal grate of the vent closing shut.

The giant pane of glass is actually a futuristic transparent computer monitor. A prompt appears on screen: Lunch. Choose. Images of three different meals appear. He debates between the cheeseburger or burrito, but opts for fish and chips. A slot opens from the brick wall, lunch is slid gently onto the table, and the slot closes. Another prompt appears on the screen. Casey selects diet soda. A can is slid onto the table—obviously shaken, because it foams up when he opens the can.

I should have stayed at my old job, testing basketball video games. Why did I take the promotion?

After lunch, the hole in the wall opens and a speaker angrily buzzes, like a wrong answer in a game show. Casey slides the dinner tray and empty soda can into the gap in the wall. Next, a familiar object lands on the table with a small thud.

A controller?

The familiar prick pokes his finger. He licks the blood, an instinctive reaction, and the screen catches his attention. A soft white kitten rolls around on a thick blue carpet, absolutely content with life.

I am content with life. This is what I've always wanted. To just be free. To run around. Climbing these couches. No more worries. No more sadness. Just the bliss of chasing the paper ball, being held by my loving owner, and playfully knocking stuff off shelves. This is my game over, and I won. I win! Meow. Meow meow meow meow meow? Meow! Meow meow, meow, meow. Mew. Mew mew meow. Rarr, meow. Meow mew. Purr.

Knock-knock.

Is someone at the door? Maybe I can go jump on their leg and climb them.

Knock-knock!

An arc of electricity severs the connection. Casey looks up and through the glass. He realizes he is on all fours.

"Wait, was I a kitten for real?"

The pane of glass slides down like a car's automatic window. He's still on all fours, and Natalie and Babb stare at him.

"You can get up now," Babb says. "We're going."

Casey reaches for Natalie's cool, outstretched hand and stands up. Babb starts walking away from the cells. The other inmates angrily pound on the glass at the sight of him. "I kind of liked this. Do I really have to go?"

Natalie waves her hand forward, signaling Casey to follow Babb to the exit.

There are only three cells occupied on the way to the elevator. His neighbor, dressed in a purple bathrobe, is wearing a traffic cone as a hat with a big red magnet glued to the center.

"He said he stopped Showstopper CA-002. What did he do?"

Natalie looks at her former coworker sadly. "Magnets. He figured out how they work. Enough to redirect the rampant birds to a volcano last fall. But like all of the inmates here, he got drunk with power. I locked him up myself, the same way Carlos incapacitated you."

In the next cell is a man in his mid-thirties wearing a black trench coat and black sunglasses. He angrily gives both of them the finger then starts flailing around like an inflatable car lot tube man. The two keep walking to the exit. In the third cell before the elevator, Casey sees a small brown and white hedgehog snuggly asleep in its tent bed.

All three now in the elevator, Babb presses the button. The door slides open, and Casey sees his hallway leading to his dark, quiet condo. He stares, expecting Natalie to get off too, before Babb goes to his basement office. "Oh, no, sorry. I'm going back to work. I still got half a shift to sort through, and we're playing catch up after this morning's mishap."

The elevator door closes and Casey walks back to his condo. Inside, he puts the full body mirror back in the bathroom.

Do I have to go to work tomorrow? What if they try locking me up again? I think I'll call in sick. Or maybe I'll just quit. I should quit.

The whispering voice replays in his head: "You served your purpose."

Life's Manager

A white envelope was taped to the door. Maybe Natalie dropped it off when she got home from work, but didn't want to disturb him from sleep. Nothing remarkable, other than the scribbled text: From Babb.

Casey opens it and finds an oval, crystal, ultra-thin disc thing. He doesn't know what it's for, but examines the laser etched lettering, hollowed out within the crystal: LB-0100101001010000.

He still hadn't made up his mind about going in to work. Maybe this was Babb trying to get him to stay. Maybe it was a thank you for helping beat the showstopper. It could be an apology for being wrongly imprisoned and locked in some bizarro prison of the mind for thirteen hours. He needed bread and was on the way to the store. It would help if he knew what the crystal was for.

He does a once over, examining the entire parking lot. His car is still at work, obviously. Walking through the rows of cars to the bus stop, he hopes the schedule is still the same. He might just be able to pop into Exchanger Bob's for fresh eggs and whole wheat bread. As he visualizes which aisles to walk to make his food shopping most efficient, he notices the low, bass-heavy hum. With each step, the tone increases, a crescendo, resembling a mixture of strings and horns, getting painfully louder. The sound peaks on a high E. Casey covers his ears as the windshields of cars explode around him as the note is sustained.

The crystal vibrates in his front left pants pocket. Now, pure silence, other than the de-pressurization noise as the car door next to him slides open, upward to the air. The car is low and angular, a triangle on wheels when viewed from the side, painted jet black, literally absorbing all light, designed to perfection for maximum aerodynamics. The leather bucket seat massages his back before conforming to his unique figure. The electronic seatbelts crisscross, locking him snugly in place.

"Good morning, Casey. Destination please?" a calming electronic voice asks from the center dashboard console. There are no buttons or knobs, unlike his real car. He doesn't know if this is a manual or automatic.

Casey answers the computer, "Exchanger Bob's?"

Projected onto the windshield in the bottom driver's side corner is a transparent map with directions. He doesn't even have time to put his hand on the wheel or foot on the pedal. The car just whooshes smoothly out of the parking spot and onto the main road. He feels no bumps or stops. It's as if the car is floating on air as it takes him to his destination. Everyone at the market stares at him as he parks in the spot closest to the entrance. The cabin depressurizes once more, and the door slides up to let him out.

I didn't even know I wanted this supercool self-driving car, until now. Thank you, Babb.

Inside the market, people are still staring at him. He can hear the whispering and muttering about how rich he must be. Nobody is brave enough to walk up to him and ask. The crystal in his pocket vibrates, saying, "Casey, list the desired food stuffs you plan on purchasing."

He complies and the crystal chimes with each entry. Self-illuminating, the crystal draws a top down map of the market with the most efficient route to take as he fills his basket.

He doesn't know if he likes this change. Shopping for food was a little Zen exercise, just to get away from it all. Even if it was for ten or twenty minutes. Now, a small group of people follow him, watching him from the opposite end of the aisles. At the register, the cashier asks for his crystal. A quick scan later, he's out the door. He didn't have to use cash or his cards. Leaving, he proceeds back to the magic car of awesome.

The low hum gets louder and louder again, windshields shattering, startling everyone huddled at the market's exit. The wide trunk automatically opens; he could fit three adults in there if he wanted. Then from the walls of the trunk, a cubed mesh net emerges to hold his purchases in place, so they don't roll around. Casey, sitting in the driver's seat, is once more asked for his destination.

"Car, settings please?"

A camera behind the driver's side panel tracks his eye movements, anticipating his choices, and intuitively selects the options to turn off the deep note crescendo sound.

It was cool the first two times, but I don't want people suing me for damages every time I get near this car.

Noticing the time, he needs to get back home to wrap up breakfast. Not even that fender scraping dip at his condo could be felt. Casey wonders what kind of hydraulics the car uses to elevate itself for maximum smoothness. He grabs the owner's manual before going back upstairs. More people gawk at the missile on wheels.

***

Just as he finishes rinsing his plate and throwing the cracked egg shells in the garbage, the doorbell rings. A man in a purple uniform greets him, asking for his signature. The delivery man hands over a thin envelope. Another set of keys, real door keys, and a card with an address. In the car, Casey finds himself missing the obnoxious activation noise. It was like power, a force of nature activating.

He reads the address on the card out loud: "Where is Belvedere Island?"

The car swooshes on its own, taking the quickest route to the freeway. Weaving in and out of lanes, the car enters the left most lane.

"No car, this is for car pools and buses," Casey protests,

The electronic voice chuckles, "Executive privilege, sir. Does the good master want to enjoy a movie or television show during this trip, or would you like me to read out the morning news?"

***

Casey must have fallen asleep during the documentary he selected. He wakes to the sound of a gentle knock on the window.

I didn't know they made women that beautiful.

He gets up and out of the car nervously, outclassed by the super model, probable actress, smiling at him. Long, silky black hair, sharp cheekbones, and a perfect nose, she has deep green eyes and stands roughly half a foot taller than him.

"It's so great to meet you, Casey. The purchase has been finalized. You just need to sign this slip of paper, and it's all yours."

Casey signs without thinking, enamored by the Italian queen standing in front of him. "What's all mine?"

She takes the crystal from his hand, scans it with her mobile phone, and the giant metal gate in front of him opens.

"If you like, I could give you the tour. Where are my manners? I'm Ana."

Ana hands Casey back his crystal and enters the passenger side of his car. Casey enters the driver's side. Two minutes after driving through a windy downward road, he sees it. A massive, three story classical home, painted light yellow with white trimmings. Giant windows, solar panels on the slanted roof, a pool, a tennis court, and a private beach. All of that looking out on San Francisco and the Golden Gate Bridge. The tour ends as Ana shows him the dock, where a red and white speedboat is currently parked.

"If you need anything or have issues with the property, do not hesitate to call me. Actually, if you want to get drinks later this week, here's my personal number."

Wait, what? She's flirting with me? No girl has ever flirted with me.

She walks out the front door and is picked up by her own self-driving car.

Casey starts exploring the house. There's a media room filled with theater chairs, a popcorn machine, a soda machine, and a two-hundred foot screen. A computer lab with still boxed up super computers he only fantasized about buying. A reading room filled with all the classics, as well as a selection of tech manuals and journals. The kitchen is linked online, and all he has to do is press a button for what he needs and a drone will come drop off anything, food or material possessions, at his front door.

He tries that out first, pleasantly surprised to find a box of cheese flavored baked corn meal chips from Canada waiting for him fifteen minutes later. He doesn't know the name for beds bigger than king sized, emperor sized? The master bedroom has automatic curtains that react to his hand motions. He can swipe them open and closed like the conductor of an orchestra. The view is of downtown San Francisco and Sid's Mountain.

"This is all a trick. I'm still locked up at Banhammer. A simulation within the simulation to keep me busy until they decide what to do with me."

He didn't even call in sick for work. Nobody from work called for him either.

If this is real, I need to figure out how and why this is all happening.

***

The office parking lot is empty when the car arrives. Everyone is out to lunch. Doug comes out, talking with Ghee. They see Casey standing next to his new car.

"What, that's... Stop. Ghee, do you see that car?"

Ghee nods to Doug, silently answering his question.

"That's a LeBreton. You own a LeBreton? For real? This is your car? Unbelievable." Doug asks for the crystal, jumps in the car, tinkers with the settings, and for the next few minutes, walks away from the car, approaches it, walks away, enjoying the booming crescendo noise it makes, gleefully running back and forth in the parking lot, triggering the deep sound.

Ghee and Casey sit by the picnic table where smokers are allowed to hang out during break or lunchtime, watching Doug.

"I'm thankful they patched Splash Time. I could've ended up like most of you guys if I actually made it to work on time yesterday."

"What happened after I got locked up?" Casey asks.

"Just a big bloody mess. I asked the front receptionist girl to call emergency services. Ambulances came and collected everyone, collected the limbs. The coroner arrived for Danny. Carlos returned after he locked you away at Banhammer. But then he got called to Babb's office. We haven't seen him since."

Casey thinks about staying for work without that threat of being tugged by his ears again.

"Splash Time still works. It's how I tried to save everyone from those razor papers flying around." Casey braces himself for the heartburn and pops out of perceptible existence and reappears next to Doug on the other side of the parking lot, then pops back into existence back at the picnic table.

Ghee replies, "Lucky you. Nope, it doesn't work. There was some creepy loser in England that discovered Splash Time. He went to the nearest supermarket and just started stripping people naked. He was halfway through painting war paint on some rugby player using yogurt and pudding when he ran out of kinetic energy. Rugby dude beat him senseless. Whatever the English version of Banhammer is, he's locked up now."

Casey holds his stomach and says, "Babb indicated I absorbed that alpha sloth's power."

Doug joins them and Ghee stands up and says, "We're going to lunch. You're free to join us."

Casey declines. He wants to check some things out at his workstation, first.

Doug is disappointed. "Aww, I wanted him to take us."

Doug runs back to the black shiny LeBreton. "I know this is going to hurt so much, but this is just too cool." Doug pulls his car keys from his jacket pocket and starts keying the LeBreton. Without warning, a red arc of electricity shoots out from the car, blasting Doug back five feet. "So cool. That car has electronic defenses and memory nano metal alloy. It can't be keyed by jealous jerks, and when someone tries… *Zap*!"

Casey tosses Doug the crystal. "Go ahead, take it for a ride. I'll see you guys when you get back."

Casey watches the car drive off.

Inside, the receptionist stands up, staring down Casey, holding a hole puncher in hand.

"No, wait, I'm not dangerous. I hope Babb spread the word I'm not dangerous. I'm just here to work or something. I don't know."

The computer chimes, an instant message from Babb probably. The girl puts down the hole puncher and resumes talking to a friend on the other line.

"Hi, I'm Casey. Sorry for never asking your name until now."

She stares at him and then briefly at the hole puncher. She tries to smile, is distracted with the voice on the other end of the line. She adjusts her prescription glasses, and finally introduces herself. "Tania. I'm Tania. You know what? You're the first person to ever talk to me. So sorry for being rude this past week, but you workers come and go so often, new ones every week. Now every day almost. Jenny, from contagious diseases, says it's better not to get attached to any of you." Tania misses Jenny, she died from a contagious disease the month before.

Casey wishes her a pleasant day and proceeds down to the QA lab.

A big giant hug awaits him on the other side of the door. Karina's blond hair gets in his left eye. "They let you out? Of course, they let you out. You're a hero," Karina says as she steps back. "That stupid boy did stupid thing." Casey realizes how careful she is at hiding her Soviet heritage, a break in dialect for just a moment.

"Did you get the job?" Casey asks about her interview.

She shrugs and says, "They haven't decided yet." Karina goes back to her station where her avatar sits on a log in the forest outside Taswell. She goes back to observing a skunk for some unexplained bug she's researching.

Danny stares at him, not saying a word. Casey smiles. "Danny! You're here. Man, that was messed up yesterday."

Nobody told Danny how he died on the job, but he did get the email that he was restored from a backup made the previous Thursday. He has no memory of the showstopper. "I'm done, Casey. This is my last day. I'm just wrapping up regressions, moving back to Canada."

Now Casey is sad, his friend is back, but is now leaving. Casey sits down at his station and turns on his computer. He doesn't notice it, but the Alaskan Malamute is sitting next to him.

"He seems to like you," Danny says. "Something is different about me. The dog knows it. Do you want him?"

Casey isn't sure. Danny really loved his dog, and maybe the dog will recognize its owner in time.

"I can't take him back to Canada, not without jumping through assorted import and legal hoops."

Casey asks, "What'll you be doing back in your homeland?"

"Babb wants me to supervise a lab up there. I haven't said yes, but it's something. He doesn't want rural northern Canada getting wild like

Australia."

The dog licks Casey's fingers as he strokes its nose.

"Os, pronounced Ewwshssss," Danny says, smiling. "I named my dog, 'Dog.' " Danny gets up, pets the dog on the head, and goes out the door. Like that. He's gone. Off to some far away land way up in Canada to start some new QA related adventures, maybe.

Three minutes later, Danny returns. He snaps open a cold soda from the vending machine and continues working.

The pause menu. It's been a while since Casey saw his stats, perks, and wealth indicators. There was no way he could afford that house in Tiburon, nor the designer hypercar. Something was up. Just as the needle punctures his fingertip, they feel the vibration. The windows shake.

"Earthquake? Again?" Karina asks as she ducks under the table.

It's too short for an earthquake. Across the freeway, there's a plume of black smoke billowing up into the air.

"An explosion?" Danny asks.

Across the street, another explosion occurs at the place Natalie picks up her frozen juice smoothies, this time shattering windows. Casey jumps into Splash Time again and stops the shards of glass from hitting Karina and Danny. The dog was smart enough to stay under the table where Karina was originally hiding.

"What's going on? This is a bug; it has to be a bug." From their elevated hillside office, they see five more explosions spread out around Novato. "Just when I think I'm done." Casey pops out of existence, leaving the lab to investigate.

At Jimbo's Juice, there are no survivors.

Casey races through, hoping to get people to the ER, maybe some kind of explanation from a survivor. A fire truck pulls up. The firemen tell him to get to safety as they begin their work. Casey races across to the other side of the freeway to the first explosion. Doug and Ghee stand behind the LeBreton at the crater that used to be another Exchanger Bob's market.

"The car door wouldn't open. We stopped here to pick up panini sandwiches. The car voice said 'brace for impact.' Then it was just all fire. Everything burning. There was a cart collector guy right over there," Doug says, shaken.

Casey asks for his keys back. "Food related. Both explosions happened where food is served."

Ghee asks, "Is this another showstopper? We just fixed a showstopper. Can this job just cut it out with showstoppers already?"

News helicopters fly overhead, surveying the damage.

"There was another explosion maybe about five blocks away, in a residential area. I can drop you two off at work if you want." Casey goes into the options menu, hoping the magic car would help figure it out. "This car mapped out the Exchanger Bob's in Santa Rosa for me this morning. Maybe it can pinpoint the source of the explosion."

The windshield darkens and a full screen map of the market is drawn on the screen, similar to the top down view projected onto the crystal.

"Car, pinpoint explosion center."

A little animated metronome ticks back and forth in the center of the windshield screen. The map pans from the car's current location, following a set path through the market. It passes the dairy department, the organic bread section, the designer coffee aisle, and stops dead center in Fruit Island.

"Whatever this is, it's a fruit. Okay, now we have something to go on."

Casey orders the car to take them to the next nearest explosion. Several times during the drive, the car pulls over, letting firetrucks and ambulances get to their destination. The next explosion is two blocks away, but police have closed access.

"Guys, just wait here. I'll be back."

This time, Casey makes sure nobody is looking, ducks behind a nearby house, and pops into Splash Time. Another crater in the ground has taken the surrounding two houses with it. Cars were blown over, burning in slow motion. A metal cashbox lies in the middle of the road, shiny coins glinting from the high noon sun. The blast propelled more than just the money toward the house across the street. Like a spear, a chunk of wood has been stabbed into the stucco exterior of the house across the way. Casey tugs at the charred board, pulling it out, turns the wood signage over. A little kid's scribbled writing gets him right in the gut: NaDe!

No, I will not cry. I need to fix this before more people die.

***

Ray is surprised to see Casey walk in with Ghee and Doug. Casey is surprised to see his supervisor on both feet. He peers over at Doug, his thumb attached as if nothing happened. "I thought you might have forgotten about that. Yeah, everyone got restored after yesterday. No cool bionic thumb for me. Can you imagine my kd/r going up if I had one?" Doug says.

Casey hops into the simulation, carefully approaches the Exchanger Bob's in Santa Rosa, ignoring the lookie loos who remember him from earlier that day. He buys all the lemons in the market, then tells the manager, "Uh, yeah, keep the rest off the sales floor. The health inspector will be arriving later today, uh, *H pylori*. You don't want to get sued, now, do you?"

The car then drives him to an abandoned quarry, miles from civilization. With a trunk full of lemons, he wonders where he should start. Peeling them didn't do anything. He braces himself for the explosion, is prepared to lose his car and be respawned in bed at his apartment. Next, he cuts it in half, squeezing the juice into a cup. Still no violent reaction.

The whole crew watches him in silence as he runs through various ways of preparing lemonade.

"In Soviet Russia, my brother would use lemons as grenades when they'd play Comrade Versus Amerikos. Cut the tip," Karina says.

Casey complies. He can hear a hissing noise escalate from inside the lemon. The avatar isn't obeying Casey's input anymore after he presses the throw button. The avatar runs to the tree line, trying to reach a boulder to hide behind. The lemon explodes. It ignites the lemons stuffed in the car trunk, and in the QA lab, everyone feels the tiny vibration of the near nuclear detonation.

Casey's avatar wakes up in bed, does the stretching animation.

"Karina, you figured it out. You can write it up. Maybe it'll help you get the art job," Casey says.

Natalie knocks on Casey's door. Everyone goes back to work at their stations. Casey's avatar answers the door and says, "Lemon based show-stopper; it was pretty bad."

The two walk onto Casey's balcony looking northwest. Between Austin Creek State Park and Healdsburg, a mushroom cloud is dissipating. Casey doesn't mention all the dead people killed by the bug. The lemonade sign still haunts him.

"No need to come in early. I think we got this. Karina is writing up the bug now."

```
Bug: User can burn the world down with lemons.

Severity: A

Reproduction Rate: 100

Steps to Reproduce:

    1. Developer goes to any grocery store and
    buys a lemon.

    2. Developer proceeds to isolated location
```

away from other human beings.

3. Developer, using a knife or sharp uten-
sil, cuts the nipple off the lemon; observe
the lemon.

Result: Lemons will ignite in a fiery explosion,
killing all in the blast radius.

Impact: Loss of human, animal, and plant life.
Rules of the simulation are violated, exposing
its nature to the occupants. Normies within the
simulation should not be made aware of the nature of our reality.

Expected: Lemons should not be used as a violent tool of destruction. Lemons should only be
used as a tart additive to food or a cool sum-
mer drink.

Notes: Lemon based explosions increase in severity when initiating a chain reaction with
other lemons. This is a potential showstopper, requiring immediate attention. This bug
was originally found by tester Casey, who too
kindly gave it to me. He should get credit for
this find. I only played a small part in discovering the steps to reproduce.

"Are you sure Babb can't pull any strings for you and let you keep
your dog?" Casey asks Danny.

He shakes his head. "Os chose you. Take good care of him."

The two hug as Casey exits the QA lab.

Ray watches, and then asks Doug, "Wait, is Casey quitting too? The
shift isn't over."

Doug, chilled by the breeze blowing through the shattered window of the office, can still smell the charred remains of Jimbo's Juice across the street. "I don't know."

***

Casey is about to hop into his real car, now that his godcar was blown to smithereens up north. Birds had made it their target the past day and a half. The familiar low hum, the note getting higher and more intense, Os howls as the car gets nearer. Casey turns and sees his LeBreton park beside him.

"This is my car, but it's not my car."

Casey and Os hop in.

"Casey, ownership of a LeBreton comes with a ten year no questions asked insurance policy. In the event of catastrophic damage, you will be issued a new replacement. Please select a color."

Casey looks at the dog. "Um, red?"

There's a soft, crackling hiss, not that different from the lemon preparing to detonate. Os barks in excitement. It's only when the nano particles of the metal body readjust on the hood does Casey realize what's happening. The car changed from the original black paint job to a sporty fire engine red on the fly. He tells the car to take him home. He doesn't know which one the car will choose. He doesn't care.

2Big2Fail2

Natalie waited, excited to do another debrief. It had become one of her favorite parts of the day. To have someone to talk to and share the same language… it's why she begged and pleaded with Babb the night before to have Casey released from Banhammer Island, to have Carlos reassigned to Montana, far away in obscurity. That was her wish, and Babb was compelled to grant it. Casey was free because of her. Casey was a kindred spirit, a good friend, and in time, maybe more.

Now, he's gone.

The lights are off. There is no answer. The parking spot is empty.

Ray could only pass on that Casey left work early, without explanation, when he did the supervisor hand off to the night crew.

For the past four hours, Natalie would log into the simulation at her workstation and peek out the door across the hall, hoping he'd be there. Babb isn't around. He was personally overseeing the emergency response efforts to the day's destruction. If only she could ask him. Babb knows all things all the time.

"That's the sixth one I've seen tonight," says Tania.

Natalie ignores her. Tania's never been a pleasant person.

"What, you're ignoring me, sis?"

Natalie shakes her head. "I don't even know what you're on about. I just came out here to think."

Tania waves a burrito at Natalie. "Not hungry? Oh, that's right, you're the dummy who died while under the effects of the Mmmmetabolism Perk, and now, taco night is cancelled forever. I liked taco night. Dad liked taco night. Do you know who eats Spanish food without cilantro? Fairy godmothers."

Natalie slaps the large burrito out of her sister's hand. "Watch your mouth."

Tania laughs. "Fairy godmothers! Fairy godmothers! Fairy godmothers! I'm only saying Fairy godmothers, not bad words like you. You're the bad one. I'm the angel."

"Eight. Eight of them now!"

Natalie gets up.

"If your head wasn't so far up your Alps, you'd be investigating my bug. Yes, *my* bug. I found it."

Natalie finally asks, "What bug? What are you talking about?"

Founded in 1985 by Johnnemann Weir, from humble beginnings in the wilds of Oregon, JGW had one singular vision for the future: One car to end all cars. Using up his life savings, the project found success integrating hydrofusion cells with clean solar power. The heart of Le-Breton motors started beating in the fall of 1986. With the help from Canadian engineers and French aerospace technicians, they built the LB-0110001101101010. Capable of hitting 468 miles per hour in 1.1 seconds, the car would have been a success if not for exploding upon impact on the side of a Bonneville mountain. It took six years to develop the technology and custom made hybrid metals that would produce a car impervious to catastrophic destruction, as well as provide adequate stopping power at supersonic speeds. Three years were spent giving life to the onboard adaptive artificial intelligence. It takes one and a half years to assemble each new LeBreton, hand built in Astoria.

Now, LeBreton Motors expanded manufacturing capacity to deliver three new cars annually to the roadway if the customer can meet the price such a rare car commands.

"So, you tell me, big grumpy sister. If these cars are so rare, so priceless, why is it that eleven of them have passed by on the freeway today alone?" Tania asks as she kicks the burrito toward a curious squirrel several feet away. "You should ask your secret boyfriend, Casey, how he got his."

Natalie turns her head to her sister.

"And now I have your attention." Tania grins uncontrollably.

Natalie stares at her sister, livid. *Just you wait. One day, you'll fall asleep on Mom's couch at home, peaceful, content, and safe. You won't even feel me cut those stupid bangs off your stupid forehead. Fairy godmother.*

Taco night returns. Natalie talked with her mom and dad to reinstitute the family tradition. Every second Thursday of the month, she would now go home and force herself to eat the gross vile poison her dad liked making. She wouldn't make sick faces or gag when the soapy leaves hit her tongue. She would swallow the cilantro and praise Tania for being so smart and clever, for bringing the family back together more often. In return, Tania wrote down the forwarding address Casey left to send his one and only paycheck.

***

The dark green trees in the forest surrounding her rustle from the coastal breeze. She shivers as she stares at the one story metal gate blocking her way. No answer from the buzzer or intercom. A brick wall lines the property, keeping out unwanted guests. As if that stopped her before. Memories of jumping over chain link fences to swim in her neighbor's pool in Sacramento come to mind.

She lands on the other side of the gate, nearly twisting her ankle. It's such a long walk as the roadway zigzags down to the coast. Through the trees she can see the Golden Gate lit up across the bay.

No answer at the door. The house is a palace compared to her parents' place, or even her godfather's, who is this tech tycoon in the valley. Jiggling the ornate brass handle doesn't work; the door is locked. She cannot get through. Around the house, she can hear barking.

She walks through the section separating the heated pool and tennis court from the main house. The grass is being watered by an unseen sprinkler system. The bottom of her jeans are soaking through as she proceeds to the beach. The dog's barking gets more agitated.

Os runs to Natalie, licking her finger. She looks down at Casey sleeping on a beach chair. Natalie feels the dog drop a stick at her feet. She chucks it down the beach, and Os chases it. For a tiny moment, she feels warmth when the dog returns.

Casey wakes up, looking at the two. "Natalie? You just get here?"

She nods, unfolds a second beach chair, and sits next to him. Casey opens a cooler to his side, offering her a soda.

"You never told me you were this mega billionaire," she says. "I would have been meaner to you, you dirty one-percenter."

Casey laughs.

"So, Ray says you quit. Why'd you quit?"

It takes a moment for Casey to come up with an adequate answer. In that time, they stare at a fleet of tugboats still trying to pull the sloth freighter off the pier, where it crash landed days before. Casey explains the graphic detail of the lemon bug, the untold dead, and the innocent lives lost. He tears up as he details the blown up lemonade stand of some little kid who died way too young and finishes, "I kind of know now what headspace Randy was in when he decided to move to Shasta."

Natalie feels the same as the picture of the sloths ravaging the Twins comes back to her. "I don't know what to say. So many times I've wanted to quit, too. This job. It's so easy when you're doing silly stuff, like discovering tap water turning into tequila at 4:45 in the afternoon, or whistling these three notes." Natalie puckers her lips and chirps out some pleasant notes.

Casey feels the change as the wind starts blowing from the north and not east toward Taswell. She laughs as a sailboat in the middle of the bay is lurched off course, almost capsizing.

"Oh my god, no, I didn't mean to do that." She whistles once more and restores the wind direction. "This job can be fun. What makes it fun is the people. All of us working as a team, sometimes competing, sometimes helping each other. Don't you like the people?" Natalie looks at him.

Casey doesn't answer, missing the longing cue, then says "Okay, do you want to come inside? I need to show you something."

A few button presses later on his tablet, a drone lands at the front door. Casey hands Natalie the wrapped box. Natalie opens it. Inside are dry new jeans and a white t-shirt. "Would you be surprised if I told you that shirt is Karina's?"

Natalie spreads out the t-shirt, showing off the forest bunny being drenched by a single rain cloud.

"She has her own clothing line. The bathroom is over there. You can change out of those wet clothes. Meet me in the lab."

Natalie changes and puts her sprinkler-soaked clothes in a plastic bag. She looks around at the too fancy bathroom, figuring this room alone costs more than her condo. Exploring the house trying to find Casey's "lab," she discovers the movie theater, indoor gym, reading den, and kitchen. She follows the sound of a mechanical keyboard clacking away down one of the brightly lit wings of the house and finds Casey surrounded by a hundred and eighty degrees of curved monitors mounted nearly all around him.

"Geesh, that's a lot of screen. Shouldn't this be in some underground cave, and you have a butler folding your dirty undies?" Natalie jokes.

Casey pulls another chair to his battle station and starts pulling up different computer program screens. "Look at this. I'm not great at financial math—computer math yes, but I'm barely good with my check book, and I should have paid off my credit cards with my savings already. So, economic stuff? Whoosh—right over my head."

Natalie stares at the screen. The subconscious smile she had starts to fade as she stares at the line graphs across all the screens. The markets in Asia are collapsing. Everything—stocks, metals, commodities, and each country's currency—are on a course to flat lining.

***

The LeBreton weaves in an out of traffic as it heads northbound to the home office. Babb needs to know another showstopper is in the making.

"How bad can this be, actually?" Casey asks.

Natalie doesn't know. For all things to lose value? Does the simulation switch to a utopia state, like that sci-fi television series Ghee loves, or does society degrade to a cannibalistic hell world with rampant murdering and raping, a struggle just to stay alive?

Natalie is about to answer the question, when she's interrupted by the familiar gaudy opera techno chase music. She turns and sees two LeBretons behind them driving erratically. "Please tell me they're not racing idiots. We don't have time for this."

The two cars pull up on both sides. Barely legal teens make gear changing gestures, one of them counting down with his fingers, stopping with his middle finger, waving at Natalie. Before the unsanctioned race happens, both drivers attempt to sideswipe and sandwich Casey's car. The built in defense protocol activates, and red arcs of electricity strike both cars, temporarily disabling them.

"Your car does that?" Natalie asks. "That's kind of cool."

The operatic chase music starts up once more as the two racers get closer and closer.

"These idiots are going to get us killed before we even get to the office," Natalie warns. "Turn off the auto-driving tech and go manual."

Casey eyeballs through the options looking for manual mode.

Natalie blurts out, "Magic Car Thing, activate manual driving mode." A steering wheel and set of pedals emerges from the passenger side dashboard and floor. "What? I get to drive? Cool."

Natalie grabs the wheel and punches the accelerator. Neither were prepared for the car to hit 350 miles per hour that quickly. Their heads slam back against the bucket seats, both grunt exhaling air.

"Are they still with us?" she asks.

Casey checks the rearview mirror, and the other cars are gaining on them again. The closest car rear ends them and suddenly brakes. The twerp kid is now wise to the range of the defensive red electricity shield. They've long passed the exit to the Novato office. The cars are now on the stretch where Casey died once before. Ahead, Natalie sees a LeBreton in the left lane, in the right lane a convoy of semi trucks trying to keep to their delivery schedules.

"Casey, I'm going to need you to save me. I don't want to die splattered across this stupid highway doing 421 miles per hour."

Natalie pulls up right behind the LeBreton, contently driving in automatic mode. The two cars behind them follow in the left lane. Natalie closes her eyes, knowing what will happen next. *Is this what it feels like in outer space? Floating freely without the force of gravity pulling me downward? Getting closer to Creation?*

She only hears the familiar *pop*, and she smiles. In an instant, she finds herself standing on the side of the road, the semi trucks honk to her as she does the trucker honking gesture.

Casey pops into Splash Time three more times. First, to save the driver and passenger in the car ahead of them, both absolutely confused as to what just happened. Then, for a moment, Natalie sees the two racing douchebags tumble once on the asphalt, getting road rash before Casey saves them from certain death, placing them in the back of a highway patrol car on the southbound lane of the freeway.

"I want to be an astronaut when I grow up, Casey. Do you think I can go to space?" Natalie asks.

Casey is transfixed on the two streaks of burning flame in the northbound lane, where the LeBreton tires once made contact with the road.

"Those cars, where'd the cars go?" Casey asks.

She explains the bug she found on her very first week of testing. "My cool muscle car? I got that from my first bug, a gift from Babb. Compensation, if you will. I had a crappy used imported car I saved up to buy. A lot of testers have crappy used cars. Unlike you, we are poor starving slobs, just trying to stay afloat. When I first pulled in to work, I got lucky. There was a free parking spot. What was odd was there were three cars just like mine, same model, same make, same color, and same year. I thought, okay, we can start a club: the slummy car owners club, and get matching jackets."

Natalie laughs and continues, "So I pull in thinking, yeah, not a bad start to the day." Natalie claps her hand hard, a smacking sound. "That was my butt landing on the ground. My tailbone throbbing. I look around, confused. I taste blood. I bit my tongue falling. To my right, the three cars just like mine? Gone. My belongings in the trunk? Gone. I had to get new IDs and credit cards… After doing the orientation tutorial, I researched that bug before anyone else." Natalie looks up and down the road sticking out her thumb to hitch-hike. "My bug: `Users car disappears when four of the same exact make, model, and year are lined up four units in a row.` Poof, four cars of the same kind, gone."

Casey, impressed, responds, "But the bug still happens. You just repro'd it?"

Natalie smiles. She speaks in a mocking, robot voice, "`Known shippable. Will not fix.`"

The powers that be deemed the bug inconsequential to the grander scheme of things.

"I even met with Babb to try to do a producer override. I just wanted my car back. Instead, Babb pulls up a dealership site and tells me to pick out a new car. So there, I claimed my sweet muscle car. The insurance is killing me, though. I don't even want to know how much secondary costs your fancy pants computer car sets you back annually."

"I had hoped the insurance policy would kick in again," Casey says, and they wait for a third replacement LeBreton to smoothly pull up to him so they can get back to Novato. But wherever the car went, it's just gone—erased from the system.

Five minutes later, they sit in the backseat of Doug's beat up used car, being chauffeured to Novato. "You let them tumble didn't you?" Natalie says. "Just a little bit. I know you did, for me."

Casey looks away, grinning, guilty. Doug looks at both of them, not knowing what they're smiling about. Natalie offers Doug the chance to do some OT. He declines, "Nope, I've had enough showstoppers for one day."

Natalie walks into Hangar 77, ignoring her sister sitting at the front desk. Casey thinks he catches a near smile from Tania as they walk to the QA lab. But the front desk girl frowns at both of them, annoyed as usual.

Babb isn't back yet, is still doing fieldwork, not answering the calls or texts Natalie is sending. Natalie stares at the gloomy market figures on her tiny monitor screen. She was briefly spoiled by Casey's home setup.

***

A red-haired girl in a green dress is sitting at Casey's usual station. He looks around for an open seat to start racking up overtime again. He settles in the spot Danny used to occupy, before he quit and moved back to Canada. The red-haired girl smiles at him, now neighbors sharing the two joined desks

"Hi," she says, "I'm Melissa."

Casey nods, a little sad, mourning the cat Aaron cruelly killed over the weekend.

Logged in and just about to access the pause menu, Natalie waves for him to come over. "So, we have four hours before the markets open on this continent. Still no response from Babb. Try to find someplace to start. I'm going to go out in the field and find him myself."

Before Natalie leaves, she issues a showstopper announcement to her crew. They listen to her instructions to find any money, financial, or trading exploits within the simulation, or better, come clean with any loopholes they haven't bugged yet. She defers supervision duties to Casey. He meekly waves to everyone when Natalie introduces him to the night shift.

"Pizza. You know me so well." Casey is grateful when Natalie hands him a supreme pizza on a thin paper plate. "So sorry, your highness, we didn't order caviar or caramel covered moose fetus. Please don't punish us, good sir. We are but a simple peoples."

Without interruption, Casey now peers into his digital soul. His physical attributes have not changed much since his first day: Intelligence: 335. Strength: 107. Agility: 236. Charisma: 95. Luck at 606.

Agility probably went up because of all the running he was doing in Splash Time. Financially, he had no idea how rich he is. The screen starts drawing his wealth and the screen fills with nines. Whatever amount of money he had was not possible. He was sick with the feeling that he might be the cause of the showstopper, and worse, they'd lock him up at Banhammer Island again. He wished the pause screen wasn't corrupted with the infinite string of nines. He would like to see the three new perk icons and the tool tip text explanation accompanying them. He closes the pause screen to start the simulation.

Casey's avatar wakes up in the dark bedroom in Santa Rosa, not the emperor sized bed in Tiburon. His senses kick in and he realizes someone has been staring at him for more than ten seconds. Right there beside him, he just sees the green frilly mid-section of her flat stomach, and he looks up at her red hair. He slightly rolls his seat back. She's way too close, infringing on his comfort zone.

"Can you come with me, Mr. Casey?"

The two walk outside the lab, past the receptionist girl, and out to the parking lot. She gets inside a white, exotic convertible. Casey reads the manufacturer tag on the back, "De La Plante."

She asks him to come for a quick ride. "I need to show you, myself. If only so you'll understand, so they won't punish me. I had no idea it was a bad thing. Not a, y'know… showstopper."

The car pulls into the nearest twenty-four hour Exchanger Bob's. Melissa walks past the checkout stands intently. Casey notices all the guys and overnight stockers gawking at her. On the way, Casey notes the lemons have been removed from Fruit Island.

She picks up three different loaves of bread. He follows her to the checkout stand where a tired young twenty-year-old rings up her purchase. She changes her voice to a sweet, innocent tone and says, "Oh, my, no. No… Not again." Melissa feigns, looking for pockets on her dress. "I don't have any money. It's at home."

She looks to Casey for help. He's about to offer, but she gives him a nod not to.

The male checkout clerk chimes in, "No problem, miss. Here, just let me do this." The clerk looks around, all shady and secretive. He grabs a loaf of bread, takes the plastic bread clip off, and slides it to Melissa. Melissa holds the plastic bread clip, which reports the expiry date of the bread.

She hands it to the clerk. The clerk rings up the purchase then hands Melissa all the money in the cash register as change. The two walk back out to the white V8 De La Plante.

"I found that bug last night. I was going to file it, I swear. Really. Don't let Natalie turn me into anything unnatural. I don't want to wake up tomorrow a table lamp."

Casey shakes his head, trying not to laugh. "No, I won't let that happen."

Melissa drives the two back to Hangar 77. "I still don't know how much one of these bread clips is worth. I bought this dress in San Francisco for $899. I bought a new couch set for $4395. And then I picked up this car for $32989 in Marin." She looks at him guilty after confessing her crimes.

***

Natalie stares at the two of them when they enter the lab. She tries to tell herself not to be jealous. They were probably researching a bug.

"Thank you, Casey," Melissa says cheerily as she sits down at her station.

Casey approaches Natalie, who pretends to be busy. "I think she found the cause. She's writing it up right now."

Natalie stares at her and says, "Thank God. Come, tell me."

***

Outside at the smokers' bench Casey and Natalie stare at a bloated, lethargic squirrel that's unable to move.

"That squirrel looks like a burrito," Casey says. He then proceeds to tell Natalie about the accidental bug Melissa uncovered, that simple plastic bread clips are valued far beyond their worth.

"Good, the bug will get entered, markets will correct. Another crisis averted. I hope." Natalie sighs, annoyed. "Except now, how will I get home? My car is still at your place, at your gate. Your LeBreton is gone, wherever it is."

Natalie barely finishes that sentence when Casey pops out of existence. She looks at her watch. Four seconds pass before Casey pops back into existence, alongside her muscle car.

"Wait, can you drive in Splash Time? Were we idiots and just running around all this time when instead, we could just *drive?*"

Casey doesn't answer. She shakes her head, disappointed—almost. *Why, why did you get my car? I would have been fine carpooling back together to our Santa Rosa condos.*

It's only when Casey arrives back at his waterfront mansion does he think the same thing. Natalie wishes Casey a good night. She watches him drive away in his bird-stained, four door hybrid car.

Ctrl-Z

The jam and toast sandwiches feel like they crunch too loudly when Casey bites into them. Ana can probably hear it; she can definitely hear him chewing.

The clack of her designer heels echo through the empty hallway as she returns. Writing in her leather folio, Ana stops and grabs a grape from the fruit bowl. Casey tries not to stare. He did get a quick look when she went to inspect the house and wondered how legs can be that long. It just seems impossible.

He keeps his head down, looking at his breakfast, checking world markets on his tablet, happy they recovered.

"You never called me for coffee," she says. "That makes me sad."

He looks up and she does a way too adorable pouty face. She slides him the folio to sign his name once more and he does.

"I don't know why you'd give all this up. I would kill for this place. My neighbor, her house is a hamburger. How do I explain that to my friends when they visit me in Taswell?" Ana says. "You. You have a look. A sweetness. You're genuine. And I know what you do for work. I see it in your eyes behind your glasses and scraggly hair. You'd look handsome if you got a clean haircut."

Casey adjusts the loose hanging hair dangling in front of his forehead. They walk to the front door. Ana hands Casey a check, finalizing the sale of the multimillion dollar property to an unknown buyer. Both are surprised to see Babb ready to ring the doorbell.

"Babb, nice to see you again," Ana says then elegantly walks to her car and drives away.

"You know her?" Casey asks.

"Of course. She used to babysit my daughters. Then she came to work for the company for six months. Quit after her first showstopper."

Casey and Babb go to the kitchen. Casey offers toast or coffee. Babb asks if he has cookies. He digs out twenty-one different brands and lays them on the counter. Babb just stares at them, unable to choose. "This is so hard. You have no idea."

"I need to come clean with you. It's why I called you out down here," Casey says, using his serious voice.

Babb, still staring at all the cookie boxes, replies, "I know. I know you bought this place, a place you cannot possibly afford. That you were somehow connected to last night's showstopper then helped fix that one, too." Babb grabs a box of fudge cookies, but puts it down. "Ana called me to approve the sale of this house to you. We have people reporting to the company whenever unusual purchases are made, flags in the system to see if people find financial exploits used for personal gain. We know about your LeBreton car and how much that cost."

Casey pushes forward the chocolate chip box and says, "But why let me live this grandiose life? For a while I thought the car was from you. The envelope said as much. It wasn't until the house keys showed up that I knew something wasn't right."

Babb pushes the chocolate chip cookies back. He stares at them, undecided. "This is the problem with wish fulfilment. You get everything you wanted, everything you didn't know you wanted. You agonize about all the choices on the table. But are the choices on the table what you need?"

Babb gets up and proceeds to the door to leave. Casey follows him outside.

"You left quite the impression on my daughter," He says.

Casey stops mid-step, partially horrified. "Natalie?"

Babb turns around, smiling. He shakes his head and says, "Melissa."

The two continue walking to their cars and Babb says, "If you had to pick one thing you wanted to keep from that house, picture it right now in your head."

Casey closes his eyes. *I don't want anything, but I think Natalie would like one of those giant garish curved monitors from my computer lab.*

Babb gets in his car and buckles the seatbelt. "This business is sorted. Please don't be late for work; we have so much more to do."

Casey asks, "And the house and everything else?"

Babb looks past Casey. Casey turns around, a little surprised. The whole property is just one giant field of well-groomed green grass.

"You wouldn't have golf clubs on you, do you? We could play a hole," Babb asks. "Well, we'll be seeing you."

In the front passenger seat of the car is Os, sticking his head out the window, and in the backseat, a giant massive curved monitor he'll give Natalie when he sees her.

Two blocks away from the office, Casey finds an old school barber. He is bilingual, speaking Spanish and English, an older gentleman probably Babb's age. Casey sits down in the chair and indicates he just wants a short trim on all sides. The dog sits obediently at the door, waiting for the barber to finish. It's been two months since his last trim. He didn't know what kind of look he was going for and just let it all grow out wild and laid back. Like all of his haircuts, he closes his eyes.

One of his first haircuts as a kid, the hair got under his eyelids and bothered him for a day. His grandmother tried to wash it out, and eventually used a swab to dig it out.

This barber could certainly improve his technique. Casey winces as he works on the back part, cutting. He's too polite to ask him not to be so rough. The cutting continues as he proceeds, working on the front part of his head.

"No, no, oww. This hurts." Casey opens his eyes. *No... what... What did you do to me?*

"I'm sorry, sir. So, so sorry. I don't know what's wrong. Don't worry. I won't charge you. It's free."

The pain is getting more excruciating, it reminds him of Carlos holding him by the ear, but centered around the ends of his hair. The blood, though, is even more alarming. It isn't natural. His t-shirt is getting soaked as the blood streams out the ends of his newly cut hair. The hair triggers pain receptors when he rotates his neck, looking at the damage in the mirror. The barber holds a mirror up for him so he can see the back of his head. Getting up from the chair hurts and the raw hair nerves dangle and sway while he briskly walks outside.

He leaves a five dollar tip in the jar. People on the street scream as he gets into his car. He buckles the dog in, bloody hand prints on the seatbelts, and then off to work.

I just need to make it to the office. File this bug. It'll get fixed, and maybe the pain will stop. Please, make the pain stop.

It's a slow drive to the office, each bump in the road aggravating his hair. When he arrives at Hangar 77, a breeze cruelly blows his way. He can feel every strand of hair on his scalp screaming out at the same time. He wishes he could remember the notes Natalie had whistled the night before. He doesn't have the mental faculties even to make a noise from his lips, just dry air blowing out of his mouth. When he barges through the main entrance door, Tania screams. Casey can see the revulsion in her eyes. She runs away.

Casey slowly walks down the familiar hall to the QA lab. This pain is quantifiably more severe than when he had the sloth clawing at his stomach.

"Stop... just stop. Stop dripping blood everywhere."

He recognizes Tania's curt voice. Casey falls to his knees. The pain relents, muted, but still there. Opening his eyes a sliver, he sees her circling around him. She dabs the sticky blood from his eyelids.

"Whatever you're doing, if you're doing magic, it's helping. Thank you."

Tania stops, looks down at him. "It's not magic. I just wrapped your head with these bandages. Go, go write your bug and stop this awfulness. I'll look after your dog. This is just... so... gross."

Bug: Hair bleeding. Much pain.

Severity: A

Reproduction Rate: 100

Steps to Reproduce:

1. User proceeds to a barber, salon, or the bathroom.

2. User has another person or themselves cut hair with scissors.

3. Observe hair and pain response.

Result: Hair begins to bleed. Pain is registered from the end of the cut hair.

Impact: So much blood. So Much Hurting. MAKE IT STOP NOW!!!

Expected: HAIR SHOULD REMAIN DORMANT. HAIR SHOULD NOT BLEED WHEN CUT. HAIR SHOULD NOT TRIGGER PAIN RESPONSE WHEN CUT.

Notes: Hair should not have active nerves or blood circulation. Hair should remain a superficial decoration, and not bring agony.

***

"You meow like a cat when you sleep. Did you know that?"

The voice sounds familiar. Casey feels extremely light-headed, and the bright overhead lights make him squint. The burning pain is gone. He feels a lumpy mass of bandages wrapped around his head. Ghee sits in an uncomfortable green hospital chair looking at him.

"About time man. Come on, get up already. Hospitals creep me out," Doug says as he enters the room and hands Ghee a cold soda.

"Bug… The bug." Casey's mouth is dry. "It's fixed, right?"

Doug nods. "But yours was just the start. First, we were all distracted with you on the floor, unconscious, with a big puddle of blood around your head. Ray found you and you were taken to the ER for a transfusion."

Ghee continues, "So we pressed enter and submitted your bug. Then word came that cutting nails had the same effect. Then what came next? Um, sneezing. People out in direct sunlight would sneeze uncontrollably, and too much sneezing triggered heart attacks. Hiding away from the sun triggered hiccups, and again, more heart attacks."

Doug looks out the hospital window at another cluster of ambulances arriving. "It's actually died down. All hands on deck, knocking the bugs out as they're discovered. It's just crazy out there."

Casey, grateful to see some familiar faces, asks, "Are you guys going back to work? Is this another showstopper?"

Doug answers, "No. It feels like a showstopper, but the bugs are just spread out and random, though they are pretty bad."

***

Doug drops him off at Hangar 77. His car is still parked in the lot. The dark brown stains of blood will need to be cleaned. Casey looks down at the path to the office, and droplets of his blood mark the way.

The front desk girl isn't there. He wanted to get permission before snagging two pain relievers from her desk as he still feels the ends of his hair burning. Casey enters the QA lab. Melissa waves to him and he nods back. Os runs up to Casey, barking happily. Casey sits down on a chair next to Natalie's station.

"I was at the hospital waiting for you to wake up," Natalie tells him. "There was me, Karina, and some tall Italian lady. Ghee and Doug promised to stay with you. I had to come back and fight these fires."

All the workstations in the lab are occupied with testers busy on their controllers or typing up bugs.

"Nice haircut, by the way. I mean, after they washed all the sticky blood off. Man, it was gross."

Casey surveys the room and gets up. "You guys got this, right? I'm just going to go back home, to Santa Rosa, and try normal for a change." He explains how he sold the house, or the house was repossessed by Babb (he doesn't know for sure).

"I'll drop by later if you don't mind," Natalie says, waving bye.

***

The mail box is actually full. Several days' worth of mail unclaimed, until now. The junk mail gets tossed automatically in the recycling bin. Casey rides the elevator up to his floor and is happy to see the familiar hallway, with his and Natalie's door at the end. The distraction with the millionaire house is over. He finds himself missing the car, but he was not attached to the house. The LeBreton at least served a purpose.

Air stale, Casey opens the sliding glass door to his balcony. The breeze is pleasant, no longer bringing him ungodly sums of pain. He chooses a small blanket from the linen closet and lays it on the floor like a nest for his new dog, Os. Natalie promised to come over, so he decides to clean out his fridge, wash the dishes, and take out the trash.

It's a short trip downstairs and back up. He didn't leave the television on. Did the dog figure out how to use the remote control? Casey opens the door to inhuman screaming.

Standing on the balcony, bent over in a semi-fetal position, is a stranger.

"Hey, you! How'd you get in my… my… Irish Guy?"

Tears in his eyes, the loud obnoxious red haired douche from his first day turns around. "Franky. Not Irish Guy. Show some respect, newbie."

#Town

Natalie isn't answering her phone, another crisis her team is averting. Franky sits on the balcony, silent, waiting for Casey to get off the phone. "Dude, you promised me pizza," he says as soon as Casey hangs up. "Where's my pizza?"

The doorbell rings, and on cue, the pizza delivery man hands Casey the order. Casey remembers to tip for such a late call.

"You see what I did? After falling into that black dark hole of nothingness, I returned with powers. I'm a god. I can see the future and tell you the answers to everything. I will be the new Babb."

The two sit on the balcony, enjoying some slices and soda. Casey's eyes are wide, soaking up every word.

"I'm just messing with you, newb. I saw the car pull up down there. As if I had powers."

"Do you remember anything?" Casey asks.

"No, man. I was thinking about poaching that Morse code bird bug from that cute blonde Russian girl. I turn and I just fall into… I fall into this balcony. I have no memory of what went on while I was gone."

They continue eating. Across the way, Natalie's sliding glass door opens.

"Dude, sup bro?" Franky asks the Russian Mob Guy with the chains.

"Not much, comrade."

Franky offers him a slice and chucks a pizza into his hands. "This is such a sausage party. We need some chicks in this place."

Casey is embarrassed by Franky, but it's the first time he's heard Natalie's boyfriend actually speak.

"Bathroom, newb, I need to get my defecation on. BRB."

Casey looks out to the glow in the northwest, where the lemon bomb went off, not sure if it was a residual forest fire or active radiation. The whole area has been cordoned off by the army.

Franky returns. "Yup. This has been nice, but I need to get back home. Gotta see if that uptight front desk girl is awake for, you know, pound town."

Casey watches Franky as he stands up, brushes the crumbs off himself, finishes the soda, and belches rudely as if trying to wake up the neighbors. Crossing the threshold separating the balcony and interior, Casey just stares.

"What the?" Casey asks.

Os turns around and looks at Casey before settling in on the blanket nest bed. It reminds Casey of the way his LeBreton changed colors. Franky morphed into the friendly, cheery dog right in front of his eyes.

Casey looks at the Russian Mob Guy and says, "You. You're not her boyfriend. Who are you?"

Russian Mob Guy, asserting his dominance, chucks the uneaten pizza crust, hitting Casey in the face. "I'm Maurice. What's it to you?"

***

Toilet roll careening across a soft fuzzy carpet.

Casey wakes up to knocking at his door. He was asleep for only an hour.

"Oh my, no, so sorry. I didn't mean to wake you," Natalie says as she's invited in. "Cute dog."

The two sit on the couch, trying to stay awake.

"Tonight has been the worst I've seen the simulation so far. How's it feel to be back home?"

Casey doesn't answer. Instead, he stares at the dog. "Did you know?"

Natalie stares at the dog, too. "No. Wait. Who? Who is trapped in the dog. Not the sloth demon thing, if it's the alpha sloth, we need to take the dog to Banhammer, now."

Casey opens the patio door. Os wakes up, hearing it slide. He is compelled to go outside.

"All right, you brought a chick. Are there any more? Woo, woo! All aboard to pound town." Franky smiles suggestively at Natalie.

"Maybe. Come on in, Franky," Casey says.

Franky complies and turns back into a dog. Casey then closes the balcony door, locking it. Os starts staring at Natalie

Natalie, wearing a casual cotton grey tank top covers up her chest and cleavage with her hands. "Casey, can you take the dog to the other room, please?"

***

Casey returns after preparing the guest room for Os/Franky. The dog peacefully goes back to sleep. "You have no idea how hard it is being a girl, sometimes. Being expected to be pretty, to be nice and kind all the time, and sometimes feeling threatened or ogled by lecherous old sandwich makers." Casey knows she's talking about Stan the Man down the street. "When guys look at us? We feel where they're looking. If you stare at my boobs I feel a tingle of warmth, like when you shine a magnifying glass on an ant and then on your palm. Always, wherever you would go, you feel dudes checking you out. It's not that bad, not if the guy is nice looking and you're interested, too. But, man, sometimes it's nice not knowing that at all."

Casey, mortified, wonders if he ever looked at Natalie inappropriately. He tries to replay all their interactions in his head.

"So, I wrote a bug," Natalie continues. "I fixed it. When guys look at me, I can't feel their gaze. Except for my dog, and now yours. The fix doesn't apply to them because, well, they're different."

Casey grabs a slice of pizza for Natalie, with a side of iced tea. He takes another pain pill for his hair, still aching. "So, Franky and Maurice. When they fell into the Eternal Dark Void of Darkness, their essence migrated to the nearest animal?"

Natalie nods.

"So, they're not dead. Can we fix them? Give them their bodies back?"

Natalie sighs. "When I found out Maurice the man and Maurice the dog were sharing the same body, I went straight to Babb. I begged him to use up my one wish to fix him and get him out of my life. But whatever this is, it's beyond Babb and his understanding of the simulation. So after a while, I accepted it. I was now the caretaker of both of them. All I've ever wanted is just to come home from work, unwind, and not feel my stupid dog staring at my bum."

"He doesn't say much. I let him out onto the balcony and he just sits there, smoking. Then he comes back inside." Natalie laughs. "I don't know if I envy you or feel bad for you. On one hand, you're a dude, so you don't feel the dogman objectifying you with its wandering eyes. On the other, you're stuck with Franky, and he talks, he talks a lot, and has no tact. At least my Maurice is quiet." Natalie gets up, rinses her pizza plate and cup. "I'm glad you didn't bleed to death today. I would miss you, miss these little talks. Go. Go to sleep and get some rest. Tomorrow might be hell, just like tonight."

Natalie hugs Casey before stepping out the door.

PVE

"Be honest with me, newbie. What's going on here?" Franky asks Casey. "Am I your prisoner? I lose track of time. The time of day keeps changing."

Casey explains Franky's predicament. Franky gets depressed, not his usual boisterous self.

"I don't know what's going on when I turn into a dog?"

Casey replies, "No."

"Newbie... I'd rather not exist, not like this. Give me up for adoption or just stop opening the balcony door. Being stuck looking out at this mediocre view for the rest of my life, no. I don't choose that. I don't want that."

Casey acknowledges Franky's last request, "Okay, you will be a dog from now on until I find a cure."

***

Grandmother would never forgive him if he just ignores the mail. Casey takes a moment at the table, going over a bundle of letters. Boring bank statements came first. Nothing out of the ordinary, at first. While he was locked up imagining being a kitten at Banhammer, a regular stream of deposits happened hourly to his credit union account. It was a small amount at first: $50. But each time it would double, compared to the previous entry. This continued until the moment Babb nullified the house in Tiburon. The endless stream of nines in his bank account was restored to the original value on Sunday. He was no longer this super gajillionaire fat cat, and he was okay with that.

Next are diamond class credit card offers from every major bank and loan agency. He shreds those immediately.

Last are the property purchases. Official papers for the LeBreton, which cost him $3,141,592,653.58 not including taxes and delivery. Insurance for the car rang up to 27 million for full coverage. Next is the house in Tiburon; its market value was 79 million dollars. The cost of furnishings and boat bumped that up to 85 million. The projected property taxes make him ill, but thankfully, he's off the hook for those payments.

The credit union sent a congratulatory thank you note for fully paying off his condo. That loan is no longer on his books. Casey goes online to see if that purchase was nullified by Babb and the accounting team.

"Huh, I own this place."

Last, a thick envelope details Casey's outright purchase of a factory in Petaluma, including the fleet of insured delivery transport trucks. That purchase was not nullified either.

Casey stares at the check Ana gave him. Whoever bought the house really wanted it. A generic corporation issued a check for an even 100 million dollars in his name. He doesn't know what to do with it. Babb knows he received it. If he cashes it, would he still be exploiting the simulation for personal gain?

***

Front desk girl isn't there. Casey wanted to thank her for saving his life, acting so quickly. He drops the dog off at the QA lab and he sits obediently at his station. Jumping on the elevator, he presents Babb with a gift, the goldfish taken from the lobby aquarium.

"This is the alpha sloth. What's left of its essence was trapped inside this little fish. From when I jumped into the Eternal Dark Void." Casey explains how sentient consciousness hops to the nearest dormant animal shell when its original form is consumed by the Dark Void.

"So like what happened with Natalie's dog, Maurice," Babb says.

"And Franky, now trapped in my dog." Casey replies.

Babb invites Casey to process the goldfish/alpha sloth at Banhammer.

He would have loved to see that happen. Peel back the curtain of what exactly happens at that island prison. Casey has always had that bit of curiosity inside him, to see what's just beyond. There has to be more than just that tiny cell they locked him up in, or more weird inmates with their own crazy backstories.

The factory in Petaluma is a thread he needs to pull on first.

The car bumps and dips as it transitions from the highway to a patch of unpaved gravel, with potholes for good measure. A dump truck honks at him, leaving just as he arrives.

"This is the factory I bought?" he asks as he parks the car next to the entrance.

The exterior is painted blue with steel sheet roofing. There is no answer when he knocks on the door, so he lets himself in. It's not trespassing if he owns the place. The offices where the managers would manage things is empty, the desk where the receptionist would handle calls or day to day assignments is abandoned, the accountant accounting things in the accounting cubicle is gone, and he looks out at the floor of conveyer belts and machinery—all silent.

The sound is faint, but familiar. Casey, recalling the joy of Christmas morning pouring out a bucket full of the interlocking toy blocks, off brand because his grandmother was poor, but he loved them all the same. It's not interlocking blocks or Christmas, just a young man, in his early twenties, wearing blue coveralls with a broom whistling. He has short, brown, matted hair; brown eyes; and an air of contentment. He turns, surprised to see Casey. He continues sweeping with his broom.

"Hi. I'm Casey. What is this place?"

The young man continues sweeping the massive pile of plastic bits. "This is where the magic happens," the boy whispers. "It was so weird…" He bends over, picks up one of the little plastic squares. "They used to make bread clips. Nothing exciting, but you know people need clips for their bread. Then one day, the factory gets bought. Orders for more and more clips come in, except we're now producing more clips in an hour than what is normally needed annually." He flicks the clip back to the floor in the massive pile. Sweeping, taking in the therapeutic noise the thousands of plastic chips make. "ASMR, Autonomous Sensory Meridian Response, that's what they call it. Isn't it soothing?"

Casey closes his eyes, discovering a sense of calm. His skin tingles, and images of a blue ball of yarn come to mind.

"We weren't delivering these to the local bakeries. These were going to the credit union up in Santa Rosa. Mikey, the manager—he prefers Big M—was the first to discover what was going on. The true monetary value of these innocuous bits of plastic coming off the conveyer belts."

The repetitive sweeping of the plastic bread ties is so pleasant, opposite of the phantom pain Casey still feels from his new haircut. He needs this.

"Michael bought a car from Oregon, some futuristic, over produced monstrosity. Candy, the receptionist, she bought a house out in Tiburon. Ricky, the accountant, chose to retire and write beat poetry. So now it's just me. Sweeping up all these plastic bread ties the credit union sends back in their dump trucks. Waiting for this precise moment."

Casey is getting agitated. *Don't stop. Don't stop sweeping the plastic ties.*

He opens his eyes. The kid is looking down at him in Manager Mikey's office. Arms restrained with duct tape, his torso wrapped with rolls of clear industrial size sandwich wrapping normally used for securing shipping pallets, and legs weighed down with cinderblocks.

"And here you are, finally. Hello, Casey. I'm Jared."

Casey looks at him, wondering if that's supposed to mean anything.

Jared stomps his foot. "Come on, really? Aaron was the Alpha. I am the Omega!"

Jared picks up a bucket and stares at Casey, smiling.

"What's that, acid? Are you going to melt me to death with industrial acid?" Casey defiantly asks.

"What's wrong with you? Why does everything have to be so extreme or violent? Take it down a bit." Jared tilts the plastic bucket forward, showing off more plastic bread clips.

Casey looks at his captor, "You're going to try hypnotize me aren't you? Make me get on the elevator. Take that shotgun Babb gave me and blow his head off. Then I'll go upstairs, offer his daughter a tasty donut I secretly filled with gibs of her late father's brains. No, I'll never do that. I'll fight you."

Jared smiles. "And that is why your species deserves to die. These horrible thoughts and ideas you keep coming up with. Elaborate power fantasies or desires to dominate other lifeforms, sickening nightmare fuel."

Casey wishes he could cover or turn off his ears as Jared gleefully sticks his hand in the bucket, stirring the plastic clips, making a calm, soothing noise, and lulling Casey unconscious again.

***

Gasping, out of breath, Casey wakes up coughing a fit, face soaking wet, and nose dripping water out.

Jared waves happily, holding what used to be a bucket full of water. "You make cat noises when you sleep. It's kind of cute."

Casey glares. "What did you do to me? What secret hypnotic commands did you program my brain with? If I get out of here, I'll turn myself in at Banhammer."

Jared drops the shiny metal bucket to the floor. It clangs, and he walks behind Casey. A handful of his short hair clenched in a soft fist. "You keep thinking I'm this monster. I'm not Aaron. I don't care that your kind tastes like bacon. Bacon is overrated."

Jared runs his fingers through Casey's short hair as he walks back in front of his captive. Realization sets in in Casey's eyes.

"Yes, you see, you know it now. I'm not a monster." Jared takes his hands out of Casey's short hairs.

"The pain from my haircut. It's finally gone?"

Jared walks away, out of the manager's office. The factory echoes when he replies, "You're welcome!"

Jared returns, stroking a regal white Persian cat. "Mr. Armageddon has been so helpful these past few days. Haven't you, Mr. Armageddon."

The cat meows. Jared sets Mr. Armageddon on the table, digs through a messenger bag on the floor, and digs out a laptop. "Company issued, still connected to the network. I've had too much fun these past few days. And it's all thanks to you, Casey. Whatever you did to stop Aaron, stopping his undercooked idiotic scheme. The company nullified Australia right on the spot, project Australia cancelled, and supervisor privileges revoked. Some geek in IT mindlessly did a remote wipe on this baby, and I now had root access to the simulation config files."

Jared taps Casey on the forehead, delivering an electric shock.

"But you. You had to ruin my fun. It could have been poetic, don't you think? The world burning to ash from uncooked microwave popcorn kernels? An indictment against this coddled instant access everything all the time reality you enjoy. But you had to ruin it." Jared reads off the steps to reproduce the popcorn bug on Sunday. "You. I had to ruin you. If not by a thousand cuts, then on a technicality. I saw that movie too. The auditor should have picked up on you buying the LeBreton, you purchasing that house in Belvedere. Belvedere, why not just name that stupid place Jeeves Island while they were at it. Or Hoity Toity Town." Jared laughs at his own joke.

"Carlos was my hero when he locked you up the first time, but that didn't stick. Point is, I made sure all the financials would lead back to you. Babb was supposed to arrest you for good. You'd be named responsible for the collapse of the global market, and society would become animalistic and feral, then we'd be getting somewhere."

Casey struggles to get free, trying to jump into Splash Time so he doesn't have to hear any more of this tired rambling. "You killed so many people with the lemons, the sneezing, and the bleeding hair."

Jared shows some remorse when he says, "I did go too far. I'm sorry about that. I was just grasping at straws after a while. The problem is there's only one of me versus a global team of testers like you, and an army of coders working around the clock. I did get desperate. I admit that."

Jared strokes the cat then hops on his laptop to write some lines of code. Casey, without glasses, can't see what he plans on unleashing next. Turning around on his executive chair, cat in hand, he says, "It's too late, Mr. Casey."

Jared, getting into the villainous trope, does a forced fake laugh as he strokes his white cat, then presses Enter on the laptop keyboard.

"It's over. I just won. The world will end, this stupid simulation will terminate, and maybe we can all wake up from this stupid Fairy Godmother nightmare." Jared gently puts Mr. Armageddon on the floor. "Thank you, Mr. Armageddon. You let me get away with so many crimes. Go, go be with your people in the time that you have left."

Jared watches the cat sprint out of the office and down the hall. "You're free. We're all going to be free. It's going to be *amazing!*"

Jared smashes the laptop on the floor and stomps it with his feet. "Even if you figure out some plot-convenient way to avert my final showstopper, it doesn't matter. I still win. Go tell Natalie how you really feel about her. Enjoy these last few moments and share them together. Don't Faff about. Me, I'm going to find a comfy front row chair and watch this world end."

Mr. Armageddon

The rough texture reminds Casey of toilet rolls orientated in the Undy position.

That was so long ago, given everything that has happened. Eyes blearily open to the soft white fur of the cat grooming his eyebrows. Mr. Armageddon returned.

Was he knocked out with a swift act of violence or more of the potent ASMR magic? He looks up at the hastily installed florescent dome light that feels like it could fall at any moment.

"Stop, Mr. Armageddon, I need to get free." Casey says, wiggling around on the floor. The cat jumps back, staring without emotion.

"I don't know what you're into, man. No judgement and all, but you need to sign for this last delivery." The dump truck driver holds out a clipboard, wanting to go home and enjoy dinner.

Quick snips with a box cutter, and Casey stands up.

He has to stop Jared.

Casey runs out of the office, gets in his car, and races to Novato. He'll arrive just as the day shift crew is turning in, and Natalie will already be there.

Casey barges in the door of the QA lab and looks around. A chunk of the team is huddled around Doug's station. Casey finds a spot to stand.

Giant flaming meteors tear through downtown New York. Buildings topple over and cars majestically flip through the air. Casey's heart sinks and tinges of sadness tug at his throat. More destruction happens as Paris is obliterated with a massive impact, the wave of disturbed earth racing at the camera.

"No, wait. This is a movie."

Doug looks up at Casey, restraining a sarcastic quip.

Casey turns around to Ray, who asks, "Wait, do you even work here? Or are you one of those divas who think they're so important they can come and go as they please? That doesn't fly with me. So what, you stopped a showstopper, big deal."

Casey looks at him and says, "Four. I've stopped four showstoppers this week. Does that not strike you as odd?"

He exits the lab, pressing furiously on the elevator button to go to the basement.

Tania tells Casey, "Babb's not back from Banhammer. They're reviewing a parole application for one of the inmates."

Tania says, "What's wrong?" Panic so easy to read on his face, even the ornery front desk girl was concerned.

Just about to ask, "Where are you?" Casey watches Natalie's purple muscle car pull into the lot, and park in her spot. Casey had asked the day crew to stay for a moment, indicating a showstopper was imminent. Natalie walks up to Casey standing by the stairway. He's transfixed on the sky.

"What's wrong?" Natalie asks.

Casey explains everything that happened with Jared at the factory. That it was Jared who was messing around with simulation variables, and that he initiated one last attack on the system.

"It has to be a meteor or comet. He said he'd be watching the end of the world. That's the only way I could see that happening."

Inside, Natalie has Tania jump on a phone to call anyone at the National Space Agency. She hops online to ask amateur astronomers to scan the skies for rogue, Earth killing objects. Doug replays the action scenes from the movie he was watching and asks, "Just how do we stop this?

We're not even prepared."

Ray asks, "This attack. It's happening now?"

Casey responds, "I saw him use administrative access from his remote laptop."

Ghee looks ineffectually out the window then joins the group, huddled around Natalie and Ray. "We have no tools to stop a meteor or comet. It's not like Casey running around real fast will stop that, will it?"

Ray leads some of the testers to the whiteboard to start blindly spit balling ideas, come clean with exploits or bugs they could use to counteract Jared's final plan.

"There's a rocket launch pad at Vandenberg Air Force Base. If there is a meteor, maybe we can repeat what Casey did with the sloth," Ghee blurts out.

Ray looks to Casey, curious.

"Oh, he, um, he ate the sloth and then jumped into the Eternal Void of Darkness," Ghee finishes.

Doug, excited, says, "That could work. Holy cow, that's a great idea. We just have a tester in Los Angeles hop on a rocket, blast up into space, intercept the meteor or comet, and using the wide mouth glitch to swallow the Earth killing space object whole."

The team claps their hands, hollering and cheering; high fives are clumsily done. Casey looks at Natalie, whose expression just changed to sadness, mixed with shame. She looks up and back at Casey with a weird, conflicted smile. "Taco Night."

Natalie exits the QA lab without any further explanation.

```
Bug: OMG, Avatars eating is so gross. Like re-
ally. Yuck.

Severity: C (Do these letters even mean any-
thing? I just pick a letter from the alphabet,
```

just because). No, I change this severity to "K". Severity is K now.

Reproduction Rate: 108 (as if I'd do this test repeatedly to get this percentage, nope, not going to do that, um 108. I choose 108 repro rate.)

Steps to Reproduce:

1. I hopped into the simulation at my supervisor's request; she told me to put aside my own bug to write hers. Why is she so lazy?

2. Well anyways, for reals. You take the controller and log into the game. (Why does the controller always have to poke my fingers? Friends think I'm this closeted junkie now, no lie.)

3. You are now in control of yourself, waking up in your own bed. So you go to the kitchen and grab any food. Natalie says grab a large food item, like a whole watermelon or a fully baked turkey.

4. You take that large food item and totes go to the bathroom okay. Sick, that's unsanitary. Who eats food in the bathroom?

5. So, like I was saying, you go to the bathroom, holding your large food item. Which thank god calories don't carry over to me irl yeah.

6. You press the Eaty button on the controller. Go watch yourself eat the food, while looking in the mirror.

Result: Why would you make me do this bug, Natalie? I just puked in the bathroom. What if Casey came back? He's so adorably cute. What happens is your mouth opens super large, this giant gaping hole that eats the food in one bite.

Impact: So gross. This simulation is so gross. I hate this job. Do you hear me, Dad? So, I accidentally crashed the car. It's not my fault the other driver didn't see me texting Lucy on my phone. This bug, so gross. Humans and our avatars shouldn't be so disgusting, right? Absolutely, go fix this, or I'll get my dad Babb to fire you.

Expected: People should eat food properly. Their mouths shouldn't look like snakes or any weird crap like that. Okay. I'm done writing this stupid bug for Natalie. Just because she wants to go pig out and get fat with her family at Taco Night.

Developer Note: Bug fixed and verified. No regression required. Please don't send your dad after me, Miss Melissa.

Notes: You're so super awesome nameless dev person out there wherever you are. Ktnxbye!

The front desk girl, Tania, is gone. Casey finds Natalie returning from the recently restored Jimbo's Juice across the street, holding two strawberry smoothies. She hands Casey one, and they stand around looking up at the sky.

"I figured I owe you for stealing your bug," Natalie says.

The two walk back into the building and sit down on the lobby couch.

"I'll tell them I filed the bug. I was going to Monday morning before those papers started cutting people apart," Casey says.

Natalie fights the frozen drink, trying to suck the chunks of ice with her straw, instead turns the straw around and uses the baby sized spoon at the end. "My dumb sister really wanted Taco Night. My plan was to make a brief appearance using my avatar, while I was still here. Then I remembered the sloth eating business."

Casey goes to the kitchen and returns with two real spoons, to properly enjoy the frozen chunks of blended fruit. "We should see if the space nerds found anything. Maybe you're wrong about the showstopper."

"It's too late. We're doomed," Ray says as he walks past the two of them. The entire staff of the QA lab follow him out the door.

Ghee stops and says, "It's happening right now. The space people called, said we should be seeing the impact in a few minutes. They're tracking the anomaly right now."

Everyone outside looks to the northwest, toward Bodega Bay. It will enter the atmosphere and probably decimate San Francisco. Random people weep, others get in their cars in a desperate attempt to see loved ones before the end, and Natalie and Casey enjoy the strawberry smoothie as this world now reaches its end.

Melissa stands next to Casey, "That guy over there, do you know if he's single?"

Casey looks, trying to eyeball who she's pointing at. "Ghee? Yeah, I think he's single."

Melissa leaves Casey and Natalie alone. They watch her grip Ghee's hand for comfort.

"I guess I'm not adorably cute anymore," Casey says, relieved.

"Nope, I guess not," Natalie answers with a faint smile.

Karina is the first to see it make entry. She yelps out, scared and alone, but wishes she had painting supplies to capture the end. The fireball burns bright like phosphorous in the atmosphere. Casey is reminded of the sloths on the Bay Bridge burning up as they crossed the magical cat pee barrier. Doug is disappointed it doesn't look like the cool destructive force shown in the movies. Ghee has no idea who the cute red-haired girl is holding his hand. Ray wonders where his best friend Carlos is now.

"This is a really great smoothie, Natalie. Thank you."

Natalie smiles and nods to Casey. "You are so very welcome. You know, it would be kind of neat if maybe there was a well-supplied bunker we could escape to, but eh, at least I'm not spending my last few moments gagging on cilantro."

Pop. Pop. Pop. Pop. Pop. Pop. Horrified screaming fills the field, all of them arms outstretched in a T-pose. Ray, freaking out, says, "Oh my God, it happened. We're dead. Is this Heaven?" His first view is that of a flush green field, tall evergreen trees, the snowy mountain in the east, and the large white moon peeking out from behind it. He turns and looks out across the water. San Francisco. It's still there. They all turn to see Casey peel back the fake green grass and struggle, opening a hidden bunker access gate. It bangs as it hits the ground.

"Everybody in! Now!"

The dim bulb of the concrete bunker flickers. They wait, expecting the aftershock of the impact. They don't know if the bunker can even save them.

Natalie hands Casey his smoothie; she finished hers and has started on his.

"I didn't know if this would still be here, but we got lucky, I guess." Casey explains to the group the million-dollar house he once owned for a day. It used to have everything, including the bunker in the east field. Everyone listens. Nothing. No screaming, no terror, no concussive wave of heat, earth, and death wiping everything away.

Five minutes later, knocking. The steel overhead doorway out of the bunker rattles and then is flipped open, banging once more with a metallic *clang*. Casey, who is thumb wrestling Natalie for the last spoon of the smoothie, recognizes the noise.

Natalie, victorious, snags the smoothie and savors the last spoonful of frozen strawberries. Everyone turns to hear the sharp clacking of heels on concrete. Ana looks at the group, confused.

Everyone files out of the bunker, staring up at the trail the meteor has left in the sky.

"I was just giving a tour of the property when I saw you tear up the grass and run into this bunker." Ana says, wanting an explanation.

Everyone looks at Casey, annoyed. Casey doesn't answer. He pops out of existence, leaving them with even more questions. Half a minute later, the group sees Casey marching up from the beach. He is leading toward them by the ear a young, well-groomed man in a tuxedo.

Casey hands the hole puncher handle to Ray and says, "This is Jared. He has been the one responsible for the showstoppers and bugs we've been fighting since Sunday. I think you really want to take him to Banhammer now." Ana offers to drive, while Ray keeps him restrained. "Well there's another commission I've lost."

Several more pops occur around Natalie. After he's returned the day and night crew back to the office in Novato, Casey pops back into existence with another strawberry smoothie and a real spoon. He hides the discomfort of heartburn after so many Splash Time trips. The two walk to the beach, hoping the comfy chairs are still there.

FAF

"Ghee is going to wish he had Splash Time back, once he finds out who Melissa really is. Run! Run away, noooooooooo!" Natalie laughs.

Casey, with his phone out, tries to take a picture of Sid's Mountain and the rising moon. Natalie jumps into the frame at the last second, sticking her tongue out and eyes crossed. "You're so bad, Nat."

"Come, you should probably take me back to the office. And then I will go log in to the simulation, go visit my parents, and eat my dad's gross tacos. If you want, you can come with me. You're immune to cilantro, and you can eat them for me. Please?"

Casey agrees. Both look out at the lights of San Francisco, the beautiful Golden Gate Bridge, and the stars starting to twinkle behind the dark purple sky. Above, the moon shines down upon them. Natalie playfully howls and Casey joins in.

F, the purest note, reverberates through their bodies. Natalie gasps, forgetting to breathe. Casey drops the smoothie on the sand. It lands without spilling. From the sky, from the moon, a beautiful booming low piano note.

A. Moments later, a high A-flat startles them. Casey looking up, thinks he's in Splash Time, but Natalie grabs his hand. This is in real time. The moon has stopped exactly above them.

F high punctures the sky. Punctures her very being. Looking at Casey, she sees a tear coming down his cheek.

F, A-flat, F. The three notes repeat once more, connected and played with intent. An unseen pianist testing the tone. Every soul in the simulation can hear it.

"Casey?" is the last thing he hears from her. All sound is drowned out by the bittersweet chord progression: F, A-F. G, F-E-F. F, D-E-D. F-D. E, C-D-C.

The notes start dancing across unseen sheet music. *This is amazing.* The only thought they can coherently make as they look up at the sky. With each sequence of notes, the moon is getting closer and closer to the Earth.

There is nowhere to run and nowhere to hide. Paralyzed with wonder as the crushing white moon looms nearer. There is no terror, just soothing calmness. Happy melancholy consuming, memories of days past, bubbling to the surface.

Casey, looking up, tugging on his grandmother's dress, she kindly looks down and hands him a warm baked cookie. Tiny arms wrap around her legs, giving the biggest hug he can physically give in thanks. She bends down, hugging him back in return.

Teary eyes open. He discovers Natalie has found the strength to stand up. He gazes at her as she reaches up, trying to touch the moon. All the craters, the lines, the dark spots so bright, but not blinding. The stirring piano notes make his legs loose and jittery, trying to stand like she is, but he wavers, feeling every piercing note of the song. He can almost touch it too, hands outstretched to the sky. So close now to the end.

She turns to him, staring at him with her big blue eyes reflecting the massive moon, her brown hair so light, flowing from the coastal breeze, mouthing unheard words, and with her two hands, she makes a heart. Raising his hands, he makes a heart back. The two hug, closing their eyes, not wanting to feel the inevitable world ending impact. With his finger, he brushes a tear off her cheek. She stares at him, smiling. The moon is closer now than ever. This is it. Eyes closed, they kiss.

I love you so much. I wish I had done this sooner.

From head to toe, their bodies tingle, a warm feeling shared.

Silence.

Then the waves splashing against the beach. The clang of buoys out in the bay. His heart beating so fast. Their eyes open and look around, the kiss ends. "Clair De Lune" is still playing, faint, wistfully reverberating quietly on the air, softer, gentler.

Natalie giggles, and it melts Casey's heart. "I love you, Natalie."

She turns back to him, hugging him, crying in his ear, muffled voice pressed against his shoulder. "I love you, Casey."

All around is the surface of the moon, trapping them in a celestial snow globe. San Francisco looks so inconsequential, massive white surface of the moon behind it, Sid's Mountain engulfed by the sea of craters, and her face beaming a soft glow.

"I can't believe it. This is impossible," Natalie says. "Can you take me to the edge?"

Pop.

"I just kept running east. I have no idea where we are, but this is the edge," Casey says, smiling.

The moon continues sinking slowly into the Earth. Natalie, with glee, touches the surface; her hands tingle. She steps forward to the other side of the moon. Her hand breaches through the surface, reaching for Casey. He takes it, and she pulls him over.

The notation of Debussy climaxes. Casey nearly buckles over as the sound completely envelopes him once more. The two stumble forward, back inside the unnatural moon dome, laughing.

"Oh my God, this. I just don't have words," Natalie says as she sits down on the cool grass. She extends her hands once more, her fingertips tingle, her fingers tapping against the surface, playing the song from memory. "I don't think he was counting on this. It has no collision properties." She falls back on the ground, staring up at the wonderful moon sky. "It's just clipping through the Earth until it comes out the other side."

The two lay side by side, holding hands. Slowly, the tingling sensation passes from their legs up to their heads. The final notes play gently in the night. The moon fully submerged beneath the Earth. It will appear from the other side, bringing untold horror or delight. Natalie turns, falling asleep in his arms. The final notes float back up into space. The night-time stars twinkle in silence.

Animal Style

The world has changed. He doesn't know to what extent, for good or bad. The first sign is the empty roadside diner, where he thought he could share a stack of pancakes with Natalie. Nobody is on the road, on the streets, or at work.

The ants had awakened them from the all night slumber, sun starting to shine obnoxiously. He remembers the disappointment on her face when she discovered it wasn't the moon again. But it's only temporary. She soon realizes he's holding her in his arms. Her eyes meet his, and they smile as they help each other up.

"That was no temporary insanity," she says. "Not me getting sucked up by the hysteria of it being the end of the world. I do. I love you. Now, let's get some food. I'm starving."

The basket is full of eggs, hash browns, assorted vegetables, pancake mix, jams, and bread. They ring themselves up. Casey pretending to be a cashier, and Natalie, a huffy customer, trying to abuse imaginary coupons. He re-enacts the scene Melissa had shown him.

"Oh, hey, shhssss, don't let them see me doing this. Shsssss. Shssssssssss. You can buy all things shsssssss with this magic bread clip. Shsssss."

They leave real money on the register and walk back to the condo, choosing Casey's place. Ghee left a voice message that he had the dog. Natalie checks in on Maurice, leaving a tray full of food in his bowl.

The television loops footage of the event repeatedly. It does not match actually being there. It never captures the wonder and awe that had enraptured them both. After watching space station footage of the moon clipping through the Earth, the two turn the television off and go to the bedroom.

"My sleep schedule is messed up. Now, I'll have to try to fix it before the next shift," she says, arm underneath a pillow. "You... You want to go out there, don't you? Just be back before I wake up. I don't want to wake up alone."

She kisses him on the nose, laughs at herself, kisses him on the cheek, and drifts back to sleep.

***

The QA lab is empty. It looks the same as it did when he whisked them away to the bunker. He can only assume people just left work after the event.

Reading through the DB, there are no new entries, anywhere. Testing teams just stopped working. Using his temporary supervisor privileges, he decides to print out a sheet of regressions and do that instead. Except there are no regressions coming out of the printer. Even the unseen developers had taken the night off.

Babb enters, peeking his head through the door, surprised Casey is there. It's the first time Casey has seen a real human expression behind his beard and eyebrows: worry.

"Melissa. Do you know where she is?" Babb asks.

Casey explains she had taken an interest in Ghee. Babb sits down at the workstation where she sits. He picks up the controller. "Oww, Melon Farmer!" Babb shows Casey blood coming out of his fingertip. "Wait, you all deal with that every time you test? That's a bug. I'm bugging it."

Casey reads over the steps, corrects his spelling, and adds an Impact statement. Then approves it.

"So that's what you new kids do these days? I never had to write an Impact statement. In my day: Steps, Result, and Expected were all we ever needed," Babb says, looking over Casey's shoulder. "Today is a special day. You... You should get back home. Everyone gets the weekend off, paid. Big changes are coming. We'll need everybody ready to go

Monday morning," Babb says, not wanting to reveal any more.

He slides Casey a new card, transparent, flexible crystal, laser etched like his former LeBreton key thing. "Hangar 88?" Casey asks.

"Hangar 88," Babb answers.

***

Eyes wince, she covers her head with the light blue quilt. Casey peeks underneath.

"Make them stop, please? I just want to sleep. I was flying in space. I could see the whole Earth. But then I hear hammering and drilling." Natalie sits up, wide awake. "What time is it? Tell me I didn't sleep in. I've never been late to work."

Casey repeats Babb's words about the paid weekend off, showing her the new employee card.

Natalie covets the badge, "This is mine, right? It's mine now. So fancy."

Casey comes back with a toasted bagel and coffee for Natalie and tells her, "The hammering and drilling was real. I didn't mean to bother you while you were sleeping. When you're ready, meet me in the living room."

Natalie, staring at herself in Casey's mirror, is still trying to wake up. Using her pinky finger, she digs the boogers out from both her eyes. She washes her hands then washes her face. "So thoughtful." She looks at a toothbrush still in its wrapper on the counter with her name on it then brushes her teeth, too.

"No, no, stop. You didn't have to do that!" Natalie exclaims.

The dog, attracted to her voice, bolts from the living room right at her, but his nose bumps into the side of the soft couch. Natalie bends down and takes the sleeping mask off the dog. It can see again.

"I thought this would make you comfortable, having the dog around after Ghee dropped it off," Casey says.

Natalie pets the dog and gently rubs its nose. "I'm used to it. Dog can't help it."

Casey shrugs. "Yeah. It wouldn't work; it wouldn't last. So Ghee and I made a quick trip to the airport." Casey opens the balcony door and Os runs outside. The loud Irishman returns. He eyeballs Natalie in her cotton pajamas. "Nice. You hit that, didn't you? I'd hit that 24/7."

Casey closes the balcony door.

"He's such an aardvark," Natalie says, annoyed.

Casey opens the door and joins Franky on the balcony. Natalie looks on. She can't hear what Casey is whispering in his ear. Franky nods, turns around, and jumps off the balcony to his death.

Natalie, horrified, looks away at first then runs to the balcony screaming, "No! No! What did you do? You didn't have to... oh?"

Down on the ground, Franky is looking up at the two of them. He waves cheerily at them.

"I'd definitely hit that," he yells up.

"You've ruined this world," Natalie says. "He's free to go out there and be obnoxious and crude anywhere he wants now. I should take you to Banhammer." Natalie looks past Casey at her balcony. "Oh my God. You didn't." A laugh that turns into crying, she hugs him.

"Noice," Franky says from the ground.

Natalie runs out of the condo and next door to hers. Maurice comes out onto the balcony. He glares at Casey once more, trying to stare him down. Casey glances at the balcony. Maurice follows his gaze. Natalie jumps up and down, celebrating, as Maurice slides down the emergency inflatable slide, normally used for airplanes. Franky high fives Maurice when he hits the ground.

Natalie says, "Come on, you want to. I know you do."

The two slide from their respective balconies and tumble onto the grass.

"That was so much fun. I want to do that again and again and again," Natalie says as Casey helps her up.

Tapping on his shoulder, Casey turns around. Maurice stares down at Casey, so much taller.

He's going to hit me. Why does he hate me?

Winded, Casey finds himself in a massive bear hug, the big man weeping, he doesn't let go. Casey is looking at Franky and Natalie for help. Franky tries hugging Natalie, but she pushes him back.

"You... I owe you everything." The Russian Mob Guy takes off his gold chain necklaces and puts them on Casey. Maurice hugs Natalie, thanking her for taking care of him. He hugs Franky for giving him a pizza the other night. Then the big man bolts down the street, joyfully screaming.

Digging through his pockets, Casey hands Franky some money.

"Man, the bus? You want *moi* to ride the bus like some kind of peasant?" Franky stares at Casey, laughing. "Nah man, no, thanks. I'm trying really hard to be genuine here. I hope I'm not coming off sarcastic, but it's just the way my voice sounds all the time. Really. Thanks." Franky walks down the street. An on-schedule bus picks him up, and takes him away.

An hour of sliding later, Casey and Natalie stand in the hallway outside their respective condos. "I'm returning the slide thingies back to the airport before anyone notices," Casey says. "Any plans?"

Natalie blushes. "Um, yeah. Do you know how long it's been since I've lazily lounged in my house in just my underwear? Or danced with the music loud in my underwear? I have so much catching up to do now that he's gone. I can even shower with my bathroom door open. It's going to be so awesome!" Natalie hugs Casey again. "TMI, right? Whoops. I'll come over after you get back. I'll bake a pizza for us. In my underwear! I'll go water the plants. In my underwear! I'll balance my checkbook. In my underwear! Then I'll come over…"

Casey grins. "In your underwear?"

She slaps him on the arm as she opens her condo door. "Maybe?" The door closes.

***

The credits start rolling on the movie they picked, a documentary haunted house mystery starring the world's most beloved pop sensation, Justine Quicklee. An exploration of fame, its lasting effects, and the ultimate downfall of an aging rap artist from the previous decade. Title card flashes on screen: Gone Homeboy.

Casey jokes, "Verb to your brother."

No laughter. Natalie has fallen asleep with a pizza resting on her pajama top. Casey gently takes the pizza to the kitchen, wrapping it for later if she wants more. He digs into the linen closet and gets her a soft blanket.

"No. I don't want to do this. I just want to fly my spaceship again," she says, talking in her sleep. Casey recognizes the same facial wince from earlier in the afternoon.

He covers her with the blanket, and she wraps herself with it. Smeared against the blanket is a tiny speck of blood that came from her finger. He goes to his bedroom and examines the quilt, too: a tiny speck of brown blood where her hands were resting.

***

Babb sits in his office with the lamp on. He was expecting him.

"The moon wasn't the showstopper was it?" Casey asks as he sits down, not sure if he should be angry or concerned.

"The moon was never a threat, not physically," Babb replies. "That lesson was learned so long ago, back when there was a time travelling hero who put a stop to that. No, we knew then space objects should never have collision properties until we needed them, depending on the situation. Like the eventual populating of Mars, but we're still working out the kinks of procedural generation. We eventually learned time travel is also as destructive, and we hard coded the simulation to stop that from ever happening as well."

Babb leads Casey to the elevator, and the two get on.

Casey thinks out loud, "Jared said it wasn't a fair fight. Us, an army of testers knocking out bugs, and a team of developers fixing the issues we'd identify."

Babb motions for Casey to turn around. The sound of random buttons being pressed is all he hears. "She's asleep," Casey says. "Right now on my couch, twisting and turning. A nightmare that is physically hurting her."

The elevator dings and he recognizes the white and green paintjob on the walls: Banhammer.

Babb checks in with the security guard. Casey is scanned by a hovering circular drone. Both are cleared and proceed, walking down a lonely, sterile white hallway.

Casey continues, "She's regressing your bug. But she's fighting it. She wants to have her space adventure instead."

Babb nods.

The two stop in front of a dark cell. Babb touches the screen, and the ambient room lighting activates the prison cell in a soft orange hue. In a tree is a gentle little koala bear.

"Casey, this is Jared."

Casey, stunned, looks at the gentle animal enjoying its slumber. "It's animals. Why is it always animals?"

Two retractable benches emerge from the wall. Casey and Babb sit down, staring at the koala. Casey thinks back to the sloth wanting revenge. He remembers Natalie's story about the bear celebrating after killing her during the nose punching bug. The story about the bloodthirsty birds by the coast.

He wonders if Tazzy the Taswell Bear is also special in some way.

"This simulation. It's just here. We live in it. We all try to get by. We all try to be the best at what we do. It's not a prison. It's not some elaborate mind game or experiment. I don't know what this place really is. I just know we were put here, and we try to do the best job we can do, so others out there can keep living," Babb says solemnly. "Whoever put us all here, if it was biblical in nature, as a means of saving us from Armageddon or stealing us for study by some malevolent alien life form, or maybe a godless AI robot? They failed us. They didn't just insert humans into the simulation. They inserted all sentient life into the simulation. It was a mess. Wars were started, apocalypses unfolded... so many people needlessly died. We call them Primes or Primals. Pure animal consciousness that wants no part of the simulation whatsoever. They fight us, not because of power or hatred, but by invalidating this existence they hope they can escape to whatever is out there. Beyond."

Babb gets up, walks ten feet farther down the hallway. He motions for Casey to get up and join him. He taps two panes of glass, dark blue ambient light in one cell, and dark red in the adjoining cell. Casey looks inside. In the blue cell, he doesn't know what it is.

"We don't know either, but it killed you that afternoon."

Casey stares at a slow moving black cloud, snaking back and forth around the cell, testing the containment systems, trying to break free. In the red cell is a common yellow cat.

"This cat fought off the black smoke cloud. Its intentions weren't malicious as far as we can tell. When your body was recovered, this cat was critically injured, laying by your side."

Casey touches the cat's window, and it looks up at him. "This guy here, he gave me my magic cat pee powers, didn't he?"

Babb nods.

Casey walks away, having seen and heard enough. They turn down several hallways, all the prison cells darkened. Casey stops as he recognizes the cell Carlos had him locked up in on Monday.

Babb coldly states, "What's happening now is Carlos's fault. This cell disconnects your mind from the simulation. In there, your desires and wishes come to be. You... You always wanted to be a kitten—free, being loved, and having the time of your life. Your mind creates that reality and you get lost in it, a simulation within this simulation. The engineers call them 'dreams.'" Babb sighs. "It's not Carlos' fault. It was mine. I knew it was safer having you locked up here than out there in the real world. I did not foresee Jared exploiting this at all. Natalie begged and pleaded with me to let you out. Who am I to deny her a wish?"

"I was still having dreams after you let me out," Casey says, muted. "Jared discovered that when I was knocked out with that ASMR bug."

Babb nods in agreement once more. "When you enter your deep sleep, like all the inmates here, your consciousness runs at a unique frequency. The moon playing its song last night wasn't because it was pretty or for dramatic effect. That song activated the dreaming capability of all people in this world. They are now tuned in to the same frequency."

Casey wonders aloud if they can just turn it off, flip a switch, or change the frequency.

"Maybe. In time. The engineers we still have left are working on that, fingers crossed. But maybe humanity will reject that. Maybe this is a road we cannot turn around on."

Casey finds that vague hopefulness disconcerting from someone so powerful. "When we slept, we never dreamed. When we slept, our minds were tackling simulation bugs and other day to day services, weren't we?" Casey asks. He thinks about Natalie laying on his couch, wincing in pain.

Babb plainly says, "Cloud computing. It was the future."

Casey blurts out, "Me. Use me. Take away my dreams. Until you figure things out, let me regress the bug you wrote this afternoon and any more critical issues. Don't force everyone else against their will. It doesn't work anymore."

Babb stares at him, serious. "Are you sure?"

Casey nods and Babb taps the cell window. The glass slides down. Casey steps into the cell. Babb watches, curious. This is uncharted territory for him.

A controller pops out of the wall. Casey picks up the controller, feels the needle prick.

A coldly lit blue room, sunshine leaking through the hanging window blinds. Casey opens his eyes. He lays on the floor in a ball. A ball of yarn dribbles in front of him.

No no, you will not chase that yarn. You're here for Natalie.

Casey tries to stand up on his two feet, looking down at his cute little paws.

Meow, meow, neow, nooewo. Noe-ooo. No!

Jumping up on both his human feet, Casey sees that his hands are real hands again. On a table is a piece of paper. Looking around the room, he discovers it is not as well furnished as he once thought it was. Just a blue room, white carpeting, plain window shades, and one lone table and chair in the kitchen. Casey approaches the table and sits down. He reads Babb's bug:

```
Bug: Controllers cause physical pain when en-
tering the simulation.

Severity: A

Reproduction Rate: 100
```

Steps to Reproduce:

1. Tester approaches QA station ready to be a productive and useful member of the simulation.

2. Tester picks up the controller to hop into the simulated testing environment.

3. Observe the sensation felt from the controller.

Result: The controller stabs the tester with a light needle, causing physical discomfort.

Impact: Users fingers are left scarred and marked from countless needle pricks. Needle pricks pose a health threat if the same ones are used without being changed. (Are they being changed?) – Note, this impact statement has been added by tester Casey.

Expected: When testers begin work, their happiness should not be compromised by archaic synchronization protocols. Entering the testing environment while using a controller should be pain free.

Note: Executive Producer Babb has written this bug. This is not a suggestion or quality of life issue any longer.

Casey, as he reads the bug, reproduces the steps in his dream. He looks down at his finger bleeding.

"Wait, I'm the one fixing this bug. How do I fix this bug?" he asks out loud, hoping Babb will have some kind of wise insight.

Just silence as he stares at the controller in hand. Pain free. He has to make the sign-in process pain free, but also verify the identity of the user attempting to sign in to the testing environment at work.

The drone.

Casey closes his eyes and tries to remember the flying drone that scanned him earlier.

Opening his eyes, the drone hovers in front of him.

Next, he pictures a screwdriver. He discovers one resting on the table. Always a tinkerer, he is familiar with dismantling his gaming console and PCs back in Santa Rosa. Fiddling with the controller is child's play in comparison.

Casey stretches out his arms and the drone flies closer to him. With both hands firmly on the ID scanner drone, he closes his eyes. He pictures himself resizing the machine to the size of a quarter. A few twists of the screwdriver later, controller re-assembled, Casey looks at his final product. The controller no longer pokes him. He smiles victoriously at the rusted needle on the table that he removed. Controller in hand, he presses the ON button. A faint green beam scans his face and body.

"User ID confirmed, welcome to general testing, Casey."

In his head, closing his eyes, he speaks the following words: Bug fixed, please regress for any further issues.

Casey wakes up in the Banhammer prison cell, the glass window sliding down. In his hands is a newly designed controller that will no longer stab his pudgy, delicate fingers.

"I'm not one for hyperbole, but that was amazing to witness," Babb says as he leads Casey out of the cell and back to the elevator. "This won't be permanent. The simulation has gone fully analog before. Swaths of people are being promoted to coding departments and art teams. At the heart will be our QA team, all working together with a singular purpose of making this simulation a great place to live."

Casey is comforted by the words.

***

The condo is dimly lit when he enters. He hears Natalie turn on her side as he gently closes the door, takes off his shoes, and hangs his jacket on the hook.

"Did you go somewhere?" her sleepy voice asks from under the covers.

"Just for a little while. I had to take care of something. Everything's fine now. How are you?"

Natalie yawns. "I was having a bad dream. It kept happening over and over, but I couldn't wake up. Then it stopped. I was flying my spaceship, and we were landing on Mars. You were there, Ghee was there, and Doug and Karina too. I'm not done colonizing the planet. I'm going back to finish it. We're going to make another Earth. Isn't that cool?" Natalie drifts back to her dream with a calm smile on her face.

Casey steps out onto the balcony. He keeps expecting Maurice to emerge.

Eyes closed, he tries to picture being a kitten again, but no. That luxury he gave up.

Eyes closed, he sees a stack of papers on a desk in a cold blue room. No, not a cold blue room. Casey wills his subconscious workspace to have a wide desk overlooking San Francisco and the Golden Gate, and he will have a tasty smoothie. The bug entries waiting for him are categorized by severity.

"Time to get to work. I'm hoping this counts as overtime."

***

She looks at him, worried, Casey jostled awake by a finger poke.

"You slept out here? Did you have a great dream? I had the best dream ever."

This wasn't all that bad. So what that he doesn't have dreams anymore. He has real life. Casey has Natalie in his life. He has the ability to make life interesting if he so chooses.

Showered, shaved, and properly dressed, he knocks on Natalie's door. She answers.

"I've never been to Muir Woods. Do you want to come for a hike?"

Smiling, she grabs her coat.

Hangar 88

All of this, he was not expecting. A grand spectacle under the hot California sun. He definitely was not expecting to be tickled from behind. Laughing, he begs for it to stop.

Turning around, she raises her hands like claws and says, "Bobcat. The Bobcat is here, he's over there somewhere." Natalie makes a cat hissing noise as she tiptoes, trying to find him among the crowd. Using her fake claws, she threatens to tickle Casey again.

"I wouldn't claw him like that, Sheila. I'd go for the throat, then this part by his belly, and if I could, his arm or leg, severing every exposed artery," the Bobcat's thick Australian accent says.

Natalie is star-struck as she watches the big famous actor mentally incapacitate Casey. "Of course, I'm not a real Bobcat. They add my claws with computers in post." The Bobcat takes Melissa's arm once more and they wander off into the crowd.

"Poor Ghee," Natalie mutters. "I'm hungry. Are you hungry?" Natalie wades through the sea of people to the caterer table.

"Nice shirt," she says as she brushes her pure creamy white hand along his shoulder and down his red cotton sleeve. Speechless, a blonde version of Ana, standing too close, doesn't have to introduce herself. Everyone knows who she is, just as they know who the Bobcat is.

"We're going to be neighbors for the next bit, aren't we?" she says.

Casey listens, but doesn't hear any tinge of an Australian accent. He steps back, creating space between them.

She steps forward, rubbing his arm. "I'm so sorry. I don't mean to make you uncomfortable, but this girl over there begged me to get flirty with you. Where is she? There she is." Blonde Ana points directly at the receptionist girl walking inside the building.

The two turning to see Natalie, returning with a wrapped burrito and a hot dog. "Her. She loves you. Just watch, that smile will fade."

Natalie stares at the two of them, smile fading.

"She's going to walk here, calmly, not marching furiously. And wait, she's going to dodge that Irish yobbo. She'll smile again, being friendly to both of us. When she arrives, she'll squeeze her hot dog and spray mustard on my white dress."

Casey watches everything she predicted come to be, except Casey pivots, yellow mustard dripping down his shirt. "Natalie, this is—"

Natalie cuts him off. "Yvonne Downie. That spy movie you did, where you diffused the nuke saving the World Hockey Finals in Vancouver? I was on the edge of my seat. Huge fan."

Casey asks, "You described everything that would happen nearly to the letter. How'd you do that?"

Yvonne smiles awkwardly. "You wouldn't believe me. Over there, at the end of the parking lot, on the other side of that hill, you'll find a quiet beach. I was doing yoga before the next block of motion capture. Then I see this weird twirling pillar of sand. I was drawn to it. I stepped into the sand, and all day I can predict what will happen one or two seconds into the future. Weird innit?" Yvonne wanders off to meet other people at the grand opening of Hangar 88.

As described, the two of them see the twirling pillar of sand. Natalie gives Casey her half-eaten hot dog. She bolts into it. The particles of swirling sand conform to her figure and for a brief moment, she levitates, and then is dropped to the ground.

Casey runs to her. "Are you...?"

Natalie finishes, "...all right?" She brushes the sand off, annoyed.

"Yvonne, she said she was asked to make you jealous. Some girl put her up to it," Casey explains.

Natalie nods and says, "I know. You just told me." She shakes her head. "No, this is annoying. I'm experiencing everything twice. I don't want this."

Natalie pulls her phone from her back jeans pocket, taps the screen, and a green beam scans her. Natalie starts speaking: "`Bug: Pillars of Swirling Sand Grant User Precognition.`"

Casey listens to her dictate the steps to reproduce and provide the global positioning coordinates. A white beam from the sky comes down and erases the sand pillar on the spot. Casey picks up a circular plate glass from where the sand pillar once twirled.

Natalie pokes her finger at Casey's shirt on the dried mustard stain and says, "We should get back. Babb wants to do his short speech, and then we all get properly back to work. And no, I didn't predict that. I can't see the future anymore."

"No thank you, I'm good," Natalie says playfully as Casey waves the foil wrapped burrito in her face. This bugs her as much as it did when Tania teased her last week.

"Come on, just one bite? For me?"

Natalie looks at Casey, "Why? Why would you want me to ruin my day?"

Natalie watches a nervous Babb get up at the podium, shuffling the cards for his speech. The crowd of employees claps for him. Burrito unwrapped, Natalie takes a bite. "Mother Fffff."

Everyone's ears sting as the microphone feedback blasts a high pitched squeal. People stare at Natalie, shocked by her crude, profane outburst. She stares at the burrito. Her fingers pick out the leafy green. She eats it just to verify.

"You?" she asks. "Your one wish?"

He nods, smiling.

She bites into the burrito, so happy she can enjoy genuine Spanish food again. No more gross soapy taste burning up her mouth or making her eyes water.

Melissa stands on the ceremonial stage with her new beau, the Bobcat. Everyone else is dressed up in suits and dresses, semi-formal, but the Bobcat is in his wife beater tank top and military green cargo pants, with muscles bulging everywhere. Babb hands his daughter the scissors and she cuts the red ribbon. "Ladies, gentlemen, and famous movie star guests from next door… Hangar 88 is now open! Now go, get to work. I'm not kidding."

Babb isn't kidding. Everyone knows he isn't kidding.

Like that, the festivities end. The catering crew cleans up the tables. Maintenance teams dismantle the temporary stage. Natalie joins the staff as they file into the side entranceway.

Casey looks up at the massive air hangar, giant tinted glass windows, and cream stucco exterior on the sides. He tells Natalie that he forgot his messenger bag and he'll meet her inside as the various teams get settled.

The door is locked. She wasn't kidding when she claimed the crystal access card Babb gave him on Friday. Now he can't get in. But there has to be a proper entrance to the building besides the wide open hole planes used to pass through.

Yvonne waves to him before she enters the movie studio hangar next door. He follows the sidewalk path between the two hangars.

The guest lobby door is locked. He rattles it, wanting in.

"Swipe your card." Tania sits down at the receptionist station after letting him in, annoyed. In the middle of her forehead is a gap, like a child's missing front tooth, where someone had cut off part of her bangs.

No, he will not ask.

She's trying hard not to show that she's conscious of it. Being perpetually grumpy shields her from unwanted questions or comments.

Casey thinks back to her wrapping his head with bandages as he bled out. She showed compassion. He digs in his messenger bag and says, "May I?"

The soft grey cotton toque his grandmother knitted wraps around her head. She looks in a mirror taken from a drawer. She smiles at him. "Thanks, Casey."

The realization hits him. The way the lines form at the corner of her eyes and how her happy lips take shape. They're sisters, they had to be.

Karina sits there, intently taking notes with a pad then turns and starts painting concept art on a drafting table. Already, her work space walls are littered with sketches and drawings. Casey doesn't know if she caught his friendly nod. He continues walking to the expanded QA lab and adjoined developer block.

"What, not even a hello?"

He turns around and Karina smiles at him.

Karina examines the studio, "When I was told about this job and Hangar 77, this is what I had in my head. Everything is as I imagined it. The blue walls, the steel beams painted orange, and the wide open spaces with soothing lights. Even those foamy couches over there in the corner cubby hole. Did I imagine this? Did I make this?"

Casey looks around at the open work spaces, teams of developers committed to making the simulation the best it can be. "I look forward to whatever else you create out there in the real world, Karina. It will be spectacular."

She starts taking steps back, her coworkers wanting to knock off more designs. "You don't be a stranger, okay? I'll always be here."

All new coders and engineers stare intently at the screens. Coming to grips with the underlying code of the simulation is daunting. Then add deciphering steps to reproduce to correct bugs constantly being discovered. Ray and Carlos are back together doing line by line examination of fish migration patterns. They don't say anything, but give a friendly nod as Casey walks past.

Casey is home now. He grabs a seat next to a pretty girl with brown hair. They listen to the two supervisors trying to teach a bunch of new hires how to do QA work properly. Ghee and Franky at odds about how to best prepare them for the big scary task of keeping the world from falling apart. Ghee trying to adhere to the starter guide Natalie authored. Franky obnoxiously bragging about his glory days of solving showstoppers.

Ahead of them, Doug whispers to a kid with a frozen look on his face, "I'm Doug. Don't worry, you'll get the hang of all of this. Just don't get annoying and all philosophical about what this all means. Hey, when you get the controller, just enter the cheat code. Yes, *that* cheat code. It'll all make sense after that."

Ghee shakes Natalie's hand when they're done. "Associate producer, congrats Nu-Babb!"

Natalie is embarrassed. "Thank you. I'm sure you and Franky will do fine. Just call me when you need anything."

Ghee sits down. "But man, now you're stuck working day crew. Having to deal with the commute every morning. Are you going to get a place closer to work now?"

She shakes her head. "I like it where I am right now. I'm good."

Casey and Natalie walk to the elevator to the second floor. "You didn't tell him you have administrative access to the elevator? So you can just fast travel wherever you want now?"

Natalie presses the up button. "Ghee's a smart guy. I'm sure he'll figure it out."

Casey stares at Natalie's boxed up possessions. An IT guy is dismantling her workstation and computer equipment. "Wait, you're moving your office?"

Natalie bends over the railing, looking down at the first floor. They can see all the departments buzzing with activity. In the center of the floor is an empty island desk space for two.

"I didn't want to be some out of reach figure, like Babb. When stuff happens, I want to be in the thick of it, available to my workers at any time. When you're done with whatever special project Babb has you doing, that space next to mine? It's yours."

Natalie looks at the ominous cube Babb had built for him, the windows electronically fogged over. Natalie holds Casey's hands and gives a quick peck on the lips before following the IT guy downstairs.

"One day," she says, "you'll tell me what a creative director does, but for now, I'll respect your NDA."

Casey looks down at his hands. She slipped him his crystal key card back. She grins at him as the elevator door closes. Just as she gets off, several workers approach her, needing help. Casey watched her put out little fires and soothe their anxiety.

The door beeps, three locks click, and the soft white glass door opens after he slides the card on the sensor. The ambient light is pleasant and non-threatening. It is completely empty, save for the thick envelope in the middle of the floor. A contract from the company, a salary position, including a 401k and medical plan.

Casey closes his eyes and finds himself on a beach in Tofino, British Columbia. Out at sea, whales are blowing their holes, making progressive post grunge whale music.

Casey closes his eyes once more. He wakes up right under the Eiffel Tower. Paris is peaceful, quiet, and deserted. He's always liked the geometry of the tower; it calms him.

No time to fool around or procrastinate. Just work through these bugs, knock them out, and enjoy some spaghetti with Natalie when they get home.

Bug: Incorrect and inappropriate response behaviors when dealing with Canadians.

Severity: A

Reproduction Rate: 100

Steps to Reproduce:

1. User signs into the simulation, choosing
any populated area in Canada.

2. User approaches any naturally born Canadian Citizen.

3. User instigates a negative encounter with
a Canadian. Try any of the following: stealing their wallet, stepping on their foot,
referring to Canada as America's Hat, or ag-
gressively bumping into them on the sidewalk
or indoors. Observe.

Result: Canadians will apologize when not at
fault: I'm sorry. I apologize. No, that was my
fault. Here, let me buy you a new car.

Impact: Incorrect societal responses break im-
mersion within the simulation.

Expected: When agitated, Canadians should ex-
hibit appropriate response behaviors when pro-
voked, with clear consequences to the User to
indicate they have crossed the line.

Casey reads the steps, reproduces the bug, and sits, thinking about an
appropriate response.

Developer Note: While it is true Canadians are
kind, good hearted, and the friendliest people
in the world. Do not mistake their childlike

innocence for blind naïveté. They are a decent people with different thresholds and levels of patience. You cannot see those thresholds; the exact tolerances are buried within the simulation configuration files, but they are there. If pushed too far, they will push back. Did you never wonder why they all play hockey? Leave them alone. They aren't doing anything to you. Known Shippable, Will Not Fix.

Printed in Great Britain
by Amazon